The

A Pride and Prejudice Story

by Timothy Underwood

Copyright © 2015 by Timothy Underwood

All rights reserved. This book or any portion thereof may not be reproduced or used in any manner whatsoever without the express written permission of the publisher except for the use of brief quotations in a book review.

This is a work of fiction. Names, characters, places, and incidents either are the product of the author's imagination or are used fictitiously, and any resemblance to actual persons, living or dead, events, or locales is entirely coincidental.

Table of Contents

My Other Books
About the Author

Chapter 1

Miss Bingley had halfway descended into a mania. "Cheapside!" She stabbed her fingers inches from Bingley's nose. "His residence is in *Cheapside*. Do you understand what that means? He can see his warehouses from his own house. How dare you consider attaching *me* to such a man?"

Darcy knew he should stop her. The snarling, red faced anger she'd reached due to frustration would not convince Bingley to drop Miss Bennet. But — it was so very amusing. She'd not started this way; it had taken ten minutes of Bingley's determined silence to bring her to it.

Miss Elizabeth would have laughed. She would have hid it while in the same room, but the instant she was alone, she would have turned her pert nose up and laughed.

Bingley hated confrontation and hunched behind a tall winged back chair. It was not enough to protect him from Miss Bingley. Her voice was now a banshee's hysterical shriek, "*Answer me*. Cheapside. How dare you?"

Without looking at her, Bingley mumbled, "Not in Cheapside, *near* it. Gracechurch Street is outside of the district."

"*It makes no difference!*"

Bingley jumped back at the savage rage in his sister's voice. His terrified eyes darted around the richly decorated walls of his drawing room. Darcy smiled and shrugged at him.

He'd always hoped to be present when Miss Bingley made her bid to enter Bedlam. Miss Elizabeth's eyes would have been so bright and delighted as she watched.

"Do you despise me?" Miss Bingley circled around the chair trying to get closer to Bingley who kept backing away to keep the chair between them.

Miss Bingley stopped and clapped her hands over her mouth. "*You do!* That is it. You hate me. There could be *no* other reason. Why do you hate me? Have I not always loved you? Have I not always cared for you? How can you hate me? Oh! Oh" — she moaned and turned her eyes towards the heavens — "What did I do to deserve such a hateful brother?"

"Enough! I will not give way. *I will not.*"

Darcy had *never* heard Bingley shout so.

Bingley's eyes were wide. Clearly he had never heard himself shout so either. He reverted to form. "*Please*, can we not stop this useless dispute? You know I hate to argue. I have never cared for another creature as I do Jane, and I will not give her up. Caroline, I — I love her, does that matter nothing to you? Does my happiness mean nothing to you?"

The longing in Bingley's eyes destroyed Darcy's glee. The situation was not amusing. Why couldn't Jane Bennet have loved his friend? Despite everything else, he could have supported Bingley if she loved him.

Still shocked by Bingley's shout, Miss Bingley blinked at him for several seconds. Then she sneered. "I shall not cease. You flirt with so many *angels* — just find another. It is never hard for men like you to switch the object of their affections."

Darcy almost winced. It was clear as day that Bingley's feelings towards Jane Bennet were stronger than any before. And to insult a man so. It struck at his honor. He needed to stop Miss Bingley before she made Bingley immune to reason.

"Miss Bingley." Darcy spoke coldly, "You have spoken. Your brother heard you. Give him an opportunity to consider your words."

Miss Bingley startled. A struggle showed on her face. She clearly wished to use whatever argument was in her mind. She snarled at Bingley one last time, "If you marry Jane Bennet, I shall never speak to you again." As Bingley blinked at that threat, Miss Bingley gave Darcy the sweetest smile. "Of course, Mr. Darcy, whatever you think best."

Miss Bingley and her sister left through the doors of the drawing room. Though she had regained most of her gentlewoman's composure and glided gracefully out of the room, Darcy fancied that the back of Miss Bingley's dress still vibrated with tension.

Mr. Hurst stood with a grunt and resettled his coat around his expansive waist. "Bingley, you care little for my counsel, so I'll not say much. Jane Bennet is a damned pretty girl, and her mother sets an excellent table. Still, they have nothing, and those younger sisters will embarrass the family terribly. However, you wouldn't marry *them*. Make your own choice like a man — you will regret whatever you do, but" — he gave a significant look towards the door through which his wife had exited — "I prefer to regret mistakes I can blame on myself to those where I trusted another."

Darcy pursed his lips and stared at the closed door as Bingley let out a long breath and sprawled himself over the royal blue couch.

"That was almost wise," Darcy said.

"What, Hurst?" Bingley had an arm over his eyes that muffled his voice.

"He's deeper than he seems. Most people are."

Darcy grunted and settled into an armchair and waited for Bingley to speak.

It was several minutes before Bingley said, without removing the arm he had over his eyes, "Knew Caroline had a temper, but this one was special. I'm sorry you saw that."

"It didn't bother *me*."

"No, I could see you were laughing at her behind that steady expression. Still, I wish you hadn't seen it." Bingley sat up. "What convinced *you* I shouldn't marry Jane? You said some nonsense about how she didn't care for me."

"I looked for evidence that she did. After I learned the neighborhood expected you would marry Miss Bennet, I observed the two of you closely for the remainder of the evening. Your partiality is clear. However, I saw no evidence of hers. She smiled and accepted your attention — but she smiled at everyone she spoke to. She treated you the same as everyone. There were no special marks of affection."

Darcy sighed. Bingley's eyes were intent on him, and he had gone pale as he shook his head. Darcy looked away. It was even more painful to break Bingley's heart than he had expected. "I am sorry. I sincerely am. But you do not have her heart. Her mother is eager to trap a wealthy man, and Miss Bennet would need to accept if you offered. It would be better for her as well as you were she to marry a man she was not indifferent to."

"No, no. Jane cares for me. I'm sure of it. She must." Bingley smashed his fist against his mouth. "Good God, you are serious. You are convinced Jane doesn't care anything for me. But, I thought — I was sure she cared for me."

"You cannot wish her to be made to marry without real affection? You cannot wish her to merely tolerate marriage to you."

"No. I would not — but I was sure she felt for me as I did for her. We shared so many confidences and talked so much."

"It is because you always approach her; given her mother's wishes, she cannot discourage you. It is painful. I wish it were otherwise. I sincerely do. But you must accept the truth. She does not love you."

Bingley rubbed his mouth and looked about like a puppy whose master had kicked him. "But I love her. How could she not —" Bingley closed his eyes and sighed. "If she cares nothing for me — I do not wish her trapped. You must be right — you always are."

Darcy was always reticent with physical touch, but he still went to sit next to Bingley on the couch and patted him on the shoulder. Bingley's manner was dejected as he stared at the floor. Darcy knew this was his fault. If only he had not been so focused on his unsuitable admiration for Miss Elizabeth, he would have seen how his friend felt before the attachment became so serious.

"I do not understand. How I could be so mistaken — when I think back on our conversations, I still see affection. She always talked eagerly to me, always with a smile. We discussed our hopes openly."

"I examined her countenance and her behavior most closely that night. She showed no symptom of deep regard for you — none."

Bingley nearly looked like he wished to cry. It made Darcy's chest and eyes ache in sympathy. He hated to see his friend unhappy. Bingley almost always was happy.

"I only wish —" Bingley stared at the mantle above the fireplace, where he had hung portraits of his parents. "I only wish I could be certain. She spoke as though she had affection for me."

"Certainty in such cases is impossible. However —" Darcy took a deep breath as he searched for the best words to convince Bingley to give up hope. His friend would not be able to leave this dismal affair behind him until he felt sure.

As Darcy thought, Bingley straightened happily. "I could ask her."

"I have already told you she will accept a proposal — in her position she must." The somberness of the occasion did not fully mask Darcy's annoyance when forced to repeat himself.

"I know *that* — I shall ask her to tell me what she feels; whether she loves me as I her. No matter what her interests, she would not lie about her affection."

"She is poor — it is not possible to trust the words of the desperate."

The two men stared at each other. Darcy grimaced. He should not have implied Jane Bennet might lie. She was a gentlewoman, and her behavior had always been exemplary. He had no call to question her character. Yet, Mrs. Younge had been raised a gentlewoman, and she lied to them. He could not repent his caution to Bingley.

"Enough. You shall not insult my Jane. If she lies, I am entirely deceived in her character and will suffer the consequence. Besides, I love her. You and Caroline may think I am a useless, flighty gentleman, but I am *not* such a man. I could not find another angel to love just because I flirt easily. I love Jane, and I will remain in love with her. I am *not* so changeable. Until she says that she wishes nothing to do with me, I will pursue her."

Bingley's sudden stubbornness surprised Darcy into silence. Why must his friend choose now to discover firmness? The consequences were very like to haunt him the rest of his life. He should have silenced Miss Bingley far sooner and not suggested Miss Bennet was dishonest.

Bingley walked to the door with his head high. He turned round, "I do not trust your observation of Jane any more. You do not understand her character. She would never deceive me in a matter of such import. You have had maybe half a conversation with her — because you were too busy arguing with Miss Elizabeth. I should trust my own observation. I am sure she loves me."

Darcy started after his friend. "Wait, Bingley — I should not have said that. Miss Bennet is a fine gentlewoman. But I beg you, be cautious."

Bingley grinned back. "I know you did not mean it. Even a man as fastidious as you can see that Jane is an angel."

THE RETURN

CHARLES BINGLEY HAD been terrified when he first arrived at boarding school as the awkwardly dressed son of a man in trade. A lump had stuck in his throat, and his stomach remained clenched for a week. Finding the nerve to greet the aristocratic children around him had been the hardest thing he ever did.

It was harder to jump into saddle and set out upon the dirt road from Netherfield to Longbourn.

At first he'd been sure Darcy misinterpreted Jane's reserved nature as a lack of affection. But — Darcy was right about so many things. Bingley's certainty that he was wrong this time could not last.

When he arrived at Netherfield the previous evening, it was too late to call upon Longbourn, but too early to sleep. Bingley tried to play billiards; he went to clean his hunting guns, but they had been packed away and sent to London by Caroline; he tried to read a book from his small library. Nothing distracted him from the swirling thoughts. For half the night he paced in fear down moonlit halls, distrusting every memory which suggested Jane had affection for him.

Darcy would prove right again. Tomorrow he would learn for certain Jane did not care for him. He would walk into the room; he would ask Jane to tell him truly if she loved him; and she would tell him no. He would be terribly embarrassed. He would have made Jane uncomfortable. He would ride back to London, leave Hertfordshire behind forever, and tell Darcy that he was right again.

But — what if Jane loved him? If only his own happiness had been at stake, Bingley never could have gone to ask.

He had been so sure she loved him the day before. If she loved him and he abandoned her, she would be heartbroken. She would cry alone to not burden her sisters with the depth of her unhappiness. The unhappiness she felt because he abandoned her.

The well-maintained surface of a turnpike to London crossed his path as he rode through Meryton. He could take it. But he needed to see Jane's face and ask her. He could not abandon her until he knew she did not care.

Jane would never lie about her feelings. He loved her and she was an angel. If the Bennets' situation was so desperate that she need marry the first rich man who came calling, no matter what her feelings, he'd rather she married him instead of someone else. He loved her.

The butler immediately ushered Bingley into Longbourn's already familiar white drawing room. A cheery fire burned, and decorative mahogany cabinets laden with brightly painted china and ivory figurines were scattered against the walls. The ladies had gathered to meet him. His eyes immediately turned towards *her*.

Jane wore a high necked blue day dress and had a handful of needlework upon her lap. Her blond hair was uncovered and pinned into a neat bun. Rather than her usual smile she looked down and twisted her hands together.

Bingley's heart sank.

"Lord — Lord! It is a very good to see you. Mr. Bingley, you are always so very, very welcome. Please sit down. Please sit down — you look very well! Girls, do you not agree? Is not Mr. Bingley looking very well?"

Bingley tried to give full attention to Mrs. Bennet. It would be polite and would distract him from his nerves. His sisters and Darcy were too fastidious. Though she was loud and wordy, he preferred Mrs. Bennet's country good cheer and hospitality to the cold civility often found in town.

"It surprised us exceedingly to hear your sisters had removed from Netherfield — I'm so pleased to see you have returned. You must come to dinner tomorrow — you had promised us a family dinner. I must have you soon — there shall be two courses."

Bingley nodded amicably, showing nothing of the flare of annoyance mention of his sisters brought. "I shall certainly attend you. I look forward to it greatly. Your table is always well worth enjoying." Though, if Jane's response was unfavorable, he would not be at Longbourn for dinner the next day.

Lydia cried, "La, there is such news. You must hear it — Mr. Collins made Elizabeth an offer and she refused him. Not that I blame her, the ugly man."

Jane spoke, "Lydia, you should not speak so of your cousin." Despite the exasperation in her tone and words, it was music to Bingley's ears.

"Well he was! He was boring. He was quite the most boring person I have ever met. It would have been no fun if Lizzy married him." Lydia returned her attention to Bingley. "Then, not more than a day later, Mr.

Collins became engaged to Charlotte Lucas. It was such a joke that he stayed with us till this morning."

Lydia's words caused the lump in Bingley's throat to grow. Certainly Jane would refuse him like Elizabeth had Mr. Collins. She would be too kind to laugh at him, but it was absurd to think a man like him had the heart of such a perfect angel as Jane. Yet, no distaste showed in the way Jane gave him quick glances and small smiles.

Mrs. Bennet had begun to speak again when Bingley burst out, "Might I have an opportunity to speak to Miss Bennet in private?" It was impossible to stand the jagged tension which stabbed his chest longer.

Jane gave him a nervous smile before her eyes returned to the hands folded on her lap. Her color was high. Bingley's heart beat as though he had fenced for hours. Miss Elizabeth gave him a bright friendly smile when she curtsied as she left. Bingley saw her wink at Jane. Mrs. Bennet volubly agreed to the audience. Jane didn't say anything.

Surely Mrs. Bennet would not be so pleased to give him opportunity to speak if she only cared for his fortune. And Elizabeth had refused Mr. Collins, whose situation was perfectly eligible. In the unlikely case Jane accepted him, it would be for himself.

Jane looked up at Bingley, holding her eyes on him as he swallowed. Bingley took one of the armless oak chairs around the card table and placed it next to where Jane sat on the blue sofa. He sat down and took her hand. It was warm and fragile, and he ran his thumb over her knuckles.

"I must have your honesty; do not pretend more affection for me than you possess. Do not try to spare my feelings. Do not speak anything but what is in your heart. I know, you have no reason to do so — I know I am in many ways a trifling man — I love you terribly. I cannot ride away and leave without asking. Do you — can you — love me?"

Jane's smile was brilliant. "Oh, yes! I do love you. I had never known it was possible to feel so much for a person. It hurt so terribly when I thought you gone, and when your sister wrote — oh, I do love you!"

Jane leaned her head close to him, and they kissed. When they parted Bingley took Jane's hand, and they greeted the family with the good news. A little part of him, which had been always jealous of Darcy, laughed: *When it mattered most, I was right, and Darcy was wrong.*

Chapter 2

The next morning Bingley arrived at Longbourn early and breakfasted with the Bennets. Everyone sat around the breakfast table together, and there was a great deal of noise and bustle. Bingley loved the way Jane darted sweet smiles at him, and his chest fluttered exultantly when once she snuck her hand under the table to squeeze his. She had always looked like an angel, but she had never looked so pretty as this morning.

He enthusiastically participated in the morning conversation, but over the course of an hour a desperate desire to have privacy so he might speak to Jane, and Jane alone, grew in him. From the way her eyes turned upon his face Bingley was sure Jane shared the sentiment. He watched her pretty red lips open to consume one last bite of pastry as they finished breakfast.

"Mrs. Bennet," Bingley began as the footman collected the dishes from the breakfast table, "that was the best breakfast I've ever had! The finest repast, the best lemon tart, and the most excellent rolls and butter!"

Mrs. Bennet smiled prettily at the compliment. "Lord! Thank you for those very kind words — though I'm sure it is not true that you have never had a better meal — I put great effort into my entertainment. And I have taught my daughters how to manage a kitchen as well. You shall find nothing wanting once married."

Bingley quickly grabbed Jane's hand. She blushed and looked lovely as he replied, "I know I shall be very, very happy when I marry my dear Jane." He pulled her ungloved hand up to kiss it and enjoyed the feel of her small delicate fingers against his mouth. Releasing her hand, he said, "I'm quite ready to burst at the seams after that meal and must have a walk — Jane, will you join me?"

She agreed, "Oh yes, there's nothing I'd like more than a walk now."

Jane looked at Elizabeth who said, "I too like the idea of a walk and shall join you — we should head in the opposite direction from Meryton; have you seen the woods thereabouts?"

Damn! He'd hoped to have Jane alone and maybe kiss her again. Oh, well. It would be too much to expect the Bennets to allow them to walk about without chaperone.

"La!" Lydia said, "Looking at woods. Well, I wish to see if Mr. Wickham has returned from London. You may enjoy the woods without me. I shall visit our aunt Phillips to hear the gossip."

Though clear, the day was cold, and when they exited the house, Jane and Elizabeth were tightly bundled up. Mr. Bingley took Jane's arm and looked to see if Elizabeth wished to walk on his other side.

She backed away with a dimpled smile and held up the huge rectangle of a book she had brought out. "I wish to compare the plants hereabouts to those in this guide to the fauna of southern England. I fear I shall be quite absorbed doing so and have absolutely no attention for your conversation or doings." She winked at them, adding, "I know this distresses you, but it shall be almost as though I were not present."

The three set off on their walk, and Elizabeth had soon trailed a fair distance behind them. As promised, any time Bingley glanced back at her she appeared preoccupied by her book. The woods Elizabeth had suggested were coppiced and at points could only be traversed through a woodsman's path. The trees deadened sound, and as Bingley animatedly talked with Jane, it felt like they were alone.

Jane stopped walking and looked back at her sister. Bingley faintly saw Elizabeth raise her eyebrows, and she lifted the large book so it entirely covered her face, removing any view she may have had of them. He stared quizzically at her form. Jane laid her gloved hand on his cheek and pulled him to look towards her. Blushing brightly at her forwardness, she stepped up to kiss him.

Bingley wanted to dance a fast jig from happiness when Jane broke their kiss and nervously looked at her sister. Elizabeth stood where she had before, with the book held up in front of her face. How long would it take before her arms grew tired?

Jane's sweet lips were red and entrancing. Bingley ran his knuckles down Jane's cheek and placed his lips on hers. When they broke off again, Elizabeth still stood with the book in front of her face. She was an excellent chaperone.

This time Jane took Bingley's arm and firmly grasped his hand. Her face glowed a delightful shade of red. It had been very clever of them all to decide the previous day they had no reason to wait more than a month for the wedding.

Bingley wanted to roar with happiness; he wished to tilt his head back and shout at the skies: "Jane Bennet loves me. The most perfect woman in England loves me." Instead he laced his fingers with Jane's and smiled gaily.

When Bingley glanced back he saw that Elizabeth, alerted by the sound of the footsteps moving away, had lowered the book and followed them again — though she pretended to be engaged by her study of a thicket.

For a time smug happiness prevented speech. The sweet taste of Jane's mouth lingered. Everything was perfect. Recollection of his sister damaged his mood.

Bingley sighed. He had firmly decided the previous night he must know. If he were to become a married man, responsibility demanded he protect his wife and manage his sister. "What did Caroline write which concerned you? I forgot to ask yesterday in the midst of our happiness — yet I must."

Jane looked away and clearly did not wish to speak of it. "I am sure they only misunderstood your feelings and plans. They must not have realized you cared for me." Jane spoke halfheartedly, as though she knew her words were a fiction.

Bingley said with a bitter smile, "It shows your good nature that you pretend to believe that, but... my sisters' behavior and thoughts are not always what they ought. Caroline knew my affections were yours. What did she write?"

"If she knew her words smacked of dishonesty. I feared that might be the case. Elizabeth believed she wished to separate us." Jane looked away. "If your family opposes our marriage, are you certain that you desire to ignore their wishes?"

Bingley pulled the hand she had entangled with his to his mouth and kissed it violently. "I am certain. Caroline and Louisa can lose themselves in a desert. I would not care. I love you; you love me. That is the only thing which concerns me. Do not feel sorry for Caroline and her disappointment — she only wishes to puff herself up before her friends."

Jane still frowned and would not meet his eyes. "You love me, do you not? You said you love me."

Her beautiful eyes flew to his. "You know I do. Do not doubt it. My affection for you is strong and steady."

"Then we shall be happy. I need no one but you."

He kissed Jane's hands again. Her face blossomed into a smile. "Oh, Charles" — she blushed pink as a carnation at the use of his Christian name — "I am so happy. So very happy. I only wish everyone — especially your sisters — were as happy as I am."

Bingley loved his sisters, but he knew them too well to have any great illusions. Until Caroline had Jane's goodness it would be impossible for her to have the pure unselfish happiness in the eyes of his beloved. For his own part, he wished nothing more than to stare into those beautiful eyes forever. And to think Darcy had nearly convinced him to stay in London. It would have been the worst mistake of his life.

He wished to kiss Jane and looked at Elizabeth to see if she watched. Her face was hidden behind that excellent book of hers. He caught Jane's eyes. She had glanced at Elizabeth as well, and with a smile they kissed. When their mouths parted this time, Bingley said, "I rather prefer your sister to my own."

Jane giggled and said, "She soon will be your sister as well."

"That she will. I hope someday we shall do her equally good service as chaperones."

They began to walk again, and a minute later Bingley sighed, "I must know all my sister wrote to you, else it will nag at my mind."

Jane looked away and sighed as she fished the letter out of the inner pocket of her coat. "I confess it had gravely concerned me, so I read it several times."

Bingley took the perfumed papers, which he recognized as his sister's stationary, and unfolded them. He read the letter with a silent frown as Jane watched anxiously. Damn Caroline! To tell Jane he wished to become attached to another. His dear angel was too trusting and kind. She must have believed the message, at least in part.

He pulled his arm around Jane and embraced her. "This letter must have pained you so — it would not be in your heart to suspect Caroline of treachery, so your only hope must have been that she was mistaken and your understanding of my character and desires was superior to hers."

Jane nodded and wriggled closer to him, "I tried to hide it. I tried to maintain some hope, but I was miserable for two days."

"I am most angry at Caroline — to do that to you. The story is ridiculous. Georgiana! Why she is almost a child."

They reached the edge of the woods and turned to walk along a low hedge, which marked the edge of Longbourn's fields. They headed back towards the house. Jane asked, "You were uncertain yesterday. Had I not given you enough indication of my affection? Charlotte — Miss Lucas that is — told me I ought to be more forward, yet I could not bring myself to show more than I did."

"'Tis not your fault. Your feelings were clear. Last night I tried to recall every conversation we have had, so I could impress them forever into my memories. I hope to never forget anything from the first few months of our happiness together. There were many ways you showed how you liked me. And I had been aware of them, some at least, before. Yet —"

Bingley frowned. It had been disloyal to Jane to doubt her. He didn't want to admit it. "You — you must understand. Understand, Darcy is a clever man who advises me well. His advice has been most useful. And he cares for my well-being. He does — he observed you most closely on the night of the Netherfield ball, and your natural reserve convinced him that you only welcomed my company out of politeness. Please do not judge me harshly — his advice is in most cases good — but Darcy's conviction nearly became mine."

"How did he expect me to act?" Jane said, "It would have been improper to openly show affection before your choice was clear. I suspect your friend would have blamed me had I done so."

"He would have — Darcy looks upon matters of the heart with the same suspicious eye he uses to judge money matters. And this summer something happened, I know not what, which left him in a thundercloud of a mood. He has spoken insultingly of people's motives since. I do not think Darcy is... qualified to judge in such a matter as this. He rarely speaks to women who are not closely connected to him. It is no surprise he would misjudge your character. He had hardly spoken with you."

Jane waved her free hand. "He thought I would accept you due to your money even though I had no particular regard for you?"

Bingley gestured in agreement, and Jane said, "I never would have. Never. To marry without affection is something I have always been resolved against. Had I not met you, I would have far preferred to be a poor surplus relative when my father died. To live on such terms of intimacy with somebody I merely liked would be insupportable."

Jane looked back at Elizabeth, who waved before bringing her book up in front of her face again. "Elizabeth's refusal of Mr. Collins ought to convince even Mr. Darcy that we Bennet girls would stand on the principle when called to do so."

THAT NIGHT ELIZABETH dressed in a long cotton nightgown and added a woolen robe for warmth. She walked to her sister's room. Jane was ecstatic, and she would marry an excellent man who she loved. Elizabeth should only feel happiness. Yet... In a little more than a month's time, in less than three fortnights, her dear Jane would be gone. These late-night conferences would be no more. No longer would she be Jane's closest confidante. She would be alone when she needed to share her deepest anxieties or hopes.

A candle flickered on Jane's nightstand, and a ruddy orange glow came from the half burnt coals in the fireplace. Jane had snuck under the quilt for warmth, and a blizzard of white curling paper floated about her head. Her teeth flashed as she sat up to greet her sister, "Is it not perfect? I still fear it is a dream."

Elizabeth smiled mischievously and hopped onto the bed next to Jane, causing it to creak. "Tell me: Was I not an exceptional chaperone?"

The skin on Jane's cheeks went dark red in the dim candlelight, and she coughed at Elizabeth's eager grin, "You were the best of chaperones."

"So, what is it like to kiss him?"

Jane flushed even redder and looked away. "Lizzy!"

"Pray tell, pray tell. If I was such a good chaperone, I must be rewarded. Do tell!" Jane was too flushed to speak. "Pleeease. My sweet Jane won't deny me, will she?"

Jane did not meet Elizabeth's eyes as she spoke, "It was so perfect. I put my hand on his jaw, and his eyes were very deep, and I leaned up and put my lips on him. I've never felt so bold. My stomach fluttered wildly, and he put his hand on my back and drew me closer. And my chest pounded so hard. And once we parted all I wanted to do was kiss him again, and I kept watching his lips and —" Jane wriggled under the covers. "It was more than I ever imagined."

Elizabeth sighed dreamily.

Watching Elizabeth's vacant expression, Jane showed her own mischievous smile. "Now we must find you a husband so that you might kiss him!" Elizabeth blushed as Jane squeezed her hand. "We must! All that is left is to find the proper man. Who amongst our acquaintance would you wish to kiss most?"

Elizabeth was too embarrassed to reply. Jane said with her cheery voice, "Perhaps it might be —" She stopped and shook her head. "No, I fear he would not do it all."

"Do you think of Mr. Wickham? For, due to Mr. Darcy's cruelty, it would be most imprudent."

"He had been on my mind, but such a match seems ill-advised. I do not believe Darcy was cruel. From what Bingley has said about his friend, he always acted with the best of intentions. Mayhap, some misunderstanding occurred betwixt the two."

Jane was naïve, and so was Bingley. The truth of Mr. Wickham's claims was shown in the open goodness of his manner. Darcy always displayed disdain for those he thought beneath him — Elizabeth recalled the first time she saw him, standing in the entryway of the assembly room with his broad shoulders pulled back and his head held high. *She is tolerable I suppose, but not handsome enough to tempt me.* It was all of a piece: his rudeness to her, his disdain for the neighborhood, and his cruelty towards Wickham.

"I expect you to think so. It is good *you* believe the best of your husband's friend. *You* have no need to judge differently; *you* shall be friends with him in any case."

Jane pressed her lips tightly together as she stared at Elizabeth, and the bed creaked as she sat higher and crossed her arms. Before Jane spoke again, Elizabeth asked, "What had Bingley to say about his sister's letter? Was my interpretation correct in the main?"

"It was." Jane rubbed her arm. "You are too good Lizzy to triumph in this. I was mistaken in their regard. Despite our friendship, both Caroline and Louisa committed themselves to convincing their brother to abandon me. They followed him to London solely to argue against return. I wish it were possible they acted from the purest of motives, but Bingley convinced me they did not. He said Caroline especially was motivated by a desire to gain a sister who she could boast amongst her friends about — and I am not. I hope we shall be friends, but I fear I will not trust her affection for some time."

"Jane! That is the most unforgiving speech you've ever made. I'm delighted you shall not continue their dupe."

"I do not like the need to mistrust their affection." Jane frowned. "Bingley was furious after he read the letter."

Elizabeth was glad to hear it. It would bode ill if he did not take Jane's side against his sisters. She asked, "What part did Mr. Darcy play? Unless you say otherwise, I shall believe he strenuously counseled his friend against you."

"Mr. Darcy acted from the purest motives. He observed me during the ball at Netherfield and became convinced from my calm manner that I did not have any strong affection for Bingley. I cannot be happy for the mistake, but it was honest. Charlotte had counseled me to show my affection more openly. I shall not hold it against him. And neither shall you. I ought to have said nothing, given your dislike for him. Bingley depends greatly upon Mr. Darcy's advice, and it proceeds from a real concern in his friend's well-being."

"I am certain you believe that. For my part, I am convinced his real objection was our want of wealth and connections. As Mr. Wickham told me, Darcy wishes everyone about him to be well spoken of."

A half-hour later Elizabeth slipped back into her bed. Her mind went immediately to the kisses she carefully had *not* watched that morning. It sounded delightful and sensuous.

She imagined kissing Wickham. After a minute she gave up. The idea was a little pleasant; he *was* very handsome. But the fantasy lacked something.

Wickham was shallow. Almost — bland. He was not bland, but he would become so with time. Marriage to him would entail decades of empty compliments, and no matter how prettily they were said, no matter how handsome the sayer, the prospect was dreary. Marrying Mr. Wickham's sameness would be nearly as horrid as marrying Mr. Collins's heaviness.

Elizabeth pulled her blankets tightly around to ward off the cold of the early December night. Wickham was like a sugar confection: He had an extremely pleasant taste, but no substance. One could not live off it. She would never marry a man like Mr. Wickham.

What sort of man did she desire?

Perhaps because she had spoken of him with Jane, Elizabeth's mind flitted to Darcy. His intense burning blue eyes and strong jaw line. The restrained anger in his eyes when they spoke of Wickham during their dance. Elizabeth's breath flew away, and her face burned hot as she imagined him pushing her against a wall and laying his lips upon hers.

Her heart pounded uncomfortably, and her body felt tight and twisted in odd places. He would push his long lean form against hers. Elizabeth forced her mind away from that image. Mr. Darcy would never be bland.

Elizabeth breathed heavily. This was such a joke. She felt nothing at the thought of a handsome, amiable man who liked her and a rush of emotion at the thought of the odious, disagreeable… handsome man who cared nothing for her. A man she hated.

If she was to be forever so perverse, she would end an old maid. At least Jane would provide nephews and nieces for her to spoil.

Chapter 3

Darcy's cousin Colonel Fitzwilliam was briefly in London on business for his regiment, and he took the opportunity to breakfast with Darcy and Georgiana. While the two men endeavored to draw more enthusiasm from their quiet cousin, the letter arrived. Darcy immediately recognized Bingley's hand and, with an unpleasant premonition, tore the envelope open. It was even less decipherable than normal, but the essence of the message was clear.

Jane loves me — she really loves me — you must wish me joy — not a mistake at all — would have been the worst mistake — how would you expect a — behave? Jane loves me! — Tuesday, January 7. Well you stand with me? Despite your — no one I more wish than you.

Most sincerely your friend,
C Bingley

Darcy hoped Bingley was right, for the marriage would only be tolerable if Jane sincerely loved him. Did she?

The letter implied Miss Bennet explicitly assured Bingley that she loved him. She would not behave as Wickham — at least Darcy did not think she would — and intentionally deceive a gentleman who had come to her with an open heart. Yet, he had seen none of those flirtatious behaviors with which ladies usually indicated their object of affection. She did not seek opportunities to touch him, or tease him, or even seek his attention when it was not on her.

He sighed, folded the letter, and tapped it against the breakfast table.

Colonel Fitzwilliam spoke, "Is it poor news? Come, you know a trouble shared is a trouble halved."

Darcy glanced at Georgiana and said, "No, it is not poor news. My friend Mr. Bingley is to be married. To Miss Jane Bennet" — he looked at Georgiana — "you must recall her from my letters to you."

Georgiana nodded. "Shall we attend the wedding?"

Wickham was in the neighborhood. He disliked disappointing Georgiana when she had expressed interest, but he would not expose her to the scoundrel's presence. Georgiana was still brokenhearted over his betrayal, and simply seeing him could set back her recovery by months. "You would not wish to go because —" Darcy's mind dashed desperately about for an excuse. "Many people will be there. You would not want to be among such a crowd."

The light which had been in Georgiana's eyes dimmed and she nodded. "I understand — might I be excused?"

Once the door closed, Colonel Fitzwilliam turned to Darcy as he took a swallow of coffee. "I do not understand that girl — it is unnatural for someone already sixteen to be that tame. Pray tell, what was the real reason you wish to keep her away from Bingley's wedding?"

"Wickham is present in the neighborhood. He enlisted in the militia regiment stationed at Meryton."

"Blast that man. I understand. Perhaps we should tell her why we wish to keep her away." Colonel Fitzwilliam leaned forward. "What is it about Bingley's marriage that made you respond to its announcement with that stormy expression. You dislike the lady?"

"No — I know no ill about Miss Bennet, except that —" Darcy stopped himself, "as you are like to meet the people involved, I think this conversation ought not continue."

"The deuce. Come now Darcy, we are cousins — I am your closest relation in terms of age and beauty. If you are not going to make confidences which should not be made with me, who are you going to give them to?"

Darcy raised his eyebrows, and Colonel Fitzwilliam grinned. "You should feel flattered that I allowed your tall noble mien to be nearly as worthy of praise as my shorter and — less striking features."

"Tall noble mien? Where did you ever hear such silly rot?"

"Your name has arisen once or twice in conversation with the ladies."

Darcy felt remarkably foolish as he reflexively smiled and stood straighter at that.

Colonel Fitzwilliam laughed and said, "Admit it, you do wish to tell me your concerns about Bingley's bride. What is that small matter that concerns you — the except?"

"Well — I suspect Miss Bennet may not really care for Bingley."

"Oh, that is a very small matter."

"She is poor. She has essentially nothing — and the behavior of her family is often abominable."

"And you fear she marries him for his money, as opposed to affection, due to her poverty. Unlike the many girls who ignore penniless colonels because they are greedy for more money, despite having a great deal already — Your Bingley is quite the handsome fellow, with charming manners. Have you considered that she might marry him, despite having no true affection, out of greed for his person and address as opposed to greed for his purse? I know if I were as tall as you, I would've had no trouble attracting some heiress."

"Please be serious — I am concerned for my friend."

"I salute you for your worry. However, all you said — besides the enormously important matter of the girl's poverty –" Colonel Fitzwilliam waved his hand dismissively. "Could be said about half the marriages in our set. If Bingley fancies himself desperately in love and imagines the lady's feelings to be similar, I daresay he has better than the average hope of happiness."

"Maybe."

Fitzwilliam laughed. "If you will not be reassured by that, let us see what else I might say to encourage you. What led you to conclude she cares for nothing but his purse?"

"When I realized on Tuesday last a general expectation had formed that the two would make a match of it, I spent the remainder of the evening carefully observing Miss Bennet. She was restrained with Bingley and showed little more enthusiasm for him than for anyone else. She did smile a great deal at Bingley, but she always smiles."

"So the foundation of your case is that she smiles no matter who she is with?"

"I looked for signs of particular regard and saw none."

"And perhaps she only displayed maidenly reserve? It is on occasion real, especially among girls who have not been regularly to London, as I imagine Bingley's penniless ladylove has not. What led Bingley to be so convinced of the affection of his lady that it overcame his usual dependence on your counsel?"

"He thought her words in their private conversations indicated affection, and after our conversation, he determined to ask her directly if she loved him. He planned to offer only if she claimed to love him. From Bingley's letter she replied in the affirmative."

"And yet you still doubt?" Colonel Fitzwilliam looked incredulously at Darcy. "You claim to think no ill of her, but you believe the young lady might lie about such a serious matter, and you trust your own observation from a distance, and for only an hour, more than Bingley's understanding of her character from weeks of conversation. Likely he is fortunate he ignored you."

Darcy smiled. "So you are convinced, based on my secondhand description of the situation, that the lady is in love with Bingley. You think yourself such a good judge as to see better in this case than me."

"Nay, do not put those words in my mouth — I would never consider myself a better judge of the minds of women than you." Colonel Fitzwilliam laughed at Darcy's embarrassment. "You may gain their attention easily, but there are few men of my acquaintance whose judgement on a lady's feelings I would trust less than yours. You have never been easy in conversation with them."

Darcy bowed his head to acknowledge the point. "I still can observe."

"True, but Bingley had far better opportunity to observe Miss Bennet. Enough of this, you can do no good by worrying about it. If I were you, I would believe Jane Bennet is sincere and resolve to feel happy for Bingley. I feel happy for Bingley and will congratulate him heartily when next I see him."

Colonel Fitzwilliam was right. What was done was done. Even if Jane did not love Bingley, she did not dislike him and was a good sort of woman. Perhaps his friend would be happy. Darcy himself could help to contain any scandal the younger girls entered in, and Bingley's temperament would not rebel at a mother-in-law like Mrs. Bennet in the way Darcy's did. The situation was unfortunate, not horrid.

Darcy at last nodded. "For once, I believe your counsel wise."

The two sat. Colonel Fitzwilliam forked several more pieces of sausage onto his plate and refilled his coffee. Darcy's mind turned from Miss Bennet to her sister. He had abandoned all thought of Elizabeth when he left. Her family displayed improper behavior, was poorly connected, and provided no dowry worth mentioning. It was insane to consider such a marriage.

Though, *now* it would make him Bingley's brother. She was not so poorly connected as before.

Her sparkling eyes were beautiful. Her mouth was pretty and begged to be kissed. And her mind was first rate. She didn't bore him like every lady he'd met during a London season. She argued and smiled and charmed. He would see her in a month more.

Could he force himself away this time?

THE NEWS OF HER BROTHER'S engagement threw Caroline Bingley into turmoil. Mr. Darcy had — unexpectedly — failed to persuade her brother to see his interest. Caroline felt too embarrassed by her brother, and her new connections, to call upon the Darcys for several days. After all the care Mr. Darcy had given her mostly useless brother, he threw it away by making the wrong choice in the second most important decision of his life.

Eventually, Darcy would grow tired of Charles's impertinence and foolishness. She had long ago. Would Charles also ignore Mr. Darcy's advice when he purchased an estate?

Charles never appreciated his great luck in attracting the friendship of a man who so perfectly combined excellence of family connections and personal capability. It astonished her that Charles treated Mr. Darcy in such a flippant manner. He even told Darcy that he could go to bed early if he was not interested in the ball! Balls and dancing were great fun, but Darcy's distaste was clear, and Charles should have respected it.

At least, until now, Charles always followed Darcy's lead in matters of importance. Perhaps this would end the steady friendship between the two.

It would be natural for Darcy to refuse to connect himself any longer with a family, which not only gained its great fortune in trade one generation ago (though the stain was reduced because their uncle had a substantial estate in Northumberland), but which also *now* had relatives actively in trade.

Certainly, this marriage damaged her hope to attach the great man to herself.

It was with trepidation that Caroline called upon Georgiana about a week after Bingley had returned to Netherfield. Miss Darcy met her with the new companion, whose name Caroline simply could not recall. It was not important; after all she was barely more than a servant.

Georgiana wore a handsome silk shawl, which she buried her hands under. Her reply to Miss Bingley's "G'day" was an embarrassed blush and a mumbled, "Good day to you too."

"We are pleased to see you Miss Bingley." The companion spoke when it became clear her charge would not take more of the conversational burden, "I know you returned to town only a week past. Has your stay been pleasant so far?"

Georgiana was an odd insipid creature. Caroline tried — she certainly tried — to make friends with her, but it was impossible to get two words out of the pathetic dear. Why Darcy doted on her was a confusing mystery.

"Is your brother well? I've not seen him since the day we all arrived in London."

Georgiana quietly mumbled. The only word Miss Bingley understood was "fencing."

The companion elaborated, "Mr. Darcy went out to his fencing club an hour ago or so. He should return within a little time, if you hoped to speak to him. We have heard your brother is to be married."

Before Caroline began her carefully crafted speech, which would show a tolerant bemusement at her brother's foolishness, but express her intention to remain above the new connections he had saddled her with, Georgiana spoke, "You must be happy — I mean very pleased. My brother said Miss Bennet is a most elegant and kind woman."

That was promising — Mr. Darcy would not praise Jane Bennet to his sister if he intended to cut them all over her. Caroline said, "I'm sure Jane will be an excellent sister."

"It is such a pleasant thought — your brother's marriage —" Georgiana spoke with an unusual fervency and glow, "I understand Miss Bennet has almost no dowry. It — it made me very happy to hear of a marriage where the man only cared for his beloved, and nothing else."

"Yes... My sentiments are... Well it is certainly true my brother marries Jane solely for her own sake." Caroline could not quite bring herself to verbally agree with the softheaded nonsense Georgiana just expressed. She almost never spoke, but when she did, it was to praise imprudent marriages.

Something had gone badly amiss in Georgiana's education — perhaps she had been pulled from school too soon. And while equally admired and well known, Georgiana's school lacked compared to her own.

"That shawl is delightful, where did you acquire it?" Her brother's marriage was not something she wished to discuss — especially not with this odd girl who approved of it.

Georgiana's awkward nature returned, and she looked away with a blush while fingering the fabric. "Do you think so? My brother bought it for me. So I know it must be excellent, but it seems almost too pretty for me to wear." The last words were barely audible as Georgiana's voice trailed away.

"Of course not, you are the most elegant girl I know. And you are so beautiful. Your brother knows that — is it not very sweet how he dotes upon you."

When Georgiana looked at her during the speech, Caroline detected a hint of a frown on the girl's face. She looked away immediately with her usual shyness. That was the worst part of it. Despite all her efforts to praise and flatter Georgiana, even though the girl deserved no such consideration, Caroline often received the distinct impression that Georgiana disliked her.

Hopefully, if that was true, she would be too backward in her brother's presence to ever mention it.

To Caroline's great happiness Darcy entered the room. His thick dark hair was damp from a bath, and he was dressed in an elegant and formfitting coat. The tan breaches tucked into his boots molded perfectly around the muscles of Darcy's legs, and his strong hands peeked out from the elegant fall of his long sleeves. He was not only the richest man of her close acquaintance but also the most handsome.

"I apologize, I was fencing." Darcy gave that small elegant incline of his head, which showed his perfect gentlemanly self-confidence and breeding. His movements were as smooth as Beau Brummell's but far more masculine and intense.

After the initial greetings Darcy spoke quietly to Georgiana. Instead of following the conversation closely, Caroline's mind wandered while she watched his perfect gestures and the flow of his clothing.

If only she could convince him to marry her, then she would be entirely happy forever....

All of her friends would be so jealous. Miss Churchill would say when they met at the theater, "My, my Mrs. Darcy, that is a *very* handsome man." And Mrs. Carter, whose husband was not worth more than half what Bingley was, would pretend to be pleased for her while seething inside. Even Lady Eleanor would be forced to admit Miss Bingley's connections were now quite as good as her own.

When Darcy suggested she display a new concerto she had learned, Georgiana scurried to the piano. It was certainly for the best that she leave the conversation. The music was beautiful, and both Darcy and Miss Bingley listened attentively while she played.

Caroline knew herself to be quite good — far better than Eliza Bennet — due to the excellent training her school gave her, but Miss Darcy had something more, which practice alone could not give. Perhaps it explained Georgiana's deficiencies elsewhere. The mind only had so much space to develop, and it was vital to receive an education which allowed the faculties to flourish in a balanced manner. Georgiana's genius at the piano had crowded out the more important conversational skills.

When Georgiana finished, the proper allotment of time for a visit had passed. Caroline had sat in the room far beyond a civil half hour. She knew they would not invite her to stay longer, so it was time to leave. She never behaved improperly in front of Darcy. Still, she had dearly hoped to directly assess how he felt about Charles's marriage. To Caroline's great pleasure, Darcy followed her out to wait for the carriage to be brought round.

His conversation was less pleasing than his presence. "I must hope you have chosen to be happy about your brother's impending marriage." Darcy stated that with the air of expressing an uncomfortable truth, not the sardonic teasing Caroline hoped for. At least he had not sought to avoid her or encouraged her to leave.

"How could I be unhappy? The new additions to the family want nothing — Mrs. Bennet is a true wit, and her daughters all proper and well behaved. I shall have Mr. Phillips to approach should I ever need the advice of a minor country lawyer — our family lacked one — and I can look forward to the warehouses of her Cheapside relations being opened to us at discount. I never wished so much for Charles. It is more — certainly more — than I thought possible for my brother."

"I comprehend your sentiments madam, but the marriage will happen no matter your desires. Your brother's honor is engaged — he could not withdraw now, even were he to change his mind, and that is most unlikely. We must hope for the best. Bingley is convinced Jane holds him in great affection, and if she truly does I will be sincerely happy for him. I have agreed to stand with Bingley and will do so with all the happiness and good cheer appropriate to the occasion."

Caroline could not refrain from speaking something of her real opinion, an opinion she knew was shared by Darcy. "No matter how Jane cares for him, it does not make Mrs. Bennet one ounce more respectable. It does not make the family one bit better managed. It does not improve their status at all."

Darcy's face was impassive. What thoughts were hid behind the elegant mask he presented to the world? At last he said, "I have thought a great deal on Bingley's behavior. He perhaps showed great wisdom. In marriage affection and true companionship is important — perhaps it is the only important thing." Darcy shrugged. "The connection will do more to raise the status of the Bennets than it will to lower the status of your brother."

"No matter who the girls marry, they always will have the aunt and uncle in Cheapside. They will still be related to those in trade."

"There are those who can never forget, nor overlook, the stench of trade." Darcy agreed, but there was that in his eye which showed her own relatives were on his mind.

Caroline flushed; her grandparents on her father's side had been entirely respectable, and no one in her family worked now. She was better than Miss Bennet. It was not hypocritical to think so.

Darcy added, "None of us would be wholly safe were the misbehavior of our relations held against us. I no longer think it well to hold the improprieties of a girl's family against her."

The carriage had waited for several minutes already, and Darcy, clearly desirous of finishing the conversation, stepped up to its door, waved off her footman, and opened it for her. He inclined his head in another perfectly executed gesture and said, "It was pleasant to see you. I hope you are well for the rest of the day."

Caroline was horrified: She'd seen how his eye followed and lingered upon Eliza Bennet. His early praise of Eliza's eyes had been to tease Caroline for seeking a compliment. But it also had been sincere. If Darcy no longer thought the status of the Bennets was reason to avoid a connection with them — if he considered following Charles's choice to marry only for affection — then he might decide to marry Elizabeth Bennet.

This was horrible. This was far worse than Charles's marriage. It was a nightmare. A sense of rejection pricked at Caroline's eyes. It had never been likely that Darcy would marry her. He was famously avoidant of women. If fondness for dancing was a certain step towards falling in love, to despise the art was an equally certain step towards avoiding the bounds of matrimony. Still, no other girl had been so close to him, with such good opportunity to appeal to him, as herself.

Since he was disinclined to marry her, could not Darcy remain a perpetual bachelor? And, if he needed to marry, could he not choose anybody besides that self-important country nobody who laughed at Caroline from behind her hand. Despite the inferiority of her wealth and consequence, it was clear Eliza saw her as a cross between an annoyance and an object of amusement.

It would be unimaginably horrible if she became the Mistress of Pemberley. It would — it would be worse than if Louisa died.

If Darcy attached himself to some Earl's daughter, it would make sense. That would be the way the world was supposed to work. But Eliza Bennet! What was so wrong with her that Mr. Darcy would prefer that awful woman, that woman who never showed him any respect?

Caroline had a beauty mark visible on her face — but it was small, and all her friends assured her it only made her appear more striking. And her face was a trifle too thin for fashion. Yet, Eliza Bennet was not a perfect beauty either. She was not like Jane whose face was perfection itself.

She was even thinner than Caroline, due to those endless — and shocking — walks. Her face was not perfectly even, and her hair was far too black. Her eyebrows were poorly trimmed. Eliza did not use her parasol consistently, and her face was unusually freckled. Caroline saw no value in lying to herself: Eliza Bennet was a little prettier. But not enough, not nearly enough to overcome her *many* other deficiencies.

It must not be!

Caroline exited her carriage at the Hurst's townhouse. How could she ensure Mr. Darcy would not marry Eliza Bennet? She suspected Eliza disliked Mr. Darcy. Perhaps that could be worked upon. If Mr. Darcy asked Elizabeth, she would accept him. Only a fool would refuse Mr. Darcy, no matter how they felt. But, if she let that distaste become fully visible to Darcy, perhaps he would withdraw.

Chapter 4

Caroline Bingley returned to Netherfield two weeks before her brother's wedding. For Elizabeth, it was not the happiest event of a happy season. To her surprise, at the first opportunity — when Jane and Bingley went out for one of their walks, and Elizabeth made to follow them with a book — Miss Bingley latched onto her arm and said, "My dear Miss Eliza, you must let me accompany you. Oh! How I adore a good walk. I have needed a good country walk since I returned to London. You shall make the best possible walking companion."

"Of course, Miss Bingley, I can imagine no better walking companion either."

Miss Bingley wore an elegant walking costume. It was made with a thin silk fabric and hung beautifully. However it would be impractical for either a long or a fast walk and would not survive much mud or dust. And her spencer would do little to protect from the December winds.

Elizabeth wondered how Jane would dress now that she would have the money to afford finer fabrics and London designers. They chatted lightly and Miss Bingley did not quickly give clue to what she was about — during the stay at Netherfield Elizabeth learned Miss Bingley was no great walker, unless it was to accompany Mr. Darcy.

At last Miss Bingley asked, after a hard gust of wind, which made her shiver, "We are to be nearly sisters Eliza. We should become the closest of friends as well."

Politeness meant, no matter what Elizabeth's feelings were, only one response was possible. In any case Miss Bingley's — Caroline's — choice to change her manner after so strenuously objecting to the marriage was quite amusing. And sensible. Dear Caroline would not wish to be excluded from the house of the future Mrs. Bingley.

"Of course," Elizabeth smiled sweetly and said, "nothing prevents us from being the best of friends. After all, my sister is to marry your brother — we all are determined to be happy about it. Are we not, Caroline?"

Caroline's eyes tightened, and she returned a perfectly fake smile. "I am delighted — a wedding is such a happy event is it not? And I shall gain a perfect sister. Your sister is so very beautiful — no one would deny *her* beauty. It pains me greatly to say, but one gentleman was so rude as to suggest — no I cannot say it, it was too awful."

Elizabeth raised her eyebrows. Was Miss Bingley attempting to insult her? No doubt Darcy had discoursed at length in private on his distaste of her appearance — obviously he was the gentleman Miss Bingley referred to. Darcy was the sort of gentleman who would make sure all connected to him knew if he disliked the appearance of a woman.

Elizabeth said, "I was made aware, by overhearing, a few months ago — why it was the very night we all met — that it is possible for a gentleman to resist my charms. You need not fear that the pool of my vanity is so shallow that it could be drained by such a thing. I am as impressed with myself as ever. It would be vanity indeed if the existence of one gentleman who I was not handsome enough to tempt hurt me."

The two walked on slowly, following Bingley and Jane. The wind kicked up, flowing freely through the bare branches of the trees surrounding them. Miss Bingley shivered and exclaimed, "It is so dreadfully cold! How do you not feel it?"

"You perhaps should have selected a heavier overcoat."

"It is a clear day, and no wind blew. I did not realize it could become so sharp. Do you always go so far? I remember you went to Netherfield when our dear Jane was sick — as we are now such close friends, I know you will not take it amiss if I admit the mud on the hem of your petticoat was most shocking."

"It was a sign of my affection for Jane — I strode into your breakfast room wholly satisfied with myself. I promise you that. I cannot be intimidated; I rise to every occasion."

"You are most forward." Miss Bingley added with a twist of her mouth, "It is your charm."

The falsity and superficial regard of this interaction delighted Elizabeth. She recalled no conversation that was its equal. Mr. Bennet would be excessively diverted when she related the story.

A further surprise was in store. "Eliza, I owe you apology. While in London several times I visited Mr. Darcy's townhouse, and once, entirely on accident, overheard a conversation between him and a relation" — Miss Bingley lowered her voice and leaned her head close to Elizabeth's — "I know it was improper for me to listen to a private conversation, but at first it was unintentional, and it is far worse for me to share the conversation with you — yet, the lack of honor shown by —"

Miss Bingley pulled Elizabeth to a stop and said, "You must promise me, on your honor as a gentlewoman, not to spread the story further."

A devious smile hid under Miss Bingley's superficial somberness, and Elizabeth did not trust her intentions. Yet, her curiosity was too great to be ignored. In a manner which showed she hoped her words to be ignored, Elizabeth said "My dear Caroline, if the situation is as you say, perhaps you should not share the story. It was gained by subterfuge — even if unintentional."

"Oh, I wish I could be silent! But my conscience, my sense that I wronged you and your friend Mr. Wickham, demand I speak."

"Mr. Wickham!"

"Yes, the conversation I overheard, it related to him. Darcy openly admitted to his relation that he had acted with unjustified cruelty towards his father's godson. Something of great value his father intended for Wickham was withheld out of jealousy. I heard Darcy say it: 'I was jealous, cruel, and unjust. Yet I will not repent of it. Wickham deserves his fate for my father loved him more than I.' I would never have imagined that Darcy could act with such a lack of honor."

"I'm greatly surprised you choose to share this with me." The story seemed odd. Yet — Elizabeth saw poor helpless Wickham, with his love for company and self-indulgent habits, denied the easy life promised for him. Darcy would have held his beautifully shaped head high when he bragged about destroying Wickham's future.

It neatly fit her picture of Darcy that he had sufficient cleverness and self-awareness to see that the source of his anger solely was petty jealousy, and yet a poor enough character to still mistreat his father's favorite.

Darcy was endlessly complex and astonishing: He could not be laughed at, but he was by far the most fascinating character she'd ever attempted to make out. If only his good features had not been paired with such arrogance and viciousness. He would've been a truly exceptional man.

Miss Bingley said, "I attacked your friend solely because I trusted Mr. Darcy. And, I fear, because I knew Wickham to be of modest birth. I had not thought a man of Darcy's breeding and education could be so duplicitous. But he is. That is what made me speak. My conscience could not rest easy till you heard the full truth about Mr. Darcy and Mr. Wickham."

Elizabeth paused a long time to digest Miss Bingley's words before she replied, "I thank you for telling me. It must have been an unpleasant shock to learn the truth about your favorite. This is no surprise to me — I had already known his character to be poor. I accept your apology. Have you attempted to warn Mr. Bingley?"

"Oh! My brother never listens to me!" The irritation in Miss Bingley's voice and pursed lips was genuine. She was probably still angry Mr. Bingley had not listened when she begged him to abandon Jane. "And Darcy is his dearest friend. He would never listen to words against him. And Darcy himself, I was never so shocked as when I heard he was to stand up with Bingley at the wedding. Before Bingley proposed, he had —" Miss Bingley caught herself and looked at Elizabeth.

She paused for a moment of clearly false consideration — during which another stiff breeze led Miss Bingley to shiver and shout, "Lord! It is cold."

At last Miss Bingley said while hugging herself for warmth, "After I have said so much, I must tell you all — Darcy spoke most violently against the marriage. He dwelt first on the disgrace of relations in trade, then he railed against what he called the vulgarity of your aunt and mother. He dislikes your mother very much. He called her a scheming, mercenary fatwit. And you as well. He despises you. He claimed you to be ill bred and rude and argumentative. Your manners are certainly not those of the best refined society, but to say such... It shocked me. And then he insulted your appearance as an argument against my brother marrying your sister."

The gleam in Miss Bingley's eye and the enthusiasm in her voice convinced Elizabeth that she — at least in part — expressed her own insults under the cover of attributing them to Darcy. Miss Bingley waved her hands eagerly, forgetting the cold. "He told us that the thickness of your eyebrows resemble the backside of the horse — an impression not contradicted by the dung like color of your eyes."

Elizabeth's hand came up with some discomfort to rub at her eyebrows, and she attempted to interrupt Miss Bingley, "Really, I don't —"

To no avail, as Miss Bingley continued with glee in her voice, "And your nose, those freckles — your freckles are so shocking. Shocking... He said, 'How does that girl not know she should use a parasol instead of walking about like a wild harridan? Why, I would be horrified if I saw my sister to act so.' And that... beauty mark on your neck, the one you did not properly cover at the Netherfield ball, why he discoursed for a full five minutes about how it unbalances your appearance."

"That is enough! We have nothing further to say to each other. Ever. And you accuse my manners of being ill bred."

Miss Bingley froze, and her ears turned red.

Elizabeth shook her head in amazement as she stepped backwards. Dear Caroline was a marvel. Elizabeth briskly walked down the road towards Jane and Bingley, who had disappeared over the horizon.

Was that mole really so bad? Elizabeth had thought it added a certain... maybe not elegance, but distinction to her neck. And Miss Bingley had her own beauty mark. It was even bigger and less well-placed.

Miss Bingley tried to catch up and called out, "It was Mr. Darcy who accused you of that — not I. Not I."

Elizabeth turned around. "I do not doubt that he also said as much." She made a derisive half curtsey to Miss Bingley. "I must rejoin my sister and new brother. Who knows that they may have gotten up to without my presence?"

Jane and Bingley were only talking as they walked along sedately. They nestled sweetly against each other's arm. Elizabeth stomped up to them, easily catching the meandering couple. "Be honest — I know I can trust you both to be honest." Elizabeth tapped the beauty mark on her neck. "Does this unbalance my appearance?"

THE RETURN

UPON THE ARRIVAL OF Darcy's carriage at Netherfield the day before the wedding, Bingley ran out to greet Darcy. He shook Darcy's hand briskly before he had even exited the carriage.

"It is *good* to see you, very good." Bingley's broad smile radiated cheer. He embraced Darcy the instant his feet were both on solid ground. Darcy stiffened slightly at the sudden close contact, and Bingley stepped back. "Sorry old man, but I am so damned pleased to see you. I am in too good a mood to give a tuppence about proprieties."

Darcy grinned and seized Bingley's forearm and, feeling a little self-conscious, embraced his friend, "No harm. No harm. I am delighted to see you as well."

"Now, I have quite enough happiness for the both of us. There is no need for you pretend enthusiasm about my marriage — I have enough pretense from Caroline."

Darcy clapped his arm around Bingley's shoulder. "It is no pretense. You are my friend, and I wish your happiness. I very much hope my advice was mistaken. You are happy at this point, a month after the engagement. It bodes well."

"I am blissfully happy. I have never been so happy — and my Jane does love me. I was a fool to imagine you able to judge in this matter. A woman's heart is nothing like an investment or a field. You can't directly calculate whether it makes sense. The areas where you are clever and wise are quite likely to lead you astray when attempting to woo a girl." Bingley laughed. "I daresay, someday you will come to me for advice."

Bingley's words struck Darcy. He had tried to push her out of his mind, but he would see Elizabeth again today. Bingley looked extremely happy. Would marrying Elizabeth make Darcy as happy? More and more, he thought Elizabeth might be worth the cost. Marrying her would be a great sacrifice, but she was beautiful and sparkling, and he would have her for the rest of his life.

Darcy replied with mock offense, "I be the one to need advice? That will be an odd day indeed."

"You know you are not perfect. And you are a bit shy with the ladies. Is that the true source of your disinclination for dancing? I have discovered it."

"Nay, that is not it."

Despite his words, Darcy thought there might be something to it. Women pretended to agree with him, while secretly thinking something else. Except for Elizabeth, none showed him their true thoughts. It made him awkward and uncomfortable.

That afternoon they went to a dinner party held at Longbourn to celebrate the marriage the following day. After the wedding itself an even larger feast would be held in Netherfield's ample ballroom.

The Longbourn drawing room was littered with a profusion of shelves and display cases. They displayed china plates and figurines and other proofs that Mrs. Bennet could waste money with ill taste. As soon as they were announced, the brightly smiling Jane ran up to her fiancé. Darcy watched the couple closely. He had promised to feel happy for his friend, but worry remained. Did Jane actually love him?

Bingley was ecstatic and devoted while Jane was radiant. Her eyes lingered on Bingley, and they were both filled with ready smiles and good nature. Darcy was shocked by the difference in Jane's behavior. She glowed with sweet affection.

He had believed Jane likely felt *something* for Bingley, but he had not imagined she felt nearly as much as she should. But no hint of anything but the strongest and sincerest affection showed in her manner. If this be not love, then he had never seen it.

Elizabeth frustrated him. When he approached, she immediately moved to engage herself in a conversation with other women. He was sure it was to avoid him. Their eyes had met before he started to walk over.

Could she not let him speak? Was she disappointed he had not followed Bingley's example? Surely she could not blame him for not lowering himself so far.

They had ended their last conversation on a poor note. She had defended Wickham. An anxious chill vibrated in Darcy's throat. Had Wickham poisoned her further against him? Maybe he ought to have been explicit about some of Wickham's misbehaviors.

No. Had Elizabeth been sensible, she would have trusted him immediately.

She was exquisite. When the company settled around the table for dinner, she sat on the opposite side of the long table, next to Jane and Bingley. A gentleman from the neighborhood whose name Darcy could not recall sat on her other side. As she ate the delicate movement of her hand half hypnotized him. She carefully pulled spoonful after spoonful from the bowl of soup to her mouth. Once the dishes were changed, the way she held her knife to cut the roast seemed perfect. It was the elegant twist of her wrist.

Once or twice their eyes met; there was strong emotion in hers, but Darcy could not interpret it. She would look away and frown. Several times Elizabeth laughed, her head rocking back and forth as she smiled at the person she spoke with.

After the dinner Darcy had no opportunity to seek her out for conversation. A group of the local gentlemen Bingley had turned into close companions dragged him away to drink during his last night as a free man. Darcy barely knew the other gentlemen, so he stood next to a stuffed deer head in Netherfield's billiard room with a glass in his hand and watched the others carouse. He drank a little and thought about Elizabeth.

He could make her play for him every evening. Those delicate hands against his body. Her slippered foot. He *did* need heirs.

She was still beneath him. Mrs. Bennet disgusted him. Miss Lydia would create a scandal. It would be a mistake, and he would regret it. He'd met the Gardiner's briefly, and while they behaved in a well-bred fashion, their situation in life was far beneath his own.

He shouldn't do it. He should not.

After everyone but Darcy was drunk, Bingley decided to refresh his haircut — though it had been done only a week before — to look his best for Jane. It was a clear night with a full moon, so they could safely ride to Meryton to wake the barber.

After Bingley's hair was done, he shouted, "Darcy, you must get it done as well. Otherwise people will think you are one of those long haired poets."

It had been well above a month. Elizabeth might like it more if he had it cut. She probably would. With a wordless grimace, Darcy sat to allow the bald middle aged man to work upon his head.

Elizabeth's poverty and disgraceful relations didn't matter. He was giving up. For once he would do what he wanted, not what he should. It may be a mistake. He might regret it someday. But he would marry Elizabeth Bennet nonetheless. It was how she laughed, that happy, unembarrassed guffaw. That wonderful sound which all the society bred ladies had been taught to disguise.

He couldn't leave her behind in Hertfordshire. He couldn't return to Pemberley and never hear her laugh

Chapter 5

Elizabeth stayed near Jane until Bingley pulled her into the carriage. Jane leaned out the window, and Elizabeth seized her hand tightly. Happy tears came to her eyes as the coachman snapped the reins and clicked for the horses to start moving. The carriage started, taking her dear, dear sister away. Jane's hand was pulled out of her grasp. Her sister smiled back at the crowd, waving her white glove. Jane appeared perfectly happy.

The carriage turned a corner in the distance and disappeared, and Elizabeth looked at the handsome figure next to her. The haircut he'd received the previous day accentuated his aristocratic beauty, and the bright blue of his intense eyes had caught her repeatedly during the ceremony. Darcy appeared impassive with a slight preoccupied frown as he stared down the cobbled lane the carriage had disappeared from.

Miss Bingley exclaimed, "Come, come! Do not all stand out here in the cold, we have an excellent feast set up in the house. Everyone come up."

Darcy handed Elizabeth his arm, and she had no choice but to take it. His expression was somber. No doubt he lamented the happy event. Elizabeth looked at the curl of his lips and the hard shape of his jaw. The contrast of his handsome form and solid mind with his horrid character fascinated her.

She had spent ten minutes this morning covering the beauty mark on the back of her neck, so that he would have no cause to despise her, before she violently washed away the white powder. She would not distort her own sense of beauty to please a man she hated.

His good opinion mattered to her, and that enraged her. She felt ugly and awkward around him. Each time he stared at her with those piercing blue eyes, she flushed and felt sick. He had judged her appearance and found it wanting. She was not handsome enough to tempt him.

She knew herself to be one of the handsomest beauties of the county. That Darcy held this control over her emotions was ridiculous.

Their eyes met again as they stepped into the Netherfield entry hall. A jolt of nervous energy went through Elizabeth. She felt his gaze in her stomach. He studied her face inappropriately long.

Breaking the moment, Darcy spoke in a pleasant tone, "The bride exemplified beauty and grace, did she not?"

"Yes, but Jane is always beautiful — everyone calls her the prettiest girl in the room. No one has ever said *she* was not handsome enough to tempt them."

From the way his expression did not waver, Darcy did not understand her allusion. Elizabeth frightened herself; the seething anger she felt threatened to take control. She had little sleep the night before. She had talked with Jane and Mrs. Gardiner for many hours. Early in the morning, she woke to a vivid dream of Darcy kissing her with those disapproving eyes.

How dare he praise Jane, when he intended to destroy her happiness? Why must a gentleman with such capability be cruel and dishonorable? How *dare* he despise her appearance when he was the most desirable man she had ever known?

She wanted to kiss him and hit him.

Darcy said, "Jane certainly was handsome enough to tempt my friend — from the first Bingley always insisted she was an angel. And," Darcy looked pained as he added, "I believe her to care for him very much. They are a happy and promising couple."

He still wished them separate; his distaste at Jane's affection for Bingley made *that* clear. And yet he pretended to approve. Hypocrite.

Their entry to the ballroom allowed Elizabeth to avoid replying. The large room had been laid out with long tables for the guests, and each spot had a label to identify who was assigned there. The tables were covered with silk table cloths.

Elizabeth's chair was next to Mr. Darcy. They were seated alone around a circular table too large for just two of them. Elizabeth took a deep breath. She would tolerate his presence; she would be polite; and above all, she would not attempt to flirt or gain his good opinion.

Jane and Bingley were to have been at the breakfast and depart afterwards, but they had decided to honeymoon at a seaside resort, which required them to leave immediately to avoid a stop at an inn before reaching their rented lodgings.

It was odd that Caroline had left the initial seating, where the wedding party was separate, intact. Perhaps she really had abandoned her obsession with Darcy and no longer would arrange to be near him at every opportunity.

Elizabeth's melancholy at being left without sensible female companionship returned. With the loss of both Charlotte and Jane, Meryton seemed barren. She should think about Jane's happiness. Jane looked divine during the ceremony. Her sister was happy, and that was all that mattered.

She needed her own husband who could absorb her mind the way Bingley would Jane's.

Mr. Darcy. Elizabeth's gaze involuntarily turned to him, and she imagined him kissing her. It was far more intense, and ridiculously more improper, now that he sat next to her. She tingled with his closeness — she could reach out and rub her hand along his well-muscled leg.

Elizabeth frowned. Odious thought.

Darcy interrupted her reverie. "I can guess what thought absorbs your attention this morning" — for a horrified moment Elizabeth thought he knew her fantasy — "you miss your sister and know she will not be so much with you in the future. You are enough of the philosopher to not be surprised that even the happiest of events brings some sadness. Your closeness is clear — as shown by your walk to Netherfield when she was ill. I was most impressed by your appearance when you arrived half breathless that morning after a three miles walk."

Elizabeth interpreted the real meaning of his smile well enough. Darcy meant to say: "Your petticoats were six inches in the mud, and by the way, do you not think you would be happier had I separated the couple?" Hateful man, mocking her, even after his defeat.

Her concern had been Jane alone; her appearance that morning did not shame her. It was petty of Darcy to mention it. This reminder of his pettiness did little to settle the tingling nerves that pooled in her stomach due to how close they sat.

"Jane's happiness and well-being has always been paramount to me. I have no concern for how I might appear while tending to it." Elizabeth's voice was sharp, and Mr. Darcy looked sideways at her.

"Of course it is. But you must put concern towards your own well-being — especially now that your sister has left the house. There must be much less to attach you too Longbourn now, and your eagerness to leave yourself must be proportionately greater. The example of marriage encourages others to enter the state, and I suspect much of the happiness you have felt at Longbourn must be bound up with Jane."

Did he hint she was unmarriageable? For that was silly. She may not be able to marry very well indeed, like Jane had, but she had already refused one eligible offer.

Rather than replying Elizabeth took several bites from the strawberry tart in front of her. It was delicious. "What think you of the pastries? Miss Bingley went to great effort to select them this morning."

Had Miss Bingley's claimed discovery of Darcy's flaws changed her behavior towards him?

"I am aware. This table is well supplied with my favorites. Miss Bingley works very hard indeed in cases of this sort." Darcy's voice was dry, and Elizabeth could not suppress her smile.

He may be a hateful man, but he was a clever one. That answered Elizabeth's question: Miss Bingley behaved as she always had towards him. At least, Mr. Darcy perceived no change.

Without being able to stop herself — she did not wish to banter with Mr. Darcy — Elizabeth said, "She works hardest in a case where it is clear success is unreachable. But, do not philosophers say the greatest value is often attained from the effort, and not the success? She will have no real cause to repine."

"I had not considered the situation in such a light. I fear *she* will not consider the improvement her endless effort makes in her character a sufficient reward." Darcy caught Elizabeth's eye and added drily, "Alas, if she chooses not to seek the lesson in her failures, they shall not make her wise."

Elizabeth smirked back at Darcy who smiled in a way that made Elizabeth's stomach flutter with butterflies. It was strange how amiable he suddenly was.

Was it wrong to disdain Miss Bingley? If Darcy did as well, surely it was wrong. Yet, it was such fun.

Darcy spoke again, "Bingley's happiness has been on my mind since I heard of his engagement. I feared he acted rashly, yet — despite everything — well — maybe he was not a fool."

Darcy looked uncomfortable and started and stopped as he spoke. He looked away from Elizabeth then back towards her. His face went from pale to red. "I had many reasons. To doubt — that is to doubt Bingley's wisdom. You cannot doubt that, and yet — despite the — despite the manners of your family" — Darcy looked to where Mrs. Bennet sat on the other side of the room jubilantly speaking to Lady Lucas — "such considerations perhaps are not that important."

Darcy's voice steadied. "It has been contrary to my character to approve of imprudent matches. But, maybe one's own happiness should be the paramount consideration in marriage." Darcy caught Elizabeth's eye and added, "This leads me to think I myself have acted amiss. I believe you understand what matter I speak of."

She did not. Elizabeth wrinkled her forehead. Surely Darcy had not changed his opinion about Bingley and Jane, though that was the obvious interpretation of his words. A Darcy who approved of Jane marrying his friend was inconceivable.

He regretted his engagement to his cousin and had decided to jilt her. That was it. Likely the girl was unpleasant and similar to him. A desire to oblige himself, rather than his family, in the choice of wife was a selfish Darcy-like thing to do.

No longer confused, Elizabeth remembered to feel angry about how he insulted her family. Despite their manners? Who was he to insult them? He had no manners. At least Mrs. Bennet never sat thirty minutes entire with a person at a ball without once opening her mouth. Quite the contrary.

When Elizabeth did not reply, Darcy added, "As you may guess, I had counseled my friend against your sister. My honest belief was that she was indifferent to him. Added to the other objections I had to the marriage that seemed reason enough."

"For truth?" Elizabeth did not believe him and did not understand why he wished to defend his behavior. "You believed Jane to be indifferent? And now that you see she is in love with your friend, you think you acted wrongly when you advised him so?"

"Not in the slightest. My counsel was the best I could give. I spoke after careful consideration of what I knew at the time. That I was mistaken in fact does not mean I was mistaken in giving the advice. It does mean I must strive to be wiser in the future. Miss Bennet, you know I openly acknowledge myself to be flawed. An unequal marriage always is an evil, but perhaps the happiness to be found in it is great enough that it is a mistake which should be made."

"You believe Bingley's happiness shall be established by his marriage, yet you still think it is an evil. A mistake. You know it is a happy occasion, yet insist you were right to advise against it." Elizabeth remembered Jane's broken expression after Miss Bingley's cruel letter had been received. "Why would you wish to destroy the happiness of my sister and your friend?"

"Miss Elizabeth," Darcy's tone was placating, "I wish no harm to Jane. I think the best of your sister and desire her happiness, both for her own merit and as she is the wife of my close friend. Yet — I do not believe disappointed hopes, the loss of an attachment of two months duration, could destroy the happiness of a person. Or, I had not believed so."

"My sister feels deeply, her heart had never been touched, had Bingley abandoned her — as you wished him to — she would have been distraught. Have you no heart?"

"You know I have. You must." Darcy's jaw was tense, and he appeared rattled as he looked pleadingly into Elizabeth's eyes. "You misunderstand my meaning. I cannot believe you would blame me for giving my first loyalty to a friend whose well-being has been my concern for many years. You naturally cared for the interests of your sister far more than those of Bingley. It is right that we look first to the interests of those connected most closely to us before extending out into general altruism."

"And what" — the pastries had been replaced by a rich ham, and Elizabeth held her fork with a white knuckle grip and jabbed it towards his face — "convinces you Bingley made a mistake when he married a woman who loves him, and whom he loves in turn. What possible consideration can overcome the importance of affection and similarity of temperament?"

"I did not say Bingley's choice was mistaken."

Elizabeth's jaw dropped open. "Do not quibble semantics. You claim unequal marriages are mistakes. I ask again: What possible consideration can overcome the importance of affection and similarity of temperament?"

"Considerations of prudence and respectability." Darcy angled his chair more towards her. "I will not pretend there are no objections to your family. Disguise is my abhorrence. Only a fool, and you are no fool, would think it proper that every time two young people feel affection towards each other they should become married. Your family lacks basic respectability, and attachment to them must make one hesitate. It must be against the better judgement of any sensible person. Only the strongest and most passionate feelings could overcome such an objection."

"Lacks basic respectability? *You* may think every merchant with a warehouse in Cheapside is to be despised, but my uncle does not deserve your contempt. He is a respectable, well-bred man. I am more proud to claim him than I would be to claim an earl as uncle. He could appear to advantage in any room. I would stake my life on that."

"The status of your uncle is unfortunate, but it was not of him I spoke. I only shook hands with him last night, and again this morning. Yet, from his appearance I believe him a respectable and sensible man. His sister, *your mother*, is not. She is who I spoke of. And your younger sisters who are totally ungoverned. Miss Lydia especially."

They both glanced to the far side of the room where the fifteen-year-old sat surrounded by three officers, giggling, drunk, and brushing her hand down the arm of a red coat.

"Your father does little to control your sisters, and I can admire no man who gives so little care for the well-being of his children. He has held this estate these twenty years. Your dowry should at least be several thousand pounds. If it were so, someone besides a besotted fool whose judgement had been stripped away by passion would be willing to connect himself to your family."

Elizabeth saw red. The tension that she felt at his nearness had turned into a rage that she no longer tried to resist. "I see. You despise us. The failings of my family are great indeed under your accounting. I only wonder that you hesitate at all in your condemnation of Bingley's choice."

"And they are great indeed under your accounting also." Darcy narrowed his eyes. "I have seen you blush when your mother exceeds her usual vulgarity and foolishness. I have seen you avert your eyes. I have seen you wish to be elsewhere. Do not pretend you do not see as clearly as I the imprudence and failings of your nearest relations. Any sensible man should hesitate to form such a connection. You know it. You could not wish for me to lie and pretend otherwise."

"You should not have said it. Had you behaved in a manner befitting a gentleman — unpleasant truths known by all need not be shared. Your friend married my sister, not my mother." She snarled into his face, "One of your cruel, unfeeling, and — and selfish disposition would not understand the difference."

Darcy went white, and the skin around his eyes tightened. He slumped in his chair. He looked hurt; his chin trembled visibly. None of his pride was present.

A spike of sympathy broke Elizabeth's anger. Surely no one had ever spoken so to him. She should not have spoken so to him. Yet he could not really care for her opinion.

He opened and closed his mouth without speaking for a full minute. A sick pit grew in Elizabeth's stomach. She had stepped beyond the bounds of propriety. She had stepped out of the bounds of Christian charity. She should not have said that. She had behaved worse to Mr. Darcy than he ever had to her.

The recollection of Wickham and Mr. Darcy's cruelty towards him — cruelty driven by what Darcy knew to be petty jealousy — snapped Elizabeth out of her pity for him.

At last Darcy asked, "Is this your true opinion of me? What have I done? How have I ever acted that would give you cause to label me cruel and selfish. Perhaps my manner is not so expressive as Bingley's, but I assure you my feelings are deep and strong. Why do you accuse me so?"

"I know of your treatment of Mr. Wickham." Elizabeth could not meet Mr. Darcy's eyes. "You cannot deny that when you stole his inheritance you acted with cruelty towards him."

Darcy was silent for a period of time. "So," he said harshly, "you take an eager interest in that gentleman's concerns. So this is the source of your dislike. He has filled your ears with tales of woe and promises of love. I assure you, Elizabeth, he will not marry you — no matter what he has promised. He is a fortune hunter and wishes to marry wealth."

"Can you not see that your words display again the petty jealousy you hold against him? That petty jealousy which led you to refuse to provide what your father promised? You do not even like me, yet cannot stand the thought I might love the rival for your father's affection. It is petty. Your treatment of him shocked me, for whatever I held against you, pettiness and dishonorable behavior had not been amongst it."

"You believe me to dislike you? You thought I was so small minded and petty as to steal Wickham's inheritance because my father held him in deeper affection than me? You think very ill of me."

Darcy pressed his palm over his mouth and looked away from Elizabeth.

She knew it was impossible that he really cared, but he looked so pained and sad. The sick feeling in her stomach returned. She wanted to touch his face and smooth away the hurt creases about his eyes. But he had mistreated Wickham terribly. "I know it is true. You may wish you acted better — I heard the story not only from Wickham, but from a person wholly unconnected to Mr. Wickham, who overheard you say that you would not give Wickham what he was owed because your father loved him better."

Darcy pulled his eyebrows tight together. "Because my father loved him better? You believe I claimed to deny Wickham what he deserved *because my father loved him better*? Can you not hear how ridiculous that is? No one would speak so. Who claimed to hear me say this?"

"I was sworn not to mention the matter and ought not to have said so much." The tension in Darcy's forehead cleared and his eyes scanned the room. An impulse led Elizabeth to hurriedly add, "I care nothing for Wickham. My interest in him is altruistic. I do not feel — he is too soft — I would not marry him. Not even if he had as much wealth as — as you. I do not have that sort of affection for him. Not at all."

Darcy's eye found Miss Bingley, who watched the two with a feral smirk. When she noticed that their attention had turned on her, she looked away and took quick bites from her plate. She glanced back every few seconds. Elizabeth realized other persons watched them as well.

"Miss Bingley determined to poison you against me. And you believed her, even though the story was fantastical and — and sublimely blockheaded. I thought better of you. I thought you too clever to fall so easily for the lies of one such as her."

Part of Elizabeth wilted. Miss Bingley's story was ludicrous. Obviously ludicrous. Nobody would say that. The other part of Elizabeth's mind rose to the challenge and replied angrily, "You deny it then? You deny that you refused to name Wickham to a living your father had promised for him? Do you deny that you acted dishonorably and with cruelty?"

"There is little point in such an endeavor, as you are wholly decided against me. I have always allowed my general character be shown through my actions and let the world draw what conclusion it may. If you are such a fool as to wholly believe Mr. Wickham's assertions, who am I to meddle with your ignorance? I might ask, however, how you became so set against me that you said after to me unquestioningly believe the accusations of a poor gambler and a jealous shrew."

"Miss Bingley is the sister of your closest friend. Ought I not trust what she says about you?"

"And Miss Lydia is your sister. Ought I trust her if she brings some fantastical story about Charlotte Lucas to me, or should I trust Miss Lucas's superior character? I see you agree with me. Miss Bingley's story only took root because it found fertile ears. So — when did you conclude my character was abominable?"

Darcy's handsome sneer looked down upon her as he waited for reply. "From the very first, Mr. Darcy. From the very first. You have shown from the first moment of our acquaintance a selfish disdain for the feelings of others. I confess I was surprised to hear Mr. Wickham's and Miss Bingley's stories. Yet, they fit with the general arrogance and contempt for those of less consequence you have always shown."

"You have always disliked me. That is good to know. A selfish disdain for the feelings of others? How did I show *that*? What selfish acts have you seen me engage in? You say from the very first of our acquaintance. What abominable act of selfishness did I perform at Mr. Goulding's dinner party when we were introduced?"

"It was not the Goulding's dinner, but at the assembly ball. Bingley approached you during the ball ... while I sat near. He suggested you be introduced to me. But ... but when..." The sick feeling, which curdled in Elizabeth's stomach, transformed into a tight sense of wrongness that grew with every word, and at last she trailed off.

She could not say it. She could not admit that the real source of her dislike was that he had called her tolerable, but not handsome enough to tempt.

A hot flash of shame burned Elizabeth. Was Darcy guilty of anything worse than rudeness?

Darcy's hard eyes bored into her. He sat upright in his fine silk waistcoat. A spotless cravat was tied around his neck. He clenched his strong jaw, and his manner showed discomposure. Next to him Wickham was a flimsy liar. Oh, why had she ever believed Wickham? Vanity and prejudice had turned her into an awful fool.

Why could she not die, or at least faint?

Elizabeth pulled her chin in and hunched her shoulders, trying to become smaller. She blushed so hard it hurt, and tears pricked at the edges of her eyes. "I must apologize — I may have made a foolish mistake. I fear I allowed a small thing to prejudice me against you."

At Elizabeth's apology, Darcy's eyes flashed with triumph. "Ha! You admit you were mistaken. What was the small thing?" Before Elizabeth replied, Darcy's mouth fell open. "Good God! I insulted your looks. You have hated me all this time because you heard me disparage your appearance. Vanity, thy name is woman.

"Bingley wished me to dance; I wished him away. I said the first thing which came into my mind. I suppose I was rude. I apologize I did not speak in glowing terms of your appearance. That I did not praise you endlessly showed enormous selfishness. And vanity — we must not forget vanity — I showed great vanity in not praising your beauty effusively after a half second's glance."

The way Darcy crowed in triumph over Elizabeth's stupidity was all of a piece with his general arrogance of character. Resentment flared back, killing her humiliation. Darcy shook his head theatrically and turned his chair fully toward the table again. "I understand. I understand the awful truth now. For a man to resist your beauty encompasses every other vice as well."

Darcy turned back towards her and asked in a resentful tone, "Is that not so?"

Elizabeth clenched her jaw.

"I insulted your appearance, so I am *selfish*. I insulted your appearance, so I care nothing for the feelings of others. I insulted your appearance, so I *steal*. I insulted your appearance, so I am devoid of all right and proper feelings."

Darcy's voice rose with each sentence, and by the end, he nearly shouted. His sarcasm roused Elizabeth to anger. "It was not that alone. You earned my ill opinion. Do not doubt *that*. You show contempt for the neighborhood. You walk about and stare at us as though you wished not to share the same air. When you insulted me openly, you behaved in the same contemptuous manner you always have."

Darcy sneered and rolled his eyes. "I act as though I am above Meryton society, because *I am*. You know I am. I shall not pretend that they are my equals. I shall not pretend *you* are my equal."

A hot anger clenched in Elizabeth's chest, and for a desperate moment she wished to stab his handsome face with her fork.

Darcy added, "You are my only mistake. I thought you better than this. I thought you my equal in sense — though not consequence. I was wrong. You are as much fool as every other ordinary, stupid girl."

The two fell silent. Elizabeth stared at the roast in front of her. Darcy was right. She *was* stupid, like every other ordinary, foolish girl. She was not clever; she was not insightful; she was not proper. How had she ever let Wickham make her such a fool?

She had thought she was cleverer than others.

Damn Darcy. He sat smugly despising her. He had acted wrongly too. He may be her superior in wit, but not breeding. No true gentleman would have behaved in the manner he did.

Darcy's cold face stared straight ahead. The white fingers of his right hand curled around a fork while the left rested on his lap out of view. His bearing was erect. There was no sign in his manner of anything but self-certainty.

Damn Darcy. Damn him for arrogance, rudeness, and poor manners.

The footman removed their plates and replaced them with slices from the wedding cake. During the disturbance, Darcy glanced around, and Elizabeth caught his eye.

Once the footman stepped away, Elizabeth spoke. She kept her voice quiet so as not to be overheard, but tension coiled in her gut at the effort of suppressing its volume. "I may be a silly girl driven by vanity. But I only returned contempt where contempt was given. Had you acted in a more gentlemanlike manner, I would not have eagerly thought the worst of you. I may be a foolish twit. I may deserve to be despised as much as you despise me. But you — you, sir, are no gentleman."

Elizabeth shredded the slice of cake.

They sat in silence. Elizabeth turned the cake into a pile of crumbs and mushed the crumbs together.

Why was not the day over? After she went home, she would curl up in her bed and never speak to anyone ever again. Elizabeth looked around, but many people's eyes were on her, and Miss Bingley caught her gaze and smirked. She did not look up again.

Another slice of cake, pushed by Darcy's hand, entered her field of view. Elizabeth looked at him, and he said, "I know not what Wickham has said to you, and I know not if you shall believe me, but I did not behave dishonorably towards him. My father hoped for Wickham to enter the church. When he died, the living intended for Wickham was still occupied. At the time he desired to be my clergyman as little as I desired to have him. I gave him three thousand pounds to support his planned study of law. He also had a one thousand pound bequest in my father's will. In exchange he gave up all claim to the Kympton parsonage."

Elizabeth's eyes widened at the sum named; four thousand pounds was a great deal of money. Darcy held up a hand to forestall any response. "That is the truth. Disbelieve it if you wish. At this moment I care not. You may wonder where the money is — I cannot know for certain. Most likely he spent and gambled it away. Such was his habit while supported by my father at Cambridge."

The breakfast was mostly over, and the other guests had begun to leave. Darcy stood and stiffly inclined his head to Elizabeth who rose with him. She gave him an almost involuntary curtsy.

He said in a cold voice, "Good day, madam."

Chapter 6

People glanced at her and talked. She heard laughter, and many of the people smiled. The argument had been too loud and obvious. Both had broken the bounds of proper behavior, but — like always in their interactions — she more than he.

She would not cry. No matter how much she had shamed herself, she would not make a further display. Elizabeth ate the slice of cake in front of her. The flour and sugar had no taste. It took an act of will to force each bite down. Half way through she remembered it had been Darcy's slice initially.

She had prided herself on her cleverness. It had been so clever to take fast dislike to Darcy. *I had thought you better than this.* So had she. He was arrogant and rude, but he was not the fool.

Why had he decided to tell her the story about Wickham?

When enough time passed to leave the ballroom with dignity, Elizabeth went to a small dressing room on the second floor. From the servant's habits during her stay at Netherfield it was likely to be open. She didn't want to be stumbled upon. As soon as Elizabeth felt safe, it was impossible to stop tears.

She'd been such a fool. She had liked Darcy all along, even if he was rude. His eyes had looked so hurt when she said he was cruel and selfish.

He wasn't cruel or dishonorable. He wasn't more self-centered than every other person. He had even approved of her. He said as much, *I thought you were my equal in sense.*

Ha! He was terribly wrong. Why couldn't she have been clever enough to realize Wickham and Miss Bingley lied to her? Why couldn't she have at least been polite?

He had seen himself as far above all the neighborhood, but he was far greater in consequence. Yes, visibly displaying feelings of superiority was a poor way to gain friends, and Darcy was not perfect. But now that she'd made him hate her, she saw him clearer, and she liked his character in the whole very much.

Too silent, too proud. But very clever, honorable, and interesting. More so than any other man she had met.

There was still movement below. She could not reenter Netherfield's ballroom with her face tear-streaked. The water in the copper basin set on a table was freezing. Elizabeth used a towel to carefully wet her face. She looked critically at the fine rosewood mirror. Much of the redness was gone, but the powder and rouge on her face was terribly streaked.

If only Jane were here. Jane would make her feel better. She could not speak to Papa about this. He would make fun of her. She knew she was a fool. She did not need Papa to laugh at her for it.

Miss Bingley entered the room. "Eliza! So here is where you went. Everyone wondered. You had a most fascinating conversation with Mr. Darcy. What ever did you two talk about? I know Wickham's name was spoken."

The fake pleasantness of Bingley's sister oppressed Elizabeth. With a step further into the room Miss Bingley gave Elizabeth's face a critical look. She made little attempt to hide her smile as she said in a sympathetic tone, "Heavens, you poor dear, have you been crying? You have been. Whatever did Mr. Darcy say to you? I'd always imagined you to be made of sterner stuff than that. That cruel man, I am sure he should not have hurt you so. For shame, to push you to tears, and on your sister's wedding day."

"Jane and Bingley were long gone, they shall be above a month on the honeymoon, and they will spend the season in London — this will be a half forgotten story when they return."

"I suppose." Miss Bingley pulled a handkerchief and blue porcelain powder box out of her bag. "Let me help you. We would not wish anyone to think something was amiss."

The day had drained her. Elizabeth couldn't find the energy to stop Miss Bingley as she dipped the handkerchief in the cold water and dabbed at her face. She would need to check any work done by *dear* Caroline before she reentered the ballroom. Miss Bingley was petty enough to intentionally damage her face.

As she rubbed the white powder into Elizabeth's face, Miss Bingley said conversationally, "You can tell me, we are nearly sisters. You took my words amiss the other day. I *do* want us to be friends. And you know I am aware of Mr. Darcy's faults — I told you of them myself."

"Why did you lie to me about Mr. Darcy?"

Miss Bingley laughed, a triumphant sound. "I lie to you? That is a horrid accusation. Why would I do that?"

Elizabeth stepped back and slapped away Miss Bingley's hands. "Do not regard the question, I cannot truly care. But if I find you lied about my sister, I swear I will find way to revenge her."

"Dear Jane! Why — how could you even dream that someone would mistreat her?" Elizabeth wished to seize the gilt chamber pot hidden in the corner of the room and dash it against Miss Bingley's head. "Oh, you need not worry for your sister." Miss Bingley wrinkled her nose in disgust. "She is my sister as well."

Elizabeth believed Miss Bingley. She had no motive to harm Jane. Elizabeth still hated Miss Bingley.

"It is too good to hide. It is too good." Miss Bingley smiled happily in response to Elizabeth's cold stare. "It may be imprudent, but I shall tell you — I *wish* to tell you — the purpose of my scheme. After how angry Mr. Darcy was as he left, it can hurt little. His good opinion once lost, is lost forever."

Elizabeth blanched. He would always remember her as the foolish girl who hated him for insulting her beauty. It was painful to consider.

Someday — someday she wished Darcy to think better of her. Elizabeth remembered when they were at Netherfield. His intense blue eyes: *I cannot forget the follies and vices of others so soon as I ought, nor their offenses against myself. My temper would perhaps be called resentful.*

Elizabeth's emotions lashed back the other direction. How dare he? Even if he hated her forever, it was no loss to her. She had cause to consider him meanly. As much cause as he had to despise her. He had no right to disdain her. None. He'd been rude to her and everyone else. He insulted Mama and Lydia and Papa — everyone in her family but Jane.

Miss Bingley laughed maliciously. "You are such a fool. He admired you! You stupid girl. You never noticed that he admired you — it was obvious. He was torn between attraction and being repulsed by your family and situation. And, with my brother's marriage, the attraction may have won."

"It is such a joke." Miss Bingley's smile was malicious. "Mr. Darcy, one of the most sought after bachelors in England, and you, a country nobody, could have had him if you'd not been such a silly fool. Now, after you praised his steward's son to the heavens, he must be disgusted with you. There is no chance for you now."

Was it true that Darcy had admired her? It must be. Miss Bingley would not be mistaken on a matter of this sort. Elizabeth's emotions were like a driverless cart, veering suddenly one direction and then the other. She felt loss and desire. What if... was it possible he would have married her?

The regret was smashed by the memory of Darcy's ringing voice: *I shall not pretend that they are my equals. I shall not pretend* you *are my equal.*

Elizabeth pulled her chin high. "I'm certain you are wrong. Further, I do not care. Even were he to lower himself so far as to offer for me, I could never attach myself to an arrogant man convinced of my inferiority and the inferiority of my family and my friends. Your lies were unnecessary. And of no value: He shall never marry you. He can see what sort of a woman you are."

Chapter 7

All this time she had hated him. How had he so misunderstood her manner?

The skin around Darcy's eyes was tight, and his chest reverberated with resentment. Maybe he hadn't always behaved as a gentleman ought. Maybe he had rudely insulted her and her family, but he cared less and less. It was impossible to relax into the velvet cushions of his carriage. He had almost decided to marry that girl. And she — she hated him. She really hated him.

She was a fool, a damned fool. She would never know what she lost due to her... stupidity. Her stupidity had destroyed his regard. Elizabeth Bennet was stupid. She was a foolish girl, solely controlled by her own vanity and not worth thinking upon.

Darcy looked out the windows at the passing timber framed buildings of a small market town.

It was breeding. He had thought Elizabeth Bennet was better than the rest of her awful family. Well, breeding would show true.

He was Fitzwilliam Darcy of Pemberley, heir to one of the best names in the country. It had been beneath him, far beneath him, to ever consider the impoverished daughter of a minor country squire. He should only regret the weakness that allowed the idea to take hold.

Flat icy fields and a succession of hedges went speedily by the window. The interior of the carriage was paneled in mahogany and kept pleasant and warm by expensive contrivances. The springs were the absolute best money could purchase. He was comfortable and happy and enjoyed luxuries Elizabeth Bennet would never know.

They overtook a farmer walking along the road. He respectfully doffed his cap to mark the passage of one of his betters.

How dare she! How could she think so little of him? He was not selfish, he was not dishonorable, and he *always* acted in a gentlemanlike manner. He was in every way superior to her and her family. *She* was unladylike. No true lady would have spoken so. She was gullible and vain.

She had called him selfish. Did she know nothing of the ways that he had protected Bingley's interests? How he always sought to be fair to others, even if it meant he suffered losses? Why, he had spent more than twelve hundred pounds the previous year on charitable causes. And that did not include the poor rates.

Selfish? Ha! He was the very opposite of selfish.

Yes, he had maintained distance from those in Meryton. But that was his proper right as a gentleman of great consequence. He had not shown contempt for the neighborhood.

Darcy winced; his inner judge refused to let the untruth pass. He had disdained their country manners and entertainments. Maybe he had felt *some* contempt.

Well, the neighborhood had deserved it. Elizabeth proved *that*. He had never behaved in an ungentlemanlike manner. Only a vain, angry girl could think he had.

Darcy's townhouse was a large modern building in Grosvenor Square. Darcy entered the vestibule and leaned his forehead against the wall. How had he been so wrong about what she thought? How had he been so wrong about her character? His judgement and perceptions were clearly faulty.

As Darcy walked towards the stairs, so he could reach his private apartments, Georgiana ran to greet him. "Fitzwilliam, I had not expected you to return for several hours more." She stumbled to a stop and asked, "Are you well? Did something ill occur at Bingley's wedding? What is the matter?"

Darcy forced himself to smile for Georgiana. "Nothing important went amiss. And the wedding itself, it was beautiful. Bingley smiled the entire time, and Miss Bennet was radiant. I said to myself, as the carriage took them away, that they appeared to be the happiest of couples. It was as perfect as a wedding could be." From Georgiana's worried expression his words were unconvincing. Darcy added, "I am well. But I do need to rest. I promise you, I shall tell you everything about the event tonight."

Darcy calmed once he entered his room. It was decorated precisely to his taste. The heavy bookshelves were packed with agricultural treatises, works of history, Latin and Greek classics, and volumes of poetry. A miniature of his father and mother, painted when they were a young couple, sat on the desk.

Darcy stared at the faces of his parents before he selected a collection of Cicero's letters from his shelf and sat down. Perhaps the wisdom of the great orator would calm and settle his mind. Darcy leaned back in the chair and poured himself a double full tumbler of brandy. With a smile, he opened his drawer and pulled out a bag of expensive chocolates. He popped one into his mouth and chewed slowly.

For half an hour Darcy worked through the passages of Latin. He had grown a little out of practice since leaving university to take on the management of Pemberley, and it was not so easy to interpret the meaning of each sentence as it had been years earlier.

Elizabeth's accusations intruded: *Your cruel, unfeeling, and — and selfish disposition. I only returned contempt where contempt was given.* He pushed the memories away.

Damn! It was impossible to focus. Try as he might to calm himself, he was still most unhappy about the conversation with Elizabeth.

Was he ungentlemanly? Had he really given offense? It was certainly true he had not cared whether he did. He had been above his company. Now safe in his room and partially relaxed, Darcy could acknowledge that his behavior had lacked something.

He winced with embarrassment as the assembly ball flashed clearly into his mind. He saw himself insult her. He'd caught Elizabeth's eye — though she was not Elizabeth to him yet — his words had been something like: "I will admit she is not plain, but she is hardly handsome enough to please *me*."

He knew she could hear. He had wished to give offense due to his ill mood that evening — it had been the first time he was properly in company since Ramsgate. Had he really wished to insult Elizabeth?

He had not acted as he ought. That was clear. It had been ungentlemanly to say *that*. He had behaved in an ungentlemanly manner the first time they interacted. It had been selfish to peevishly injure the feelings of an unknown lady due to a poor mood.

Darcy rubbed his forehead and looked out the window. Despite the lateness of the season and hour, a few persons walked vigorously along the road, and a man and woman decked in heavy coats meandered arm in arm through the garden in the center of the square.

He had behaved poorly. Darcy finished his brandy and poured another into the fine crystal glass. He would not drink much, but he needed to mellow himself if he was not to be a bear when entertaining Georgiana later.

There was a lesson: Never insult a lady's appearance when she might hear it. *See, Elizabeth, I can admit my behavior was not perfect.*

She'd hated him. Every time Elizabeth spoke with that arch smile and her sparkling eyes she had thought, "This man does not think I am handsome, so I shall be as disagreeable as I can."

The situation was absurd. It was ridiculous. The woman he'd formed an infatuation towards had hated him because she thought he found her ugly. Well, it had been foolish of her to pay no attention to his later behavior and manner.

Darcy grimaced and slid down in his chair. That gave himself too much credit and Elizabeth too little. She'd accused him of showing contempt to the neighborhood. He'd felt contempt. Perhaps his icy politeness was *proper*, but it was no surprise she did not like him. He'd not like someone who openly showed a disdain for his friends and family.

Before it had all gone wrong, when he tried to hint he wanted to marry her, he'd talked about how poor the manners of her family were.

What had Elizabeth said? *Unpleasant truths that are known by all should not be shared.* Elizabeth had, from his behavior *after* he'd insulted her beauty, perfectly good reason to dislike him.

Well, she was still a fool. She admitted *that* herself.

She probably behaved like every other foolish girl with a man she liked. No doubt, when she was with Wickham, she acted the way Miss Bingley did with a rich man. She probably fawned over him, laughed at his empty nothings, and agreed with everything he said, no matter how silly she thought it.

Worse, maybe she found Wickham's inanity clever: *Oh, Wickham, tell me more about how that mean Mr. Darcy stole from you! I am wild about you, even though you are not as tall and rich as he!*

That was not fair. Darcy finished his brandy. The woman who shouted at him this morning might have been Wickham's dupe, but he could not imagine her slobbering over him like a dog. He had observed enough of her behavior with others to know her manners were always light and playful. She may not have flirted with him, but her charming manner was not solely due to dislike.

She was a fool, but he was a worse one.

I only returned contempt where contempt was given. He had thought meanly of Elizabeth, of her family, and of her friends. He had held her in contempt.

He had fallen short of his own ideals.

Elizabeth's forthright anger taught a valuable lesson, and he should thank her for it. In the future he would strive to think more kindly of all persons and less highly of himself.

Beyond that, he was done with her. He had hesitated for the wrong reasons. He did not need money, and if he were happy in Pemberley, it could make little difference to him what they did in Meryton. How could it actually matter if he called a tradesman uncle?

But Elizabeth loathed him, and *he* no longer thought her a flawless creature. It had been blockheaded to fancy himself in love. He had not known her well enough to enter marriage.

He only hoped they could meet civilly when he encountered her as Bingley's sister.

Darcy pulled out the watch he always kept inside his desk. Dinner was in only another hour. It was time to bathe.

Georgiana was eager to hear about the wedding, and as soon as they both sat in the drawing room after dinner, she asked, "What did the bride wear? You promised you would give me a detailed description of the wedding."

Darcy had made such a promise before he set off for Hertfordshire and had tried to impress details of the ceremony onto his mind, so he could relate them to Georgiana. "Miss Bennet wore a silvery silk dress. It was most elegant. Her shawl was white with this embroidered flower design. The flowers were made with yellow thread. Miss Bennet wore the shawl like so," Darcy gestured with his fingers trying to produce a picture while Georgiana laughed.

Darcy added, "She wore a cap, which I thought pretty. The cap was more gray than white, and it had a great deal of lace — you shall have to meet a lady who was present to get a proper description of the lace, it's amount, and type."

"No, do not disparage yourself." Georgiana immediately reassured her brother, "You are an exemplary describer. What did Mr. Bingley wear?"

Darcy frowned and looked to the side. Elizabeth's face and figure had been so pretty she near glowed in his eyes. Their gaze had met many times. Her eyes had been intense. He had been sure it meant she desired him. He had wondered what she would look on their wedding day.

It was odd. This morning he had seriously contemplated marriage, and now he felt nothing of the sort. What did she think about their argument?

Georgiana jostled his arm. "So Mr. Bingley was nondescript? I begin to fear I will need to ask Miss Bingley."

"No — my mind had wandered, Bingley wore a black coat with long tails. Bingley's pantaloons were white as well. With a hint of yellow. And, of course, he wore a white cravat. He'd had his hair cut the day before and forced me to join him."

"It is a handsome look."

"What about Miss Bennet's — I mean Mrs. Bingley — what about her sister? Wasn't it Miss Elizabeth who was her bridesmaid? The one who walked three miles in the mud to care for Mrs. Bingley when she fell sick?"

Darcy stomach twisted. He saw her blazing eyes as she spoke: *Had you acted in a more gentlemanlike manner.*

"She wore a blue dress, her hair was arranged in curls that fell around her face. She had done something with her eyebrows to make them thinner… Some pink rouge was rubbed into her cheeks."

Georgiana looked curious — perhaps his detailed description of Elizabeth's face gave her ideas that would have been true this morning. "It was a beautiful ceremony; the parson had been at Longbourn since before Miss Bennet was born, and it clearly pleased him to see the girl well-settled."

Georgiana asked more questions about the ceremony and afterwards. Darcy's replies became vaguer as his thoughts refused to abandon the argument with Elizabeth.

"Georgiana, what do you think of Miss Bingley?" Darcy spoke abruptly, ignoring the preceding topic.

Georgiana looked at him with a deep frown and in an endearing gesture bit her finger as she thought. If Mrs. Annesley was present, she would have attempted to break his sister of the habit. Darcy only smiled.

"She is a fine lady," Georgiana began cautiously. "She always praises me and is most attentive." Georgiana ended in a rush, "You are far better than me at judging people's intentions. You would never make such mistakes as I have." Georgiana frowned. "I mean I shall think as you do of her."

"What do you believe I think of her?" Darcy held up his hand as Georgiana opened her mouth. "I can tell you do not like her; that is good. I wish you to be cautious in her presence. She wishes to marry me, and I have learned she will lie in the pursuit of her goal."

Georgiana gasped. "You mean she *is* like Wickham!"

Darcy opened his mouth to deny that claim. Miss Bingley was a well-educated lady with a large dowry. Simply because she wished to marry well.... Miss Bingley had lied in the most ridiculous manner for the cause. Maybe the comparison was apt.

"I should not have said that. She is the sister of a friend and a real lady, unlike me."

"What? You are a real lady. A far better one, I daresay, than Miss Bingley – her behavior *is* similar to his. I do not think we shall be at home for her in the future."

"You need not coddle me Fitzwilliam. I know how you see me — I know that you expect me to misbehave if ever given an opportunity. And you are right — I should never have let that horrid, horrid scoundrel — I can't believe I was so foolish, and naïve, and bad —"

Georgiana began to cry, as Darcy asked in surprise and confusion, "Whatever gave you that idea?"

"It's why you would not let me be in a crowd for Bingley's wedding. You are afraid of what I might do if people who are not our intimate acquaintances could see me. I know you've been kind by keeping me with you and spending so much time with me since it happened — but you need not pretend you trust me. I know I deserve your scrutiny, but you'll see. I will never do anything wrong again. You'll see."

He had been remarkably foolish. Darcy pulled his crying sister into his arms and stroked her hair as he tried to figure out what to say to undo the damage he had — stupidly — done to her. He had believed he knew what she thought and then proceeded to make a mess of things.

He'd also believed he knew what Jane and Elizabeth thought. He *always* was mistaken when he interpreted a woman's thoughts. Much as Elizabeth's rejection hurt, Georgiana's well-being was his responsibility, and he'd failed her once already. He *couldn't* allow that to happen again.

"I do not think that Georgie," Darcy said when she ceased to sob. "I am proud of you, you are becoming more elegant and pretty every day. I know you would not behave so foolishly again — you know what is right, and I trust you to do it. The fault was mine, and Wickham's — and I suppose Mrs. Younge's. Not yours. I don't blame you at all."

"You should. I was foolish: He told me I was pretty and mature and clever — and I believed him. I knew all along an elopement was wrong — but I would have done it."

Darcy sighed. "He deceived our father as well. You were fifteen; you do not realize how very young that is. I will give you leave to think you ought to have behaved a little better, but not to think you should behaved perfectly."

Georgiana sat up so she could look at his face, and Darcy flicked her nose. "Why do you think you had a companion and were not yet out? It is because fifteen-year-olds cannot be trusted to make serious decisions. You behaved no worse, and perhaps a little better, than most girls your age would when their appointed guardian had been subverted."

"If you are not scared I would embarrass you, why did you not let me go to Bingley's wedding?"

Darcy still worried about what might happen if he discussed Wickham with Georgiana. "Perhaps I made a mistake. I did not wish to remind you." His face went stiff, and he said in a cold voice, "Mr. Wickham is in Hertfordshire. He enrolled as an officer in the militia regiment stationed in Meryton. I had not wished to risk you meeting him."

"Oh." Georgiana asked in a small voice, "You thought he might convince me to run off with him?"

"No!" If he had spoken more with Georgiana and not been so scared to talk about Wickham with her, she would not have developed these ideas. "I did not fear *that*. I trust you. I know you would act as you ought. I thought you still heartbroken over his betrayal and that it would hurt you were you to see him again."

"No! I hate him — I was naïve and foolish, but it was terribly wrong of him to pretend he loved me. I know it was fictitious. He only wanted my fortune — why else would somebody attempt to gain my affection?"

Darcy missed his parents. Mother would have known what to say to Georgiana.

Georgiana took the way Darcy froze as agreement. "See, you know the only reason a man would wish my affection is due to our wealth. I wish I were penniless."

"Do not be ridiculous. Such a wish is melodramatic and silly. You are a kind, elegant and highly accomplished lady. Only a fool would not see your worth."

Darcy's sister sat tall and pulled away from the arm he had had around her shoulder. "I am backward in company, and besides our family, other girls only seek me out to become closer to you. And Wickham only — if I had no dowry he would not have treated me so."

Georgiana allowed Darcy to pull her close again, and she started to cry. He let out a long breath — Wickham lied to penniless girls all the time. That was a topic impossible to discuss with his little sister.

Darcy murmured comforting nothings to Georgiana. He needed to fix her unhappiness, but could find no words which would work.

His mind drifted back to Elizabeth. Something in her manner when she denied affection for Wickham had convinced him she was sincere. Elizabeth had called him soft. Darcy smiled. She may be his dupe, but she was not his conquest.

He shouldn't care.

When Georgiana stopped crying Darcy asked, "Do you feel better?"

Georgiana nodded her head, and Darcy said, "It is not just our family relationship which makes me think well of you. Were you to act as — as Miss Bingley acts, I would care for you as my sister, but I hardly could *approve* of you."

Georgiana giggled wetly. "Did she really lie to you?"

"Not to me, but about me." Darcy added, grave and unhappy, "Her lies were believed."

"Oh." Georgiana's voice resonated with a quiet sympathy, and she squeezed Darcy's hand.

The two had been silent awhile when Georgiana suddenly spoke, "Do not think so ill of Miss Bingley's victim. It is often easy to be deceived."

It was partly his fault in any case. He said his general character should have protected him from such stories, but he saw himself during the weeks in Meryton. All he did was stand about the edges of rooms and think upon how great his consequence was. Hertfordshire was far from Derbyshire where his reputation was well-established.

"You are right. I should not."

Darcy yawned. He had been awake quite late the night before, and in a few minutes more he and Georgiana stood to return to their rooms.

As they parted Darcy called out, "Georgie, I know I —"

Darcy swallowed, feeling very uncomfortable. "It is hard for me to say such things, but I — I am glad — most glad, you are my sister. I always have been. And — this is not only my opinion as your brother, but as someone who lives in society and has seen many young women — you are growing into a very fine lady. There is nothing important I would wish changed about you."

Georgiana ran up and gave him a fierce hug that convinced Darcy he somehow had said the right thing.

Chapter 8

While Elizabeth managed to avoid company the evening after the wedding, she needed to sit with her family the next morning at breakfast. Lydia laughed at her and exclaimed again and again, "La! What a joke! To quarrel with that dull Mr. Darcy. What a joke."

Mama was worse.

"Lord!" She cried out to Lady Lucas when her friend arrived to commiserate on both losing a daughter so close in time together, "You saw my Lizzy put down that horrid ill-mannered man. Was it not good of her to do it? Miss Bingley said Mr. Darcy tried to keep our Bingley from marrying Jane. Horrid man — Lizzy will not say what they argued about — but he slunk off defeated. I've never seen such an arrogant man give up the ground so."

Elizabeth blushed and blushed at her mother's foolishness. Lady Lucas turned a more critical eye upon her and said, "It was quite the spectacle — nothing of the sort happened after my Charlotte was married. Though — Lizzy, was it wise to argue with him so? I heard from my dear son, Mr. Collins, about how grand his estates are. But nevermind, we all know you never look towards your interest first. It is a virtue, and one all those around you must be pleased at."

Maria Lucas had called at Longbourn with her mother and cried out, "Oh Lizzy, do tell us — please, do tell us! What was it about? I am so terribly curious. Was he so terribly angry about Bingley marrying your sister? I heard you use our dear Wickham's name. Did you rail at him for stealing Wickham's inheritance?"

Elizabeth plastered a fake smile on her face. "Really, Maria, you would hardly wish me to reveal what was said in a private conversation?"

Lydia prevented Maria's answer by exclaiming, "La! I certainly would. It would be such a joke! Besides, your conversation was hardly private — did you declare your undying love for our handsome Wickham, and Darcy stalked away because he realized how despite his ill humor he would not prevent the dashing officer from finding happiness?"

"I do not care a whit for Mr. Wickham. *Not a whit.*"

There was a startled moment of silence. Lydia had a mischievous smile and with a lilting voice said, "La, methinks the lady doth protest —"

"Enough!" Elizabeth stood. "Do *not* suggest such things. I will have you spread no such stories about. I would suggest you behave more cautiously around your *dear* Mr. Wickham. I will say this — I have grave reasons to doubt his character."

Elizabeth exited the room with a poor imitation of intact dignity. She heard Lydia's voice cry out, "La, this is such a joke. She likes dull Mr. Darcy now!"

Elizabeth stalked to the side door. She went out, slamming the door shut, without putting on her pelisse and gloves. She passed next to the window of her father's study. Their eyes met, and he raised his eyebrows sardonically and gestured for her to join him. Papa had gone home immediately after the departure of Jane and Bingley's carriage, so at least he'd not seen their argument. But by now he had heard enough of the story to laugh at her.

She did not wish to talk to him. She was already ill tempered, and he would be displeased that his most sensible — ha! — daughter had made a spectacle of herself on such an important occasion. Worse, he would make her an object of sport. Elizabeth entered the study by a side door. It would do no good to put off the interview.

Mr. Bennet smiled jovially and fitted a piece of paper into the book he was reading. He wore the thick woolen cap he preferred during the winter to keep his ears warm and his reddish-brown dressing robe. He waved his hand at the narrow brown sofa kept in the room. "Sit down. Please, sit down."

Her face flaming with embarrassment and anxiety, Elizabeth settled onto the sofa cushions.

Mr. Bennet made a dramatic production of it as he pushed his spectacles down his nose to peer over them at her. "Lizzy, tell me, what horrid crime of Mr. Darcy's led you to quarrel so publicly with Bingley's rich friend?"

Elizabeth scowled. Mr. Bennet smiled. "That is a most ferocious expression. Why, I have been deluged with reports of your behavior. Surely you would expect me to demand explanation of what you were about. Don't be Missish — do tell me."

Elizabeth rubbed her hand back and forth on the couch and examined the pattern in the rug as she decided what to say. "Several sources had informed me that Mr. Darcy had been vocally opposed to the match, so when he commented on how happy Jane and Bingley looked together, I asked him to explain himself."

"Capital! Capital. You decided to confront the rich man with his hypocrisy, and I daresay, since your mother tells me he slunk away in complete defeat, you succeeded at making him appreciate the errors of his way. A good job of it Lizzy, very good. Men of that sort rarely listen. And you would not have been able to pick a more momentous occasion than after your sister's wedding for your triumph over that unpleasant man. Pray, how did Mr. Wickham's name end up mixed in this?"

"Must you make sport of everything?" Elizabeth said in exasperation and began to cry.

Mr. Bennet was startled by her tears and rose from his armchair to sit at Elizabeth's side. "My dear, if it has been that distressing, do tell me what is the matter. Your real unhappiness can never be a matter of fun for me."

"It ought to be — I deserve it to be. You will laugh when you hear how stupid and silly and vain I have been."

"Whether you deserve to be laughed at or not, it will not be by me, not until you can look back on it with amusement yourself." Her father's shoulder smelled comforting, and Elizabeth took a deep breath when Mr. Bennet embraced her. "Now, how were you silly and vain? For I am sure you were far too clever to be stupid."

Elizabeth sighed. "I was not clever when I chose to dislike Mr. Darcy for so slight a cause."

"So slight a cause? Why, you are not the only young lady who would declare eternal enmity over such a *serious* cause as being declared merely tolerable."

At Elizabeth's forbidding expression, Mr. Bennet apologized, "I had promised not to make fun; my habits have led me astray — it will not occur again."

"He was rude, but — that would not have bothered me had he not injured my vanity. Then everything, every interaction, I used to justify my dislike of him. It did not matter what he did — he was that hateful, odious man. And I believed those awful stories about his behavior and character from Miss Bingley and Mr. Wickham."

Mr. Bennet raised his eyebrows. "Miss Bingley? I knew that Mr. Wickham wished to blacken Darcy's character, but I imagined Miss Bingley to be quite, ah, intentioned towards him."

When Elizabeth made no immediate reply, Mr. Bennet said, "So you chose to think the absolute worst of Mr. Darcy, encouraged by a woman who hopes to marry him and the son of his father's steward. And you did not have any thought these stories might be false, as you knew him to be the most horrid sort of person — proven by his having declared you not handsome enough to tempt him. Lizzy, you view yourself rather more the fool than you are."

"You do not understand — he did not dislike me!"

All of Elizabeth's self-recriminations poured out suddenly. "He admired me. That was why Miss Bingley told me that ridiculous story, and his feelings are obvious now that I know. That was why he always watched me and sought conversation — it was not to look for imperfections, but because he liked my company. I think he wished to marry me."

Elizabeth's misery returned. "And now he must hate me. I called him selfish and cruel and insulted him horribly. It was cruel of me — I saw how much it hurt him. He looked so shocked. Now he knows what a petty, vain fool I am. And I realize I liked him very much. He is not a horrid man; his only failing is that he is too quiet among strangers and has too low an opinion of those whose status is lower than his."

"Wait —" Mr. Bennet blinked at her. "You mean to say that, after insulting Mr. Darcy horribly to his face, you decided you had an affection for him."

"No! Perhaps." Elizabeth wailed, "I don't know."

Mr. Bennet wore the solemn face he showed when he was amused but did not wish to reveal it to the object of his amusement. She pointed and accused him, "You said you would not laugh."

Her father pressed his lips tightly together and looked away. "You are right. This is not a matter of sport because you are distraught and confused. It would be unfatherly to think it amusing while seated next to you. Perhaps I can help you see what you feel. I can hardly understand your claim to like him, for as everyone knows, he is a proud, unpleasant sort of man — a point you admitted yourself merely a minute ago — so why do you nonetheless like him?"

Elizabeth cried out, "I was such a fool! Now that I know he spoke out of friendship and even admiration, I realize that when we conversed, he was perfectly amiable. Amongst those he likes he is a pleasant, if disputatious, man. I thought he was rude, but I relished our conversations about the difference between country and city or how desirable it is to be easily persuaded by friends. He is proud, that is true, but he has great reasons for pride."

"Besides, he is so tall, and his face so very handsome, and I want him to —" Elizabeth's cheeks flamed hot as a fire, and she stumbled to a halt. She absolutely would not describe to her father how Mr. Darcy's presence made it impossible for her to turn her eyes away from him, how simply touching his arm would give nervous jitters in her stomach, and how she had dreamt for the past month more nights than not of him touching her intimately.

The way Mr. Bennet raised his eyebrows and peered at her made her suspect that he knew *exactly* what was in her mind. She looked down to avoid his gaze. Her blush creeped down her neck and onto her chest. This was the most awkward moment, including after the argument yesterday, in her entire life.

"Well," Mr. Bennet drawled out the word very slowly. "I have solved the mystery of why you like him. And why you took his insult so much to heart."

It was impossible for Elizabeth to feel more embarrassed, so Mr. Bennet's suggestion that she only took Mr. Darcy's indifference to heart because she had been attracted to him improved her mood. She had behaved like the fox with the grapes in Aesop's fables, disdaining what she could not have. It was a common, ordinary failing. She may be as much a fool as every other girl, but she was not more foolish.

Elizabeth frowned at her father with mock annoyance. "You had promised not to make sport of me. I believe you just did."

"It did cheer you — why then are you not sure you like him?"

"Oh, I do *like* Mr. Darcy, but not enough to regret him. He is too arrogant — I could never marry a man who disdained my family and birth, no matter how much I may appreciate his virtues. He should not have insulted Mama and Lydia; he thinks the marriage between those of unequal stations is always an evil. He would never make an offer to a creature with so disreputable a family as to have relatives in trade and a vulgar mother."

"He insulted your mother during your conversation?" Mr. Bennet asked with a smile. "That was quite rude of him. You have less to be ashamed of than you imagine, for a man who would openly insult you and your relations has no right to complain when insulted in turn."

Elizabeth felt a flare of anger at Darcy suddenly. She clenched her fist. That was right. He no doubt thought she was a fool, and she was, but he probably believed he'd never behaved ill. And he had. He didn't have a right to hold her in contempt. She needed to feel angry, otherwise she would cry again.

Was their argument the worst mistake of her life?

Mr. Bennet embraced her. "Don't look like that Lizzy. It feels awful, but things turned out for the best. I recall how your Mr. Darcy appeared when you two danced at Netherfield, at the end of November. He might have asked you despite believing it to be a mistake."

The humor normally in her father's eyes was absent, "Youthful passion drives men to act against their better judgement and contrary to their normal character. But those feelings rarely last, and when they are gone, what is left is regret. It is a poor basis to build a life together. I beg you never to enter marriage under such circumstances. I would not wish to see you made unhappy for life with a husband who resented the marriage."

Elizabeth remembered a snatch of the conversation. *An unequal marriage always is an evil.* Her father was right. She didn't want to marry a man who thought himself so far above her that their connection must be a mistake.

THE RETURN

"Mr. Darcy used almost those very words!" Elizabeth flushed. "It was when he insulted Mama — he claimed that a connection to us would be against the better judgment of any sensible man and that only the strongest passion could overcome those objections." Elizabeth's hand flew to her mouth. "He actually would have asked me, and I would have needed to refuse him. And perhaps I wouldn't have. Maybe it is for the best. I only wish I'd not given him good reason to despise me."

She had acted inappropriately and been a fool. But at least as she had not destroyed her best hope for a happy marriage. She could not have married Darcy anyways. "I acted a fool, but it really was for the best. I shall take the lesson and never judge so quickly in the future. But I have no cause for prolonged unhappiness."

Mr. Bennet smiled at her. "I am relieved to see your reaction is so sensible."

Elizabeth embraced him. "Thank you Papa."

He patted her shoulder a bit uncomfortably and smiled. "There, there sweet girl." At last Elizabeth released him, and with an affectionate look in his eyes, he left the sofa to return to his chair and book.

Elizabeth smiled at the middle aged figure of her father. He was a little short and had put on weight over the years. He tended to smell of port and tobacco; he was indolent and should manage her sisters and mother better. Darcy was correct that he should have accumulated a dowry for them. He wasn't perfect, but she loved him dearly.

COLONEL FORSTER GREETED Elizabeth when they sat next to each other at a dinner party, "I hear you defended the honor of one of my officers the other day Miss Bennet."

This was the worst part. They all thought she was in love with Wickham and had done something wonderful. Except Lydia who, more perceptively, teased her about being in love with that awful mean Darcy.

The gossip and market town foolishness of Meryton had always been so amusing. This was not amusing. Not at all. Maybe it would be funny if it happened to someone else. Papa found it hilarious, though he never teased her about it.

Even if it was funny, *must* they think she was in love with Wickham? Would it cause so *very* much difficulty to speak kindly of Darcy? His pride did not make him dishonorable, and much of his rudeness was discomfort in company.

Oh! If only she had not insulted his character herself. Then she could properly despise the neighborhood. But she was no better than any of them.

"Colonel Forster, I *assure* you I did nothing praiseworthy."

He responded as Elizabeth expected him to, as everyone had, "You are far too modest. Lieutenant Wickham is a good man, and he was cruelly wronged by Mr. Darcy. Few persons would challenge a man with Darcy's consequence for the sake of one with as little material worth as Lieutenant Wickham."

Wickham had used her. He was as petty and miserable in character as she had imagined Darcy to be. He deserved to have his true nature made known, and he deserved to be disliked by everyone. However, Elizabeth did not dare repeat Darcy's accusations. It would be the absent and disliked Darcy's word against that of the present, handsome, and charming Mr. Wickham.

Besides, she was too embarrassed. She could not say it straight to all of her friends and acquaintances that she had been a vain fool and was wrong about both Darcy and Wickham. She ought to but had not yet found the nerve to do it. If she did, they would all know she was a nitwit. Her vanity still refused that.

Elizabeth had the perfect idea. She turned to the Colonel with sparkling eyes and said, "You will not believe what stories Mr. Darcy told about our dear Wickham. They were horrid. Why, Darcy claimed he had paid out to Wickham an inheritance of four thousand pounds and that Wickham spent the entire sum in a few years. And — if you believe it — he accused Mr. Wickham of spending extravagantly everywhere he went and leaving behind large debts to tradespeople."

Elizabeth wrinkled her nose and shook her head with an exaggerated expression of disgust. "Darcy even, and I only tell you this because your own observation of Wickham's character will absolve him from the accusation — Darcy claimed Wickham would gamble to excess and not always pay his debts of honor. Surely, you see why I had no choice but to defend our dear Wickham's honor. Any person would have spoken under such provocation."

Colonel Forster had a troubled expression, and Elizabeth asked sweetly, "What bothers you? Surely you have not seen anything in Wickham's behavior to justify Darcy's accusations?"

"Of course not — only —" Colonel Forster pursed his lips than shook his head. "I'm certain it is nothing. Wickham does enjoy a good game of cards, but there's nothing amiss in that."

"Certainly not. Certainly. And I'm certain that a man of Wickham's talent, drive, and indefatigable application will quickly rise in the service. You have watched him perform even the smallest task you give with a relentless desire to do well. Small extravagances *now* are likely to be paid back out of his future fortunes. He shall have many opportunities to distinguish himself."

Colonel Forster half smiled at Elizabeth, "You mistake us. We down twenty lines wake up are the militia, not the regulars. Unless Boney should land on the shores of our merry England — and let us all pray to God that he does not — there are few opportunities for finding distinction or advancement in our ranks."

From his manner, it was evident that she had unsettled Colonel Forster. Elizabeth smiled with better cheer than she had felt in days. "I am certain you do yourself a disservice. I would never doubt the bravery of those who stand and wait for the attack of the French. Should the worst befall us, it will be your efforts that save us from rapine and pillage."

Now it was Colonel Forster who flushed with embarrassment, and with a vindictive glee Elizabeth spent the remainder of her conversation exaggerating the risks and bravery of the militia.

Over the next days Elizabeth had enormous fun spreading the story of how Darcy had paid out a large inheritance to Wickham, which he spent and gambled away. She pretended to disbelieve the story entirely, and she always added that she was certain her hearer could refute it by their own observation of Wickham's virtues. It was pleasurably dishonest to attack Wickham in this manner.

Soon Wickham himself approached Elizabeth, at another card party given by her aunt Phillips, and begged her to stop. Elizabeth pretended to be pleased when he came to sit next to her, but the sight of his smirking handsome features made her gut clench with anger. He had taken and used her vanity and foolishness to further his own ends. She deserved every censure for her failings, but he was the liar.

"My dear Miss Bennet — by the way, have you enjoyed the added distinction of being *the* Miss Bennet? I know it can be so pleasant to be the first among anything."

Elizabeth returned a fake tight smile. "I have enjoyed it — my dear Jane likely is less thrilled when called Mrs. Bingley than I am when called Miss Bennet."

Though his smile did not waver, Mr. Wickham was taken aback by Elizabeth's sharp tone. At first they talked about the weather, and Wickham politely asked questions about the wedding. Elizabeth mostly restrained herself, but her anger towards Wickham showed in her manner.

At last Wickham reached his point. "I was most pleased to hear you defended me in conversation with a certain gentleman. I salute you for your forwardness in doing so."

"Of course I did." Elizabeth forced a smile. "We are friends, are we not?"

"We are friends. Very good friends I believe, and I understand your desire to see that certain gentleman be shamed. He did fill your ears with a shocking deception. However, perhaps it might be best to be silent on the matter. When people hear such stories secondhand, they can be easily misinterpreted. Reputation is such a fragile thing."

"I do sense your meaning. Had I thought you anything to fear, I would never have spoken. Your goodness, which shines forth from your face and manner, and the general upright mode of your life must be applied to any accusations against you. Those who know you, your friends, will always see the truth in your behavior."

Mr. Wickham smiled and inclined his head at Elizabeth's praise. "I thank you for those kind words, and you are far too kind to think otherwise. However, I have learned through hard experience that wealth often speaks louder than goodness, and one has few true friends when poor."

"I, Mr. Wickham, am I not your true friend? Is not Captain Denny? And has not Colonel Forster become your true friend? Are we not all your friends here in Hertfordshire? I will not have you speak such calumnies — unintended though they were — against this neighborhood or yourself. Your happy manners will gain you friends wherever you go, and your virtues will keep them. You have nothing to fear here."

Wickham's face spasmed with frustration as she spoke. It quickly cleared and was replaced by his habitual easy smile. "You are far, far too kind, Miss Bennet. I —" He turned slightly away and wiped at his eyes, "I am brought to tears to know I have such friends as you. It — I do love this neighborhood and its society, and I acknowledge your virtues." He brushed at his eyes. "I have never had such good friends as I have found here. Except for" — Wickham gave a long sigh — "except for my very dearest friend, my first patron and my Godfather, Mr. Darcy's father."

Wickham seized Elizabeth's hand and said, "I misled you when I suggested it was my reputation for which I worried. Mr. Darcy is my dear benefactor's son. It is for him that I worry. No matter how he may hurt me, I can never forget the beloved memory of his father. I feared, given your rightful anger against Mr. Darcy, that your sympathies could be better aroused if you believed I worried for myself, and not him. I know your kindness will not take offense at this."

Elizabeth drew her hand from Wickham's and brought it to her mouth to cover her smile. To use that argument. And after he had defamed Mr. Darcy himself. Mr. Wickham was a marvel. "I can take no offense at that, for your reticence was generated by the highest and most selfless of motives. I do understand, and I salute your desire to protect Mr. Darcy from the consequences of his actions. The love you hold for his father is a model. However, I cannot do as you wish."

Mr. Wickham's smile became chagrined as Elizabeth continued, "A man who deceives a gentlewoman, out of a desire to gain revenge against a man he ought to treat as a brother, ought to be punished. The love you bear for your Godfather binds your tongue. I know I shall never hear you speak against Mr. Darcy in any way — that love does not bind mine. An attempt was made to use my vanity to turn me into fool. Surely you see why I must spread the story about?"

"I understand you perfectly." Mr. Wickham's smile was fixed, but his manners did not fail him, and he showed Elizabeth a broad bow before he sought a new conversational partner, "Your goodness is remarkable and a model to us all. I shall speak no more on the subject."

Following this Wickham showed a marked disinclination for Elizabeth's company. He also ceased to acquire new clothing and the quality of his table deteriorated markedly.

Chapter 9

Months passed. Elizabeth was not often present in Darcy's mind. He had learned a lesson, but the affair was past. He did not view Elizabeth poorly; she had been governed by vanity and prejudice, but he had been governed by an excess of pride and selfishness. It would be hypocritical to judge her harshly, but not himself.

However, she had disliked him the entire time. His behavior had been reprehensible, but hers had been foolish. It was a cold splash that doused the flame of ardour.

Beyond that, Darcy thought little about the matter. His mind was filled with the welfare of his sister and the entertainments of the season. Following their conversation on the night of Bingley's wedding, Darcy always sought to ask Georgiana her wishes instead of assuming them. Under this increased consideration she blossomed, and the melancholy which had lingered since the previous summer disappeared.

After their honeymoon Bingley and Jane settled in London for the season. At the first moment convenient for the couple, Darcy and Georgiana dined at Bingley's rented house. Georgiana and Jane immediately took to each other, and the next day Georgiana filled Darcy's ears with exclamations on how gracious, elegant, and sweet Mrs. Bingley was.

Soon Georgiana and Jane were the closest of friends, and they shopped together, exchanged confidences, and visited each other several times a week. Soon Georgiana started to imitate her older friend, adopting the same mannerisms and wearing gloves pushed down to her wrists in the same way as Jane. It amused both Darcy and Bingley. The friendship would be good for Georgiana. Jane was an excellent woman, and Georgiana needed female companionship closer to her own age and station than a paid companion.

In the middle of March, the Bingleys dined at Darcy's townhouse. It was a small party, just the four of them and Georgiana's companion, Mrs. Annesley. Near the end of the evening, Jane and Georgiana sat on the couch planning the alteration of a hat, and Darcy and Bingley had drawn up around the card table and set up a game of checkers. It was a dull way to spend an evening, but except Georgiana, they were exhausted due to a ball held by Darcy's uncle the previous night.

"I say" — Bingley yawned, tapping the back of his hand against his mouth — "have you any plans for Easter? Jane and I plan to get up a good party and hire musicians."

Darcy grimaced and pushed a piece forward. "I shall be out of town for two weeks; my annual visit to my Aunt Catherine. I leave for it in only a week's time."

"I forgot — you visit her every year. Oh well, we would have had an excellent time."

"I know. The entertainment at your house would be superior. But, blood and family."

Bingley rolled his dice. "Aye, even when you wish otherwise, you cannot escape them, not completely. At least I convinced Caroline and the Hursts to make their own party for the season."

Jane heard something of the conversation and walked to stand next to her husband. "You are to visit Lady Catherine at Rosings Park? In Kent?" At Darcy's assent she said, "You must give my greetings to Lizzy, she is visiting Charlotte — that is Mrs. Collins — I believe you know that our neighbor Charlotte Lucas married your aunt's parson."

"Miss Elizabeth? She is at Rosings?" She had not crossed his mind for several weeks, and now he was to meet her again.

Jane laughed merrily. "Nay, she is at Hunsford Parsonage. From Lizzy's letters, I understand it to be almost ten minutes' walk."

Darcy smiled at Jane's jest as his composure returned. He had known he would meet her again and was wholly prepared to greet her as an acquaintance. He was eager to see how she would behave. Would she appear different now?

Darcy said, "I will be happy to give her your greetings at the first opportunity. Might you wish to use me as a courier? I could save you the postage on some letters or bring some small object or gift."

"That is very kind. With your permission, I will also ask my aunt. Lizzy is a great favorite with her children, and they have produced some drawings for my sister that were to be given to her when she passes through London on her return, but are not worth paying the postage on."

Darcy nodded agreeably. Jane turned to his sister, who still studied the hat they had discussed. "Georgie, shall I lose your company for a few weeks?"

Georgiana almost shivered and shook her head vigorously side to side. "Lady Catherine frightens me — I never visit her if I can avoid it. Fitzwilliam does not make me anymore." Georgiana blushed and said, "I ought not to have spoken of my aunt so."

Bingley laughed. "No harm done, we all have difficult relations. She frightens me as well. I once went to a dinner here when she was present" — Bingley showed his friendly grin — "like the best dandies I decided I wouldn't change out of my riding jacket. I thought I was at the height of fashion. Lady Catherine delivered such a blistering lecture that the next week I was too terrified to wear my riding clothes even to ride and wore evening dress from morning till sup. Ruined a good coat and tails that way and made myself the joke of the week."

Everyone laughed at Bingley's manner of telling the story. Darcy remembered how embarrassed he had been by his aunt's behavior. To make such a speech; to another man's guest. It showed a great want of sense on his aunt's part.

Darcy said, "I apologized then, and I will apologize now. She should not have spoken so to you. But Lady Catherine is not to be gainsaid. When she wishes to speak her mind, she always shall. No matter the situation."

"Lizzy, in one of her letters, said your aunt is celebrated for the frankness of her advice." Jane smiled sweetly and patted her husband on the shoulder. "It was merely that. She realized how handsome you are in a white cravat and waistcoat."

Georgiana hugged herself. "I do not wish her advice. No matter how sound."

"Have you any plans for while your brother is in Kent?" Jane asked.

Georgiana shook her head.

"For it may be lonely with only your companion. If your brother is willing, I would like to invite you to stay with Bingley and me. I grew up with four sisters and would enjoy the company of another lady again for a few weeks."

Georgiana's eyes lit at Jane's offer. "Oh, please Fitzwilliam, might I?"

Darcy grinned at Georgiana's enthusiasm and after a quick glance at Bingley to see him nod and smile gave permission.

JANE WROTE THAT MR. Darcy was coming to Rosings. He would visit her to give his greetings and deliver her next letter. Elizabeth definitely would see him. What manner would he show? She had offended him badly. Likely he would treat her with an icy politeness and hidden contempt.

She did not want him to despise her.

Yes, she had misjudged him horridly. She had thought far worse of him than he deserved — yet, the idea of him thinking ill of her filled Elizabeth half with resentment and half with hurt. She had been prejudiced and vain. But, *he* had shown persistent rudeness towards the neighborhood. He did not have the right to despise her for her failings. Yet, she shied away from the next meeting; she would feel terribly rejected when he proved to hold her in contempt.

The day came when Mr. Darcy and his cousin, a Colonel Fitzwilliam, made the trip to visit their aunt. Mr. Collins stood out at the edge of the road by his garden gate, so he could doff his cap and show them respect as the carriage passed. Given her curiosity to see Mr. Darcy again and perceive his manner towards her, Elizabeth had a brief urge to join Mr. Collins when the hour of their expected arrival drew near.

She was stopped by horrible embarrassment. What would Darcy think if he saw her waiting out for him?

Charlotte watched Elizabeth's agitation as she could not settle down and would look out the window at Mr. Collins standing next to the lane every few minutes.

Twenty minutes after Mr. Collins went out, for the third time Elizabeth stood up, looked through the window, sat back down, and ordered herself to focus on the needlework she did for the poor box. This time she really would think no more on Darcy.

Charlotte asked, "Eliza, pray tell, what has you so fascinated with Mr. Darcy's arrival? You dislike him."

Elizabeth threw the needlework to the side. "I do not. It was a mistake to dislike him. A terrible one. I believed Wickham when he attacked Darcy's character simply because Darcy had offended my vanity."

"So charming Mr. Wickham lost your favor? I expected he would in the end. He seemed insubstantial, but *I* was not the object of his attentions, hence *I* could hardly trust myself."

"In that you were my superior — for I took his attentions as confirmation of the wisdom of my preference. I see myself clearly now. Vanity and prejudice drove my behavior, not reason. I had not imagined I could be so foolish. I can see that you laugh at me." Elizabeth grinned back at her friend, enough time had passed for her to see the humor in the situation. "I admit the discovery of my own foolishness is humorous, but it was not pleasant."

Charlotte pursed her lips. "Poor Lizzy — she discovered that she is not always right! Why, as your friend, I had hoped you to at least reach thirty before that awful truth dawned upon you. I would not have believed you could take it so calmly."

Elizabeth stuck her tongue out at her friend.

Charlotte laughed. "How did this astonishing realization come to you? Perhaps it had something to do with that famous argument at your sister's wedding. The one my mother, and sister, and even my brother wrote me about?"

Elizabeth's cheeks flamed. Since Charlotte had made no comment on it before, she had hoped the story had not reached from Hertfordshire to Kent. To distract herself from the embarrassment, she teased back, "John wrote you a letter? I believed him not to know the art."

The oldest Lucas brother was famed amongst the intimates of the Lucases for writing home only twice in the entirety of the four years he was away at university, both times for money.

"Yes, it shocked me exceedingly as well. Your argument was a better joke than any he heard while away." Charlotte tilted her head to the side. "Though what prompted John's letter were the rumors of Wickham's debts and depravities, which had spread through Meryton. He found it terribly amusing that the clever Eliza Bennet had defended the gentleman just before everyone turned against him."

"*I* began those rumors."

"Yes — I heard *that* from my mother. She was impressed by how cleverly you did it."

Elizabeth blushed; the praise pleased her a little.

"Come, Lizzy, tell me the whole story. You wish to — and even if you do not, I wish very much to hear it. My curiosity has eaten at me for the past three months — I beg you to end my suffering."

"Just for that, I ought not to tell you." Since Elizabeth would likely see Darcy soon, she did wish a confidant besides her father. She looked away from Charlotte. "I chose to lecture him for all his failings when we sat together at Jane's wedding."

"You did?" Charlotte's eyes lit with enthusiasm. "I can see it clear. Elizabeth Bennet, full of a righteous fury, defending the honor of her dear friend Mr. Wickham from the despicable Mr. Darcy. At a wedding no less. Her own sister's even."

"I held off until Jane and Bingley had left — you cannot claim I lack affection for Jane. In fact, that began the argument — you see, your view of the situation was proved out. Mr. Darcy thought Jane indifferent to Bingley and discouraged his friend on those grounds — the ill-bred behavior of our family, except for myself and Jane, was an additional cause for his friend to avoid the entanglement. I proceeded to prove that all of us but Jane could show ill-bred behavior. Jane, of course, never shall."

"Oh my, if he were so rude as to say to your face that your family was ill bred, perhaps you had an excuse for incivility."

"No, the excuse had been his — I accused him of caring only for money and connections, and lacking all good Christian feeling."

Charlotte raised her eyebrows.

"He did attempt to detach Bingley from Jane. Was it unreasonable for me to think it was a matter only of money? And *poor Wickham* had told me this dreadful story about how Darcy stole the inheritance intended by his Godfather for him."

"And Mr. Darcy defended himself by claiming to believe Jane indifferent and your family improper?"

"Yes. And I would not believe him, for I knew he was cruel and unfeeling. Oh, I should not have said that — beyond the impropriety, it was not true, and I hurt him. I could see it in his eyes. Miss Bingley later told me that he had admired me. It must have been a terrible shock, and the worse for being undeserved."

"Miss Bingley? *She* told you that? What had she to do with the matter?"

Elizabeth laughed. "It is very ridiculous. Caroline — as she insisted I call her — became worried that Darcy's admiration might lead to marriage. She claimed she overheard Darcy admit he stole Wickham's inheritance because his father loved Wickham better. She did so to rouse me further against him in hope I would offend him and end any chance that Darcy's admiration might become more. Well, she succeeded. Though Jane wrote that Darcy refuses to speak to Miss Bingley or admit her to his house, so hers was a Pyrrhic victory."

Charlotte's mouth hung open. "Well, I cannot fault her for lack of audacity. I thought he admired you when he asked you to dance at Netherfield." Charlotte smiled smugly. "I told you not to offend a man with a hundred times Mr. Wickham's consequence."

Elizabeth waved her hand dismissively. "The reason you gave was not why it was a mistake."

"*You* would think that." Charlotte asked cautiously, "Have you some fear or hope for his behavior?"

Elizabeth shook her head vigorously. "Oh, he would see the effort of treating a silly girl such as myself as anything but an indifferent acquaintance as beneath him. I do not care how he treats me. I behaved abominably towards him, and he was right to call me a prejudiced, silly girl. The superiority of mind I admired in myself proved to be empty vanity."

Elizabeth violently stood and threw her hands in the air. "Lord! He acted quite as poorly as I. He is a clever man, perhaps he can see how his behavior gave us good excuse to dislike him. Yet, I imagine that he despises me and views himself wholly blameless. Oh, it makes me angry to imagine that arrogant sneer refuse to acknowledge any fault."

Charlotte turned away with a smile. Elizabeth flopped into one of the chairs around the writing table. Charlotte bit her lip and tilted her head in the manner she used when seeking a clever phrase to tease Elizabeth with.

It was silly to care what Mr. Darcy thought about their argument. Charlotte was a good friend. Elizabeth would never act as her friend had with Mr. Collins, but she had no right to look down upon her for it. After all, she could behave foolishly too.

At last Charlotte said, "I perceive you care a great deal for that gentleman's good opinion." Elizabeth grabbed a cushion from the sofa and threw it at Charlotte.

"I shall take that as confirmation. Do invite me to the wedding."

"Do not forget, that he is still rude, arrogant, un-talkative, and excessively fastidious."

"Oh, I had not!" Charlotte said with wide innocent eyes. "Still, if *that* be your sole objection — I daresay his tall handsome person and ability to argue you down will overcome those considerations."

It was ridiculous, but maybe the jokes would prove true. No reasonable man would maintain an infatuation to a woman who had called him cruel and selfish. She knew that.

But maybe — maybe he would treat her as he had before.

Chapter 10

As early as practicable the next morning, Darcy and Colonel Fitzwilliam wound their way down the neatly mowed lawn to call upon the parsonage. Darcy carried a bulky package filled with letters and drawings Mrs. Bingley had entrusted to him to deliver to her sister. It was as though he brought her a gift.

It would not matter. She probably despised him yet and still thought him the cruel gentleman who destroyed Wickham's hopes and endeavored to separate her sister from Bingley. Well he would prove her expectation false. He had practiced showing friendship to those socially beneath him for months. His manners were enormously improved — and to his own benefit. He could be polite.

He would show Elizabeth.

The parsonage was a solid timber framed building with two stories, and as they stepped towards the entry way, Darcy's eyes caught that an addition had been built to the kitchen since he passed by the parsonage last. The vegetable garden had been expanded and neatly fenced in. Knowing his destination for the morning, Lady Catherine had described the improvements she made when Mr. Collins took the parish and again when he had married. Darcy did not like his aunt's taste in ornamentation, but she was a sensible woman, and Mrs. Collins must appreciate many of the changes.

The fresh-faced young maid showed them in. Upon entering the drawing room, Darcy's eyes uncontrollably sought out Elizabeth's form. He felt a shock at seeing her, and there was still a glow around her pretty face and figure. But it was a quiet whisper compared to what he had felt at Bingley's wedding.

Elizabeth's face was red and she did not meet his eyes. She wore a yellow dress with a white lace collar around her neck. Darcy collected himself and stepped forward and sat near her. "Miss Bennet, you look well. I have been instructed by your excellent sister to deliver this."

Darcy handed her the wrapped parcel. "I understand it contains not only her letters, but also a collection of drawings from your young cousins. I can assure you from my own observation that your sister was in the very best of health only yesterday morning."

Elizabeth at last looked at his face, her blush darkened further, and she looked away again immediately. He recalled how striking her eyes could be.

Elizabeth said with a smile that did not reach her eyes, "I am glad to hear that. You are well enough acquainted with Jane to know that she would *claim* to be in the best of health until quite sick. I hear your sister stays with mine."

"Yes." Darcy filled his voice with amiability and good cheer. "They have become quite close. My sister has developed quite an enthusiasm for yours. Georgiana decided she must imitate Mrs. Bingley in every respect not expressly advised against by your sister."

No doubt, Elizabeth expected him to show disdain for her sister, due to the contempt he had shown before. But he would prove his feelings were quite the opposite. Darcy added, "I am grateful to your sister for allowing mine to come under her wing. Georgiana is backwards in company, but has blossomed under your sister's guidance. There is no woman I'd more like her to pattern herself after than Mrs. Bingley."

Elizabeth replied with a real smile, "Jane adores Miss Darcy. Since they met all my letters from her have been filled with her piano playing, their shopping trips, and their visits to various London sights. I begin to grow quite jealous."

Her manner did not show any ill will towards him, but he had before proven incapable of interpreting Elizabeth's emotions. He would not trust himself. He had greeted her warmly and politely, she must greet him in a similar manner no matter her feelings. He still had to prove that he had changed for the better and no longer held those of lower station in contempt.

After a few more polite requests after family and news had been exchanged, Darcy introduced Elizabeth to Colonel Fitzwilliam and started a conversation with Mrs. Collins. Darcy had only spoken with her a few times in Meryton, but he had always seen her as a sensible woman.

They conversed about parish topics and the parsonage. Darcy enjoyed the conversation. She was a clever woman. It was to be expected: She was Elizabeth's particular friend. Elizabeth's attention was partly on them. Likely, she expected him to suddenly revert to his former behavior and become silent and rude once again. He would disappoint her. He thought well of Mrs. Collins.

Colonel Fitzwilliam made Elizabeth laugh, and Darcy forced himself to not look. He no longer was infatuated, and he would not act as though he were. He still felt himself smile, and his spirits lift at her laugh.

Besides, Colonel Fitzwilliam had a plain square face and was short.

When it was nearly time for them to leave, Mr. Collins returned from a clerical call. Darcy remembered that he had thought very poorly of the man. Mr. Collins had presumed to introduce himself and proceeded to give a long winded description of the felicities he found as Lady Catherine's flatterer.

Surely his mood that evening had made him think worse of Mr. Collins than he deserved. If he'd been quite as much a fool as he remembered, a sensible woman such as Mrs. Collins would not have married him. On the man's entrance Darcy quickly said, "I am pleased that our call allowed us an opportunity to greet you. My aunt depends on you greatly, and you must be about a great deal."

Mr. Collins's eyes widened and he almost swooned in pleasure at Mr. Darcy's friendly greeting. "I thank you for those kind words. Like your aunt, you are all affability and condescension. My humble abode and dear wife and cousin do not deserve the visit of such an august personage as yourself. But, it shows the way your family graces and elevates its high rank that you nonetheless condescended to grant it. None in England deserve respect more than those of your blood."

He turned to Elizabeth and Mrs. Collins and said, "My dear ladies, are we not all very grateful for the visit of Mr. Darcy and his noble cousin. You must admit your gratefulness for the condescension."

Mrs. Collins calmly told her husband that they had already thanked their visitors for the friendliness they showed. Colonel Fitzwilliam's eyes were a bit wide as he stared at Mr. Collins. Elizabeth frowned and did not look towards them. Her color was high. Did she expect him to disdain her cousin as he would have before?

Darcy could freely admit that was the most toadying speech ever directed at him. But Elizabeth watched. He would prove he could treat Mr. Collins with respect. "Sir, you underrate your own merit. A visit to this parsonage could never be a burden. I do not feel so far above you."

"You are too kind. Far too kind. But I know my place. I am happy to be your humble servant. Her Ladyship, your estimable and gentle aunt, has done so very much for me. All of my present happiness is owed to the patronage I have been so fortunate as to receive from her liberal hand. Every respect is due to her and to every person so profoundly blessed as to be connected to her great personage. Even all of my daily comforts depend upon her."

Mr. Collins made a minute description of every change and modification made to his home by Lady Catherine. It was dull. Why ever did Mrs. Collins marry him? Darcy recollected that Mr. Collins was to inherit Longbourn, and at twenty and seven Mrs. Collins must have grown desperate. It was a pity for her, though fortunate for Mr. Collins.

Darcy normally would have found some way, polite or otherwise, to escape the conversation. But not in front of Elizabeth. After ten minutes Colonel Fitzwilliam stood. "We shall head back to Rosings."

He saw Elizabeth gaze in his direction, as she stood with Colonel Fitzwilliam. Did she think he desired to escape conversation with her cousin? Darcy held up his hand. "I wish to wait a little longer — Mr. Collins, I meant to ask you about your sermon last week. On what subject did you speak? I shall not leave until I hear a full description of it."

Mr. Collins glowed from within, and he clutched his chest and looked at Darcy with an adoring smile. "You, sir — you are as good as your magnificent aunt! Of course, one of your noble blood would have a proper respect for matters of religion. You need not worry, I followed your aunt's instructions on how to prepare the sermon in every detail!"

Everyone else stared at Darcy in frank amazement. Elizabeth began to smirk and brought a hand up to hide it. Darcy found himself beginning to smile as he was forced to listen to Mr. Collins's detailed summary of his sermon, which included long digressions on the wisdom Lady Catherine had imparted on the art of writing sermons.

Nobody, except Lady Catherine, would ask Mr. Collins a question of that sort. At least Elizabeth must know he wished to be polite.

As soon as they escaped and stepped back into the sunlight, Colonel Fitzwilliam exclaimed, "Darcy! Have you taken leave of your senses? That was the most ridiculous man I have ever heard. I have never seen someone who better fit the type Lady Catherine seeks when she hires. Never. And you encouraged him."

Colonel Fitzwilliam shook his head, as Darcy made no reply. Elizabeth had shown no ill will towards him. Maybe she believed what he told her about Wickham. Perhaps they could meet as friendly acquaintances in the future.

"It was not a loss for me — I did have an opportunity for ten more minutes' conversation with that pretty Miss Bennet." Colonel Fitzwilliam halted and grabbed Darcy's arm, "Did you attempt to impress her? Is that why you pursued conversation with her cousin? You succeeded. She saw very clear how ridiculous you can be."

"No." Darcy replied stoutly, "Of course not."

"Ah. Of course not. Fitzwilliam Darcy would never make a fool of himself for a lady. It was absurd of me to suggest it."

ONCE THE TWO GENTLEMEN left, Mr. Collins exclaimed, "Were Mr. Darcy and Colonel Fitzwilliam not the very epitomes of affability? Did they not show the very essence of civility? I should never have expected such a compliment as for them to call upon us the day after their arrival. And Mr. Darcy showed a serious care for his own soul and those of inferiors. It is most becoming for one in his station. I have never been so pleased by an encounter. We must not expect such attentions in the future. As you know, Mr. Darcy is a very great gentleman."

Elizabeth decided not to undercut Mr. Collins's ecstasy by pointing out that Mr. Darcy had been required to visit so quick due to an errand entrusted to him by the wife of a dear friend. Elizabeth opened her parcel as Mr. Collins exulted in the triumph of the call. She set aside Jane and Mrs.

Gardiner's letters for when she would have greater leisure and looked with a smile at the pictures drawn by her cousins.

Whatever did Darcy's manner mean?

Mr. Collins at last left the room and hummed a horribly off key tune as he walked down the hall to his study.

Charlotte exclaimed, "Lord! He must be in love with you. I can imagine no other cause which would make such a man seek conversation with my husband."

"I do not think so." Elizabeth had paid much attention to Darcy during the call, but he rarely looked at her. He talked with Charlotte and Mr. Collins far more than herself. That showed indifference. "He must realize he behaved a little wrong in Hertfordshire. He wished to prove to me he could behave better. It showed more resentment than admiration."

A part of her wanted to cry, but she would not let herself. She had made her choice. His behavior showed he could acknowledge when he behaved poorly. Perhaps he could have learned to respect her. Perhaps a marriage between them would have been happy if she had not destroyed his affection.

Charlotte peered at Elizabeth. "That is a perverse notion. You must truly wish to believe he dislikes you. I am sorry, but you are not right. He desires your good opinion and was most interested in how you took his conversations. You should find opportunity to apologize and see if you might rekindle what interest he had."

"Do you really believe that?" Elizabeth shook her head. "He is too silent and grave. I will not obsess over this, and I will not make myself unhappy over him."

Charlotte smirked. "There was nothing silent and grave in him *today*. He eagerly questioned my husband, and his conversation with me was amiable. You must find better objection."

For the next days Elizabeth saw nothing of Mr. Darcy. Rosings had more activity due to the guests. It affected Elizabeth mainly because with the presence of her nephews, Lady Catherine was not so inclined to call the Hunsford party to her side.

Elizabeth was not surprised. She could not blame him if he did not seek her company, or even if he avoided it, not after her treatment of him. But his evident indifference still stung. She did not let it make her unhappy though. She walked a great deal; the changing season showed the area to great advantage; and the conversations and calls made with Charlotte occupied her mind.

A little less than a week after Mr. Darcy and Colonel Fitzwilliam had called upon the parsonage, Mr. Collins returned from a consultation with Lady Catherine to give them the momentous news — tomorrow they were to dine with Lady Catherine and her esteemed nephews.

Elizabeth set out for a walk. So she would dine with him tomorrow. How would it go? No doubt he would follow the pattern set when he called at the parsonage. Politeness to her and everyone else, but no special attentions. She wanted that. Anything else would unsettle her.

When Elizabeth reached a grove which had become a particular favorite of hers, she saw Mr. Darcy. He stood along the path. He could not see her because he studied trunk of a thick old oak tree. Darcy's hands were pulled behind his back, and he stood firm and tall with the tails of his green coat hanging behind him.

He was so handsome, and she had made such an awful fool of herself. Now that they were outside of company, he would treat her with the contempt she had earned. Elizabeth nearly turned to walk the other way. That would be silly; he would not behave that way, for he was not cruel.

She had no good reason to avoid Mr. Darcy, and she would grow quite frightened of him if she let herself. With a light step Elizabeth quickly walked towards Darcy and called out, "I can see you enjoy yourself this fine morning, Mr. Darcy."

Darcy blinked at seeing her and grinned. "I confess I do," he shouted back. "It is a fine day, and this grove has always been a favorite of mine when I visit my aunt." His smile showed in his eyes and cheeks, and he bowed as Elizabeth came near to him. "You look well this morning Miss Elizabeth — pardon me, I mean Miss Bennet."

Elizabeth laughed. At least he would treat her politely. "You may trust me not to take offense should you fail to give me proper precedence."

"I am pleased to hear that" — Darcy took Elizabeth's arm and they began to walk along the path — "for I once knew a girl, the sister of a Cambridge friend, who was terribly offended if someone referred to her as Miss Iphigenia after her sister's marriage."

"Oh, you can hardly blame her — Iphigenia is quite a mouthful, and was she not the girl who was burned alive by her parents to ensure good sailing to Troy? If that were my name, I would wish to escape it as well." Elizabeth laughed nervously and looked at Darcy, who showed an impenetrable smile. "That was Iphigenia? Not Antigone, or some other girl."

"Iphigenia was Agamemnon's daughter. Antigone was Oedipus's daughter." He frowned and added quickly, "Many women would not recollect the story at all."

"Oh." Elizabeth nodded. He was as handsome as ever. He'd once liked her. Did he now despise her? She would show him her best self. Elizabeth said gaily, "Antigone is another name with most unfortunate implications — should I marry, I will decidedly put my foot down and disallow classical names for any girls. Should he wish to saddle his sons with such stories that might be his prerogative."

Why had she spoken about children's names?

Darcy seemed entirely unruffled, and he replied with that steady manner of his, "Some classical names have fortunate implications — for example, Fortuna."

Elizabeth giggled. "That would be a fortunate name, I admit. Still, the best names for girls are those of reigning British monarchs. Such as, Elizabeth."

Darcy smiled. "Perhaps you are right — my mother's family agreed with you: an Anne in each generation, and Georgiana is almost the name of the reigning monarch. Catherine though is not." Darcy turned to Elizabeth with a serious expression that made her smile and asked, "Do consorts count? Three of Henry VIII's wives were named Catherine."

"Perhaps, but they are of an inferior order to those who actually reigned." Elizabeth froze. Even when she dearly wished to be friendly her conversations with Mr. Darcy would go astray. "I apologize, I mean no insult to your estimable aunt."

"None taken, of course. You need not fear I will mistake an attempt at levity by you as an insult. Quite the contrary."

There was something like resentment in Darcy's tone, and Elizabeth's stomach squirmed unhappily. Her behavior last autumn had been abominable. They walked along a shaded path. There was a mottling of light on the ground where the sunlight broke through the leaves.

Darcy snorted. Elizabeth turned to look at him, and his eyes were bright and mischievous. He said with a serious expression, "Perhaps you ought to discuss whether the name of a monarch regnant is intrinsically superior to that of a queen consort with my aunt when you dine with us tomorrow."

Elizabeth raised her eyebrows. "I shall. Your aunt is a sensible woman, who has always been praised for the soundness of her advice. She shall set us right. We may trust her to not let the small matter of her own name not being that of a reigning monarch to bias her"

"I eagerly await the enlightenment I shall receive from your discussion."

Tension fell over the two, or at least over Elizabeth, as they silently walked through the woody thickets of Lady Catherine's estate. She had behaved badly. The horrible accusations she'd thrown at Mr. Darcy weighed on her. She would have been prickly and offended had he shown the reserved contempt she had half expected from him, but Darcy's unusual amiability left Elizabeth uncertain and guilty.

Elizabeth pulled away from Mr. Darcy and, wringing her hands, burst out, "Mr. Darcy, you must allow me to apologize, most profusely, for the abominable way I treated you in January. I accused you in the most vile manner with absolutely no justification and showed my poor judgement and extreme vanity. There is no justification for what I said, and I have long since realized that you are far better than what I accused you of being."

Mr. Darcy's deep blue eyes searched her face with a serious expression Elizabeth could not interpret for a seeming eternity. "Please, sir! I must know that I have not lost any hope of your good opinion forever — you once said you can be resentful. Please tell me I have not earned that resentment. I deserve it, but —"

"Elizabeth, do not fret so. You have quite as much to forgive as I do. More. While much of what you said was rude, it was amply justified by my own rudeness. And of what you said, little was not true. I did not, out of a selfish sense of my own superiority, give proper consideration to the feelings of others. I had given you cause to feel offense and made no effort to correct that offense. Mr. Wickham is a practiced liar, and I have no right to blame you for believing his stories, as I had given no reason to trust my character."

"Yes, but — there is ample evidence of inconsistency in Wickham's stories. Had I not been blinded by vanity, I would have seen it and seen your worth. I was blinded by prejudice. Before I thought myself clever. One who would not be so easily duped. I — I learned a great deal about myself and my own weaknesses. I can only hope to be less nitwitted in the future."

After completing the speech Elizabeth looked down in shame and then glanced up shyly to see how Darcy had taken it. His clear blue eyes met her gaze. "And I learned much as well. I found that I thought meanly of those with less consequence than myself. Since then I have striven to improve my manners, and I hope to never act or think as I did in Hertfordshire again. It was not pleasant to examine my own behavior and see so much to regret."

"You were not so very bad!"

Darcy replied with a broad smile that made one of his cheeks dimple and started butterflies fluttering in Elizabeth's stomach. "I was so very bad. And you knew it *then*, whatever you think now. Miss Bennet, as we both learned a valuable lesson from the occasion of our quarrel, I cannot regret it."

"I must. I could never look back on what I said with that much easiness. It was wrong of me and foolish, especially when I called you cruel. The way you appeared has burned in my memory for these many months. I have heartily regretted it."

Darcy smiled somberly. "I am glad you do not think that still."

His manner convinced Elizabeth he *had* felt the accusation deeply. Elizabeth's shoulders slumped, and she could not look at him. She had unjustly hurt him.

Darcy touched her shoulder. "Do not feel poorly. Please, you must come to see our argument as I do. I cannot have you remain unhappy. I will not allow it." Elizabeth looked into his eyes, and they were warm. "If I were the perfect gentleman" — he smirked at her — "I would claim your behavior was unexceptionable, and hence that you had no need to censure yourself. But that would not be true. While you did nothing immoral — Miss Bingley's story was *very* ridiculous."

Elizabeth giggled. Darcy's smile was broad and pleased. Elizabeth felt as light as a hot air balloon. He took the sting out of her guilt by making her laugh. She said, "It always sounded odd. I thought it a mark of how very fascinating you were that you would say such a thing."

"So I fascinated you?" Elizabeth blushed, and Darcy's smile was a little lopsided. "Well, you have taken your lesson, and I have taken my lesson, and we both have committed to doing better. You have nothing left to feel guilt about. At least, you can have no more to be ashamed of than I do." Darcy showed a handsome smirk. "For myself, I would prefer not to feel *too* deeply shamed."

"You mean to say, if I insist on strongly feeling my misbehavior, you would take that as an insult to yourself?"

"That is a fair interpretation of my words."

"I had believed my true failing to be a propensity to willfully misunderstand everyone." Elizabeth smiled happily at him. The awful feeling she'd had because she wronged him had dissolved.

Darcy smiled back at her. But he then looked away. "Miss Bennet, last year I believed us to be friends." Darcy looked Elizabeth straight in the eyes. "I would very much like it if we were friends in truth. Can we be? Would you start afresh?"

Elizabeth felt another stab of guilt and an upwelling of hope. "I would like that very much. Very much indeed."

Darcy replied with an infectious smile that lit his eyes and made him yet more handsome than ever before. Elizabeth exclaimed, "Wait, if we are to begin afresh, we must be introduced anew. The trees will hardly do a creditable job, so we must do the honors ourselves."

Darcy's pleased expression made Elizabeth's heart skip. He said, "That is a capital idea."

Elizabeth thought she appeared as happy as a loon when she stepped back and gave an elaborate, deep curtsy to Mr. Darcy — such as those she had practiced with Jane years ago for an imaginary presentation to the Queen — "Miss Elizabeth Bennet, of Longbourn in Hertfordshire. Very pleased to meet you."

Darcy made his own elaborate bow. "Fitzwilliam Darcy, of Pemberley in Derbyshire, at your service. *Very* pleased to meet you."

The two smiled at each other. She felt so light that her feet were barely tethered to the ground. He still smiled. She could not look away. At last Darcy spoke, "Tell me Miss Bennet, do you as a rule never talk about books in a wood?"

Chapter 11

Elizabeth felt as though she could fly like a sparrow until dinner the next day. Even if Darcy only wanted her friendship, *he still wanted that*. It made life perfect. She was so happy. And he'd looked at her with those smiles. Perhaps he didn't admire her, but she didn't need that. She just needed his respect.

He'd chosen to improve himself. He completely forgave her. He hoped to be her friend. He made her laugh. He was near perfect, with only a few flaws that accentuated his other virtues.

Did he still admire her? If he did not, might she contrive to reawaken his admiration? Did she desire to?

Papa had feared he would regret the choice. But, if Darcy came to admire her again — surely he no longer cared so much about connections and wealth. He claimed he would never think so meanly of those beneath him in station again. Elizabeth believed him.

Further, the thought was disloyal, but Darcy was a better man than her father. He would not allow himself to treat his wife in a similar manner to how her father treated her mother.

At dinner the next evening, Elizabeth was seated next to Colonel Fitzwilliam. Darcy had been placed between his cousin Anne and Charlotte. Colonel Fitzwilliam was an excellent partner, and she enjoyed his conversation greatly. He had an easiness of manner that charmed, and he supplemented it with a well-informed mind.

Darcy always stayed in her attention. Colonel Fitzwilliam made her laugh, and Elizabeth surreptitiously looked to see how he took it. He glanced briefly in their direction and returned his attention to his conversation with Charlotte.

No sign of jealousy.

Damn.

At least he showed little interest in Anne. He had attempted to converse with his cousin, but when she responded in monosyllables he gave up with a tiny shrug. Though Mr. Wickham had said they were to marry, Elizabeth had long since come to disbelieve that story as she did every other given by him. Elizabeth liked to see her belief that it was a lie confirmed by Darcy's manner.

Their eyes met a few times when she glanced in his direction, and her heart skittered. She pushed out a bright smile each time, and he would smile back a little before looking away. She was being silly, but it was impossible to stop herself. She just wished he would look at her as he used to.

When the parties separated Lady Catherine settled on her throne-like chair in the middle of the drawing room and lectured or questioned the ladies in attendance upon her. Elizabeth had far less attention for her than usual. She mixed ecstatic high spirits with disappointment. He did not look at her as he once did, but he was here and her friend.

Darcy had spoken amiably to Charlotte as they talked about parish business. She had never seen him so friendly, not even when they were at Netherfield. If he often behaved so, her sole remaining objection to him, that he was too solemn and grave, would disappear.

But he did not admire her anymore. That was no matter, it was not as if she loved him. She just liked him. Very much.

Hopefully he would converse with her. They had promised to be friends.

The men did not linger long over their port, and while Mr. Collins immediately went to attend Lady Catherine, the other two gentlemen approached her. Colonel Fitzwilliam spoke first, "I have been informed you play. You must indulge us with music later tonight."

Elizabeth smiled and immediately tried to involve his cousin in the conversation. "Mr. Darcy can swear to the inferiority of my playing, but if you insist — I might be prevailed upon." She looked at Darcy with an arch smile. "*You* can vouch for me — *you* know I am not one of those girls who imposes her meager talents upon the listening public with no regard for their boredom. I know the limits of my skills."

"On the contrary, I have heard few performers I enjoyed more."

Darcy's smile was genuine. Elizabeth could not reply. She wanted to make him admire her. He had asked her to favor him with music several times at Netherfield. His admiration for her must have distorted his judgement, for his manner made clear he had really enjoyed her playing.

Colonel Fitzwilliam spoke, "Then, I look forward to your playing very much. Miss Bennet, I want to gain a clear understanding of your character. We have established you play better than you believe. At dinner you revealed your enthusiasm for Shakespeare and told me that you found the spring in Kent to be quite as green and wet as that in Hertfordshire. Tell me, what do you read besides the Bard?"

Elizabeth grinned at Darcy. "Your cousin can reveal what I do not read, for he knows my dreadful ignorance of Greek mythology."

Darcy smiled back, and she turned to Colonel Fitzwilliam. "Yesterday, I encountered him in that delightful grove of your aunt's — the one… oh, a quarter mile south of the house, where the trees grow together above the pathway to form that delightful bower —"

Colonel Fitzwilliam nodded his head. "I know the one you speak of."

"When I encountered Mr. Darcy in that pathway, I revealed to him my general ignorance of the classics. I confused Iphigenia, who was Oedipus's daughter, with Antigone, who Agamemnon burned to convince their wind God, Zeus, to give him good sailing to Troy."

Colonel Fitzwilliam smiled. Darcy said, "Do not believe her, she pretends greater ignorance than her real level."

Elizabeth laughed at him and smiled impishly. "I will admit I have not yet forgotten that you specified Antigone to be Oedipus's daughter." She shook her head and looked at Colonel Fitzwilliam. "He will teach you not to trust a word I say. I had hoped to pass myself off with some credit here, but as a *friend* Mr. Darcy knows enough of my character to puncture my pretensions."

Darcy smiled widely, and Elizabeth lit up in response. He replied, "Were he not my cousin, *as your friend*, I would not have revealed your petty deception, but allowed Colonel Fitzwilliam to discover it on his own."

Colonel Fitzwilliam asked, "What is your real opinion on the classics? I, like all true warriors, keep a copy of the Iliad under my pillow while out on campaign."

Elizabeth laughed. "Do they all? I had not known that."

Darcy replied, "It was only Alexander the Great."

"I admit, I occasionally engage in petty deceptions as well." Colonel Fitzwilliam grinned. "I do not have it under the pillow I sleep on — that would be uncomfortable. Instead it is under the pillow in my room at Matlock, and all the servants have strict instructions to leave it in place. I do dearly love Homer and thought it a good luck charm to follow Alexander's example. But I wanted the charm at a distance to avoid attracting his fate of a drunken death while still young."

Elizabeth smiled. "I must confess — I know this is horrid — my tastes have always been more for modern novels and poetry than history or classical literature."

Darcy replied, "That is a pity, for antiquity produced the most sublime and beautiful works of the human mind."

"Ah — I knew you would say that. For every university educated gentleman — with a scholarly bent — who I know is mad about them."

Darcy's eyes lit. "It is a sign of their greatness, and the virtues of our system of education that we all agree. In this case the rush of the madding crowd of Cambridge and Oxford students have settled upon the correct opinion. You will not shake my view by suggesting it to be popular."

"Ah. Then I shall fail. For I had intended to turn you against them, and now I have no idea what to say."

"That you intend to read the classics from end to end yourself, so that you might discover details with which to insult their lovers."

Elizabeth laughed in reply. "I am glad for the challenge. 'Tis a clever way to encourage me. And more like to succeed than the simple repetition of how sublime and beautiful they are. But I have attempted them in translation and found no pleasure."

"Perhaps —" Darcy began.

Elizabeth interrupted him and smiled happily into his face. She loved how he immediately entered the dispute with her. "I know what you mean to say. It is what you all say. That it is better in the original than when translated. But I do not know Greek nor Latin. You cannot blame my father in this — he did try to teach me when I took a notion to learn as a child — I had no taste for the level of application necessary."

"Perhaps," Darcy repeated with emphasis and a smile, "were you to find a better translation — there are many of Homer. This time, you cannot accuse my opinion of being too popular, for most such scholarly gentlemen, as you imagine me to be, would not admit any translation could have value."

Then he showed a smile that made his eyes warm and bright. "That image is very charming. I see you as a little girl struggling over declensions for a week or two before running to Ann Radcliffe or Frances Burney for easier entertainment."

Elizabeth laughed. "Your imagination drew a good picture, for as I recall that is how it went, except it was Robinson Crusoe I turned to. So you think I should find a superior translation. That does destroy my objection. Once someone has already learned the ancient language and translated the poet's words into readable English, what excuse could I offer for not putting forth the much lesser application to read their efforts?"

Colonel Fitzwilliam spoke, "There is no excuse — it is Pope's translation that sits under my pillow; I can heartily recommend it."

"I attempted Pope's Homer already. I have begun the Iliad in more than one, though less than three, translations." Elizabeth gave Colonel Fitzwilliam an arch smile. "We disagree on the merit of Pope. I have never liked him — the heroic couplet is too refined and constricted for my taste. Unnatural — I see you both smile, you think I speak like every girl with an enthusiasm for contemporary poets. And I do. I own the ordinariness of my enthusiasm freely."

Darcy shifted about and said with a half frown, "You have a potent charm solely your own. Even should your opinion be shared by many other persons, it has distinction due to the possessor. I smiled because I agree about Pope. The poets between Milton and Cowper are rarely to my taste."

He had once said she was a fool like every other girl. And now he praised her in this manner. Elizabeth's spirit soared birdlike, and she exclaimed, "Ha! We *have* read the same books, with the same feelings."

"*I* never doubted it; *you* suggested the opposite."

Darcy's grin flashed his teeth, and Elizabeth replied, "Never have I been more pleased to be wrong."

Lady Catherine called out from where she sat on her stiff chair, attended by Mr. and Mrs. Collins, "What do you speak of? I must have my share of conversation."

Elizabeth saw a flash of irritation in Darcy's eyes. She held up her hand to stop him and Colonel Fitzwilliam from replying to Lady Catherine. With a mischievous smirk at Darcy she spoke, "We spoke of names, and I wished your advice on the matter. I think Greek or Roman names should be prohibited. The other day Mr. Darcy told me about a young lady named after a girl burned alive by her father. This lady forced her sister to marry a man she fancied not at all so that she could escape being Miss Iphigenia and become Miss...."

Elizabeth looked at Darcy for help. She hoped he was not offended by the levity with which she'd chosen to treat his aunt.

He grinned back at her. Elizabeth felt warm and happy. "The lady became Miss Webb."

Lady Catherine cried out, "Miss Webb, is she one of the —"

"No Madam, her father is a cousin of theirs though."

"I have met the man." She then said to Elizabeth in a firm voice, "You wish my advice on names?"

"I do."

"It is wise you put thought on this matter. Naming a child is a momentous consideration. The name influences how a man is perceived and through that changes their character and destiny. However, your opinion is wrong. Classical names are appropriate, even if the story is tragic. But, there is a common practice you must swear to avoid when you marry. Do not allow your husband to add a feminine ending to a man's name. It is silly. I never permit anyone I can prevent from doing so."

Elizabeth blinked, a little surprised by her vehemence. "Is not your niece named Georgiana?"

"I tried to prevent it!" Lady Catherine slammed her hand against the cushioned arm of her chair and directed her speech to Darcy, "Nephew, I counseled your father to seek a different name. But he did not listen to me. An illness of Sir Lewis's kept me in Kent at the time of your sister's birth, or else I would have prevented that horrid name. When I had opportunity to speak with him, your father was convinced it was too late to change. She had already been registered and baptized. I will have your promise that you will never act so."

Elizabeth watched Darcy to see how he would reply. He turned to her before he replied and smirked. His eyes were bright and mischievous, and he was very handsome. Darcy adopted a somber look. "Aunt, I apologize and must beg your pardon. But Fitzwilhelmina has a delightful ring in my ear. I have long desired to have a daughter named so."

As Lady Catherine sputtered in response, he looked around and caught her eye. Elizabeth was a foot behind him so he did not face Lady Catherine when he did. He winked at her. "Miss Bennet, I appeal to you, do you not think it a beautiful name?"

Lady Catherine ranted about how horrible of a name Fitzwilhelmina was and demanded he drop the notion. Elizabeth barely heard any of it, as she stared at Darcy with an astonished smile. She was lost. Perhaps he no longer cared for her affection, but this brilliant man who wished to make her laugh had it.

Chapter 12

Following that evening, regular intercourse grew between the gentlemen of Rosings Park and the ladies of Hunsford parsonage. Darcy met Elizabeth while out walking, and often he called on her at the parsonage. The Hunsford party dined at Rosings a further three times.

On the final day of Darcy's stay with his aunt, he walked out with Colonel Fitzwilliam quite early to call upon Elizabeth and Mrs. Collins. It was a damned shame Colonel Fitzwilliam needed to return to London, so he could visit his parents for a few days before he rejoined his regiment. Lady Catherine remained a terrible bore, but Elizabeth's presence had made this visit an actual pleasure.

Near every day he had spoken with her on a call or a walk. The infatuation which led him to desire to marry her was gone, but he'd found in her an excellent friend whose mind worked in a sharp yet charming manner. She was different from any other person he knew. If his own wishes were solely consulted, he would stay in Kent until Elizabeth returned to London.

Even with the presence of Bingley, his clubs, society, lectures, races and so many other entertainments, London was never half so enjoyable as Kent with Elizabeth in it.

Elizabeth sat in the parsonage's small white parlor and wore a bright sprigged muslin dress. He was struck again by the regular features of her face and how deep Elizabeth's eyes were when she looked at him and smiled. However, she was paler than normal, and her smile not so bright.

He pulled a chair next to where she sat on the couch. "Are you well Miss Bennet? Your spirits appear low. Is something the matter?"

Elizabeth flushed and bit her lip, looking away at Darcy's question. She rubbed her cheek as though she were embarrassed. "It is nothing, only a headache."

Darcy frowned and peered closely at her face. "Are you certain? You must care for your health. If there is anything I might do to help, I am at your disposal."

Elizabeth's eyes brightened, and she turned to him with a sweet smile. "I assure you, I am perfectly fine. I know the exact cause of my indisposition, it is nothing dangerous."

Her smile lifted his spirits. Her smiles always were warm and genuine. Perhaps Elizabeth really was well. He replied with his own smile. "I am glad. It would distress me greatly if something was amiss with you. Your friendship is dear to me. I shall miss your presence in London. Neither Bingley, nor any other friend of mine, can argue near so charmingly or cleverly as you."

Elizabeth glanced at where Colonel Fitzwilliam patiently listened to Mr. Collins speak on the other side of the drawing room. "I shall miss your company as well. Excellent as he is, my cousin's conversation lacks something present in yours."

The animation in Elizabeth's face left with a sigh. Her affliction seemed more melancholy than headache. "Miss Bennet, something does bother you. If you do not wish to speak on it, I shall importune you no further, but if anything is the matter which I might help, I beg you ask."

Elizabeth looked down and chewed on her lip. It was a pretty gesture, but she looked discomposed. Darcy wondered what could be the matter. "Is it something amiss with your family, I know Jane and Bingley were well as of a few days ago, and —"

Her clear eyes met his, and their corners crinkled with amusement. "I assure you, it is not an issue of *that* sort. No one is ill, no one is bankrupt, no one is — well whatever horror your imagination constructed."

While this relieved Darcy of any serious worry, the way Elizabeth sighed and looked down, almost avoiding his gaze, did not satisfy him. What was the matter? She did not want to speak on it; that was clear. He pulled in a deep breath. "So long as you are well, and I can be of no help, I am satisfied. Though only because you assured me the matter is not dangerous."

Elizabeth laughed quickly. "I did claim it was not." She studied his face and then said, blushing and looking at her hands, "I — in truth I am melancholy at parting. Your conversation has been very dear to me."

"Oh." Darcy felt the rope of affection that bound him to Elizabeth tighten. He made her life happier. Elizabeth's embarrassment kept a bright unstoppable smile on his face. He said enthusiastically, "We must see each other when you pass through London. Might I hope you will stay for some period of time? There are a great many sights in town you must see. I shall call upon Bingley while you are resident — I wish Georgiana to make your acquaintance."

"That is an enticing plan. There is nothing I'd like more than to meet Miss Darcy and laugh about town with you." Elizabeth sighed and shook her head. "The melancholy truth is I shall be present one evening alone. My father dearly wishes my presence at home before my summer trip with my Aunt and Uncle Gardiner. I do not think it shall be possible."

He'd counted on seeing Elizabeth in London. They would dance at a ball, and she would be in his box at a play. She and Georgiana would meet and become friends. None of that would happen. She would be in Hertfordshire and then the north for months. The season would end; he would return to Pemberley; and he might not see her for a long time.

"I shall find some expedient to call upon you, even if it requires I behave quite rudely towards your brother and sister. I shall not allow our friendship to be broken up so long. I will not. I promise to see you in London."

The depression in Elizabeth lifted at this. "There is the Darcy spirit." She laughed, her fine dark eyes sparkling. "I now have no fear I shall miss you. You are a man to run over all obstacles in your way once determined. I shall depend upon seeing you."

Her confidence in him and eagerness to see him again made him feel as good as making her laugh did.

Eventually their call ended, and he was forced to walk slowly back towards his aunt's house.

The lawn was kept clipped short, and one of the mowers was out in the middle sweeping the long scythe through the grasses. It was a foolish extravagance to cut it as often as his aunt did. His aunt was often extravagant, mistaking expense for substance.

Elizabeth's eyes brightened and she showed that impertinent smirk whenever Lady Catherine asked one of her overbearing questions. She always responded in a playful manner that punctured the pretension without giving offense.

He would miss Elizabeth while they were separate. How he cared for her now was very different from the desperate desire to touch and possess her he felt in the autumn, but the affectionate closeness had more meaning, more permanence. She was burrowing into his soul.

He would find a way for them to meet again after she left London far sooner than Elizabeth expected. She would smile and look at him with warm approval before teasing him when they met again. She liked him quite as much as he liked her.

Darcy stumbled to a stop. Might Elizabeth have a romantic affection for him? Could her sadness at their parting have been due to deeper feelings than only friendship? She had been very affected. Maybe Elizabeth loved him.

He saw Elizabeth bite her lip as she watched him with those large eyes. She had watched him so many times in the past weeks. He had thought she studied whether his manner had actually improved since the autumn. But, if she loved him, she watched because she liked to look on his person.

In his mind Elizabeth stared intently at him through those pretty lashes and spoke in a breathy whisper, *I want you to kiss me*.

Ridiculous. They had become friends, but her determined dislike of the previous autumn could not become affection so speedily. Before he thought she flirted with him when her true intentions were the opposite. He would not go down the same path again.

Only a foolish man would rush to think a woman had affection for him. Only a foolish man would think friendship meant love.

The next morning Darcy and Colonel Fitzwilliam left quite early to make the journey to London. For half an hour the two sat in silence while the carriage swayed as it bounced along the road. Was it possible Elizabeth loved him? He could say it was ridiculous many times, but the idea refused to leave.

They had sought each other out on walks, and Elizabeth always treated him warmly and preferred his conversation to that of any other. But that was only because their minds worked similarly, and she found his conversation highly engaging. Darcy smiled. For once he had entertained a lady better than his cousin.

Ha! When a woman was sufficiently clever, he could charm her.

What if she did like him? Did he want to marry Elizabeth? The flush of desire that had raged back into his body shouted yes. He yearned, like a drunken sailor stumbling about for his grog, to make her laugh again. His every emotion said yes.

Yet, he could not trust himself in this matter. These feelings were powerful, but they misled him last January. Should he trust them now? Was his desire rational?

Colonel Fitzwilliam broke Darcy's deepening reverie. "That Miss Bennet — she's a damned fine woman. Damned fine. Don't you agree Darcy?"

Darcy frowned at his cousin but nodded.

"It amazes me she is not married yet. The gentlemen in Hertfordshire must be fools to have not hunted her down. Even with her small dowry, a woman like that would be worth it — don't you agree?" Colonel Fitzwilliam nudged Darcy.

When no reply was made his cousin continued, "That will change soon. Her sister's marriage to Bingley will bring her out into a broader society. Some clever gentleman will find a superior wife in her."

Of course Bingley would want to do Elizabeth a good turn. He and Jane would introduce her around in town at the first opportunity. Thank heavens she would return so speedily to Hertfordshire and her father. It had depressed him that he would have little opportunity to see her in town, but now that seemed an excellent situation. He'd seen that no gentleman in Hertfordshire impressed her.

"I had a thought." Colonel Fitzwilliam pushed Darcy's shoulder. "I want your opinion on this scheme, so pay attention — I have fifteen thousand settled away, and with my salary it would hardly be *impossible* for me to marry, even if the girl had nothing. I know I have always declared an —"

"You cannot marry Elizabeth! You cannot!" Darcy roared into his cousin's face, baring his teeth, "I will not —"

"Hahahaha!" Colonel Fitzwilliam slapped his leg. "I had wondered how much it would take to make you admit you liked her."

Darcy flushed and the tense anger left him as Colonel Fitzwilliam laughed. "I wish you could have seen your own face. That was near the most terrifying look I have ever seen. Well, are you going to act on it? You would be a damned fool not to."

"I don't think Elizabeth likes me."

"Seriously?" Fitzwilliam peered at Darcy and laughed again. "This is perfect. I always knew you could not tell what women think. But this proves it — I have rarely seen a lady so eager for a man's esteem as your Miss Bennet is for yours. What ever made you think she disliked you?"

Darcy sat stiff and didn't reply. He'd told Colonel Fitzwilliam months before about how he'd argued with a lady he nearly decided to marry and that it had convinced him he thought too highly of himself. Colonel Fitzwilliam had thought it was hilarious. He *would not* admit to his cousin that the lady he'd argued with was Elizabeth.

The admission was unnecessary. "Wait — I should have realized it before — the lady who said you'd behaved as a crowing rooster must have been Miss Bennet. Oh, I wish I had seen her railing at you. She has such bright eyes. I assure you, that lady no longer holds the manner you insulted her against you."

Darcy glared at Colonel Fitzwilliam. Bingley would have ceased to speak if shown that gaze, Colonel Fitzwilliam grinned wider. "You cannot scare me. I have known you since we both were lads jumping in puddles — she most likely argued with you because she liked you."

"That makes no sense." Darcy felt a spasm of rejection again, as he remembered that horrid moment when Elizabeth called him selfish, cruel, and unfeeling. "She thought most ill of me."

"Don't feel bad about it. You have improved, and she likes you *now*. That is what is important — had some ordinary person offended her she would have laughed and been done with it. Our aunt and her cousin try their best to offend her, and it arouses no dislike."

Colonel Fitzwilliam smirked. "But when insulted by the tall and handsome Mr. Darcy — the man whose noble mien she admired — that was different. Miss Bennet would not have thought ill of you if she did not think well of you."

That made a startling amount of sense. It explained so much. Perhaps when they argued in the autumn, she'd tried to impress him. Elizabeth thought him a friend now, and she argued even more. Hardly an opportunity was lost to challenge him or make him defend some silly hypothetical.

Darcy grinned, not caring that he looked like a lovesick fool. He loved Elizabeth's manner.

He loved Elizabeth. It was that simple.

Colonel Fitzwilliam laughed again. "Now that is a silly smile. So will you marry her?"

"I am still not certain she cares for me," Darcy said plaintively.

"Love, it makes the best of men fools." Colonel Fitzwilliam said, "Ask her. You are no coward."

"I think I will."

ONCE THEY ARRIVED AT Darcy's house, Colonel Fitzwilliam took off to his father's townhouse. Without Georgiana or a guest, the house was empty. Darcy rarely minded solitude, but it now oppressed him. He'd have so little opportunity to see Elizabeth when she was in London. Should he ask her then?

It was late for a call, but Darcy set off for Bingley's house. He more wished to see Elizabeth's sister than Bingley or his own. It would connect him to her. It was near dark when Darcy knocked on his friend's door. It was improper to call so late, and the butler who had been rented along with the house looked askance at him. Darcy stared back firmly though he felt a little guilt.

The man brought Darcy's presence to his master's attention, and Darcy was ushered into the dining room, even though the Bingleys were in the middle of a meal with two guests. He recognized them from Bingley's wedding as Mr. and Mrs. Gardiner. Darcy went stiff and tall at seeing himself the object of everyone's attention due to his unfashionable intrusion.

Georgiana burst up from her chair and ran to embrace him. She then looked embarrassedly at the people around the table who grinned at her.

Bingley also stood quickly and stepped forward to heartily grasp Darcy's hand. "I'm so pleased to see you. Very pleased. We had not expected you until tomorrow morning."

Darcy began to stammer an explanation, but Bingley cut him off, "Nevermind that. It doesn't matter why. I am glad to see you. Have you dined yet?" Darcy shook his head no. "Excellent, excellent. You must take a seat with us. It is no imposition — right dear?"

Jane immediately added her assent to Bingley's and said in her soft voice, "We are glad to have you."

Darcy was seated between Mrs. Gardiner and Georgiana. The footman arranged a set of plates and silverware, and Bingley eagerly carved additional slices from the roast goose for him. The cook was informed to produce an extra plate for dessert.

Georgiana peppered Darcy with questions about his stay at Rosings. Half the questions had been answered before in his letters, but after several weeks absence Darcy was happy to entertain his sister. Many questions related to Elizabeth, who Georgiana had developed a lively curiosity about. Prompted by this Jane also asked Darcy questions about how her sister did.

It was a comfortable, pleasant gathering. Jane and Bingley exchanged small smiles and almost indecent marks of affection. For the first time Darcy near burned with envy for the good fortune of his friend. To have a wife to smile at him and share his concerns and entertain his guests. To have a wife at home instead of empty parlors and bedchambers.

He always smirked at those gentlemen who longed for domestic bliss. The pleasures of independence had never palled before. Yet, Bingley was so happy, and Jane so sweet. Darcy wanted Elizabeth. He understood why Bingley preferred Jane, but Elizabeth was immeasurably superior. Jane smiled, Elizabeth laughed.

After the dinner it was determined they would spend another hour together in the drawing room and Georgiana would return with Darcy. The sudden realization that she would leave the roof of her idol sooner than originally planned caused Georgiana to abandon her brother in favor of conversation with Jane.

Darcy sat next to Mr. and Mrs. Gardiner. They both were neatly dressed with excellent taste. Mr. Gardiner was a vibrant, balding man of about forty.

He had a quick smile, and from his manners it would be impossible to tell that Mr. Gardiner was in trade. Or that his sister was Mrs. Bennet.

Darcy had not seen them since the wedding and guiltily suspected his oft mentioned distaste of the Bennet's connections, prior to Bingley's engagement, may have been the cause. Had he not chosen to intrude rudely upon Bingley, without invitation or notice, quite likely he would not have met them again for some time.

From the conversation at dinner, Darcy found they had been regular visitors during the past three weeks, and Georgiana was now on familiar terms with the two. Darcy wished to become friends with them as his sister thought highly of them and they were Elizabeth's favorite relations.

After a few pleasantries, Darcy said to Mrs. Gardiner, "I understand you spent your childhood in Lambton. It is a mere five miles from Pemberley. I do not pass through more than a dozen times in a year, but it is a neat town, and the dining rooms at the inn are excellent. I always stop in when I have business with my tenants in the fields thereabouts."

Mrs. Gardiner had a lively smile, which, despite the absence of a blood relation, reminded Darcy greatly of Elizabeth. "I consider that corner of Derbyshire to be the best in England. The weather, the forests and meadows, the society — perhaps it is only the fond memories of a girl, but I have never so liked a place. That inn — my father was friends with the proprietor, old Mr. Brown. I remember they argued politics and business each time my father stopped in for a meal. He always ensured I had a fine bit of pastry. He would be quite old today — but tell me does Mr. Brown still live?"

Darcy shook his head. "Nay, a fever took him in the winter some three years past. He was well mourned. But his life had been good, and he lived far past the three score and ten years allotted to us. His son-in-law Mr. Kendrick now runs the inn. The food — and pastries — are as excellent as ever."

"Oh." A little depression was in Mrs. Gardiner's eyes. "'Tis strange how life goes. He saw notice of my father's death in the paper and sent us a kind letter. Yet I had no knowledge of his passing. And the lawyer, Mr. Pyne, do you know if —"

Darcy smiled. "Mr. Pyne is alive and well. He recently won a suit for my neighbor brought against me about water rights. A most clever and capable man. I admire him greatly. The manner in which he beat my lawyers, several who were distinguished London solicitors, showed him to have a genius for his profession."

After the names Mrs. Gardiner wished to inquire after were exhausted, the two compared anecdotes about the region and memories of particular locations.

A wonderful idea came to Darcy. Elizabeth had told him that she would travel with the Gardiners this summer when they toured the north of England. Might he convince them to stay, perhaps for a substantial period of time, at Pemberley? "Your affection for Lambton is clear, you must wish to see the neighborhood again. Have you any plans to do so?"

Mr. and Mrs. Gardiner exchanged a glance, and Mr. Gardiner shrugged. "We had not, we intended this summer to go on a tour through the Lake District. But in the last week a matter of business arose that will require my presence in London for several weeks past the date we hoped to leave. We no longer have time to explore that far north."

Mrs. Gardiner nudged her husband. "*He* wished to fish and sail on the lakes. However, I have determined to make the best of the situation and have near convinced him to take us to Lambton instead. I have desired to see the neighborhood again for some months now. I only worry that Lizzy will be disappointed at the reduction in our plans, for she is to travel with us."

This fit neatly with Darcy's hope. "If you choose Lambton, it would delight me to host you at Pemberley. While we cannot offer sailing" — Darcy grinned at Mr. Gardiner — "the fishing in my ponds and streams is first-rate. And they are always perfectly stocked — I have fished at the Lakes, and there is no comparison. The park at Pemberley is superior."

"That is a strong inducement," Mr. Gardiner said.

"Do promise to make a plan of it. From Pemberley you could easily visit your acquaintances in Lambton and survey the land about. Besides, you remember from your time in the neighborhood how beautiful the park at Pemberley is. You must make the circuit around it."

Mr. and Mrs. Gardiner both looked intrigued by the idea, and Mr. Gardiner tapped his cheek in thought. Darcy suspected he hesitated at accepting his hospitality so quick after they had become properly acquainted. Bingley and Jane had begun to play a game of cards with Georgiana and Mrs. Annesley. Darcy called out, "Bingley, can I convince you to visit Pemberley this year? You must let me introduce your wife to its beauties. Last year it was I who visited, it would be unsporting to not let me return the favor."

Bingley replied, "That is a capital idea. You merely need command me as to the date, and I will be there."

"Would you confirm for Mr. Gardiner that my claims about the excellence of my fishing and sport are not merely the fond exaggerations of an owner, but honest truth?"

"I will freely confirm that the fish in your ponds are large and clever and that a fox hunt on Pemberley's lands in November is close to perfection." Bingley said to the Gardiners, "I see towards what Darcy's requests turn. If you add Derbyshire to your tour of the lakes, it would make an excellent scheme. We all should set out together and travel to Pemberley together. We could stay a few weeks before you set off to the lakes. You can save much of the fare on rented horses."

Bingley added to Darcy, "I must have you and Georgiana at Netherfield for a few weeks before we leave. You could lodge at Netherfield once the season ends, and we all might leave from there for Pemberley once Mr. Gardiner has wrapped his business in London up."

Darcy smiled. The opportunity for several more weeks with Elizabeth was perfect. It would give him ample opportunity to improve her opinion of him if anything was wanting. Then once she had seen Pemberley, he would ask for her hand. Even for a girl as sensible and unimpressed by wealth and consequence as Elizabeth, Pemberley must make him more attractive. "That is an excellent extension of the plan. I will happily follow you to Netherfield."

Bingley shouted, "Gardiner, accept this plan. It's perfect."

Mr. Gardiner smiled and said, "It is impossible for me to object further. I shall hold you to your promises about the fishing. I gained a taste for stream fishing as a boy in Meryton, but in town there is little opportunity to engage in the sport."

The details were soon settled, and Mrs. Gardiner promised to write a letter that evening to inform Elizabeth of the change in their plans. But as a shortening of the trip was unavoidable, she would vouch for her niece thinking it an excellent modification.

Even if she did not — yet — feel affection for him, Darcy knew Mrs. Gardiner was right. Elizabeth had asked him many questions about Pemberley and would love to see it for herself.

She loved that sheltered grove on the edge of Rosings's park. Many walks about Pemberley were considerably superior. They would delight Elizabeth. She would smile and look about with eagerly darting eyes as he held her arm and pointed out the varied beauties of his estate.

Chapter 13

Despite the briefness of Elizabeth's stay in London — only one evening — Jane was determined to do her sister a good turn and provide for her an opportunity to see something of the pleasures of London before returning to the rustic life in Hertfordshire.

Jane had become stubborn since her marriage. She never used to be so pushy. Protests were useless, and despite having been in a post-chase a full five hours, Elizabeth's comfortable day clothes were stripped off, and she was bathed and placed in a gorgeous yellow ballgown Jane had purchased as a gift. It was almost extravagantly expensive. Then Jane stuck her on a chair in her dressing room, and they talked while Jane's superbly trained lady's maid spent a half hour turning her hair into something that was pronounced barely acceptable.

Jane forced her to borrow a necklace with real diamonds and pushed Elizabeth into the carriage. She was quickly driven through the streets of London's most fashionable districts before they arrived at the destination. It was a large ball held by an Earl who was a friend of Darcy's and an acquaintance of Mr. Bingley's. By the time they arrived at the large house Elizabeth's fatigue and soreness had been replaced by excitement.

Would Darcy be there? She'd been too embarrassed to ask Jane, but she desperately hoped he would. He'd promised to try to see her during the day she was in London, and the ball would be his best opportunity.

It would feel awful if he was not there.

When Darcy left Rosings, Elizabeth had been depressed. He'd not watched her with the intense stare he showed in the autumn, and she started most of their conversations. She'd come to love him after she destroyed his esteem. It was what she deserved for the horrid way she behaved in the autumn. But over the fortnight since, Elizabeth concluded matters were not hopeless.

The scheme, which Mrs. Gardiner claimed to be Darcy's idea, for them to spend three full weeks at Pemberley had been hatched. Darcy had liked her once. It was hardly impossible for that feeling to be renewed with greater intimacy. Nothing would be more natural. Between his stay at Netherfield and the trip to Pemberley, she would have more than a month of his regular company.

The ballroom was crowded and a little too warm. Hundreds of candles burned on an endlessly branching chandelier hung from the center of the room. The expense of clothing and decoration was greater than Elizabeth had ever seen. What would they be like?

She had seen the aged great in Lady Catherine. Now she would see how the young London set behaved.

So far this only appeared to be a better dressed and more crowded version of the Meryton assembly balls. Elizabeth bit her lip with amusement as she looked about. Surely the possessors of all this wealth would prove *somehow* more interesting than her neighbors.

Several gentlemen looked at her and Jane with clear appreciation. Elizabeth felt her spirits jump yet higher. She looked *very* well this evening. If only Darcy was here, it would be perfect. Any admiration he'd once felt must be rekindled if she could smile at him while dressed this way.

Lord Carrington, the host, gave a smooth bow when he greeted them and begged a dance from both Elizabeth and Jane. Several other gentlemen began to approach for introductions.

There was Darcy. Elizabeth lit up like a bright lantern.

He looked at her as he strode towards them, elegantly dodging the people about him. He almost floated through the crowd. His hair fell a little over his forehead. The tightly fitted breeches and perfect fall of Darcy's coat took her breath away.

Darcy had an eager smile as he stepped next to her. "Miss Bennet, you look especially handsome and tempting tonight. You must promise to dance with me twice. Name any sets which appeal to you, for I am unengaged at present."

Elizabeth planned to be bold. But that was impossible. He was so very handsome, and she loved him. She felt a sudden shyness and could not meet Mr. Darcy's gaze. She looked down. His dancing slippers had a silver buckle. The fabric of his stockings clung firmly to Darcy's muscular legs.

"Miss Bennet, are you well?"

Elizabeth forced her eyes up and hurriedly responded, "I apologize. I was — briefly distracted. If you will let me choose any, then the first and — I would say the last, but I'm not sure if I shall be awake that late. I was woken quite early this morning to begin my journey from Kent. Perhaps —" Elizabeth looked at her card and pointed to a set an hour and a half before the ball was to end, "Would this please you?"

At Darcy's nod she penciled his name in. Elizabeth's spirits rallied, and with a smile she said, "You must promise to dance most sets tonight. There never are enough gentlemen, and it shall be your duty to help those ladies who are slighted by other men."

"I shall do as you command. I have failed in this duty before, but it shall never be said that I am incapable of improvement. I am even prepared to be introduced to someone in a ballroom. I shall be more forward and dance more than I ever have before."

Elizabeth laughed, but before she could speak a handsome man about Darcy's age, who dressed with a dandy's care, approached them and cried out, "Darcy! You must introduce me to this delightful creature next to you. My eyes have not been able to leave her since she entered the room."

Elizabeth hoped that was frustration — or better jealousy — in Darcy's eyes when he hesitated before performing the ritual. After this Elizabeth and Jane were surrounded with gentlemen seeking an opportunity for a dance, and she had no further opportunity to speak with Mr. Darcy before the music started and they went out to the floor.

Elizabeth was happy to dance with Darcy. She fancied more was present than just friendship and platonic admiration in his eyes. It made Elizabeth nervous and a little quiet. The novelty of the setting also left Elizabeth off balance: The roof was thirty feet above them, and this one room in a private house in London was larger than the assembly hall in Meryton. The other couples were very fine, and many dressed far more expensively than even the gown Jane had gifted her.

Darcy noticed nothing of that. He had been born into this society. Was any hope she might have to attach him a delusion?

Though he did not dance a great deal, Darcy was capable at the art. After a few minutes of mostly silence, he teased Elizabeth into a better mood with entertaining anecdotes of persons in the room. Darcy's eye for character and inconsistency was as good as her father's, and by the end of that dance, she had relaxed.

Immediately Elizabeth was claimed by her next partner, and for the next hours she was passed from gentleman to gentleman. It gratified, but while many were excellent and handsome men, and some possessed even more wealth and consequence than Darcy, none were near his equal.

It was great fun to watch his progress through the room. He danced all but one set during the evening, and that he spent in conversation with several dowagers, who sat on the edges of the room to chaperone their daughters for the evening. Darcy was a handsome figure of a man.

Elizabeth could see that the conversations wore at him. Near the end of the evening, their eyes met as he went to a side table to acquire a glass of wine for his partner of the moment. Darcy looked at her and smirked and shrugged, as though to say, 'Behold I have followed your commands. I am able to put myself to the trouble.'

Their dance arrived at last. Elizabeth's feet hurt, and Jane and Bingley planned to leave after this set. The crowd had thinned greatly, and the number of couples on the floor was a little less than half what it had been at the start. Elizabeth saw Darcy was fatigued, so she smiled at him and held his hand a little tighter than appropriate when he led her to the dance floor, but said nothing.

Darcy smiled at Elizabeth, and for the first minutes of the dance, they enjoyed the sense of contentment and silent companionship together. They were good enough friends it was not necessary to speak. At last Darcy said, a hoarse rasp in his voice, "I feel I have finished a hard day's journey and arrived safely at the inn. I can be myself with you. It exhausts me to make conversation for a half hour with someone I barely know. I do not know that I have ever spoken so much to strangers and bare acquaintances as I have this night."

Elizabeth winsomely smiled at him as she stepped through the next figure of the dance. "And yet, you did so well at it."

"A most excellent lady set the task upon me tonight. I had no choice but to perform."

Elizabeth felt warm and gave Darcy a sparkling toothy smile in reply. He appeared taken aback by Elizabeth's happiness and with an almost embarrassed smile added, "Of late I have attempted to be more social at such gatherings. I do not wish to stupidly stand about the edge of a room always. I find I enjoy it in small quantities. But even if I did not, I ought to practice the art of conversation with strangers."

This resolution on Darcy's part felt almost a compliment to Elizabeth. She smiled too happily and roundly praised Darcy, "It delights me to hear this. That you strive to improve yourself shows your superiority. It shows how excellent and fine of a gentleman you are."

"Shows my superiority?" Darcy's eyes gleamed. "You ought not to praise me so well, for I shall begin to think too highly of myself — excess of humility is by no means my failing."

Elizabeth laughed. "I have my own vice. By no means praise me for my cleverness."

"Then I shall only think highly of your cleverness and never praise you direct for it."

They beamed at each other. The horrid argument in January had turned into a mutual jest, which helped cement their friendship and — she hoped — affection.

As the set continued Darcy acted uncomfortable. He uncharacteristically stumbled over a step, and his face took that stiff expression he used to hide emotion. He opened his mouth to speak once, but nothing was said. What could he possibly find such difficulty with? Elizabeth felt tense and unsure whether to hope or fear.

At last Darcy said, "It has been on my mind of late that I ought to marry."

Elizabeth swallowed, and the odd idea that he might of a sudden ask her here, in the middle of this crush, came to her mind. Or would he, as all his words to her had been of friendship, beg her to speak her opinion on some other lady he liked.

When Elizabeth's face froze, Darcy added hurriedly, "There are general reasons. It has been on my mind. I have seen your sister and Bingley. The happiness of their marriage does make me long for similar bliss. I have reached the age where a man ought to marry, Georgiana needs a sister..." Darcy trailed off and cleared his throat.

Elizabeth's heart stuttered uncomfortably, but she forced herself to speak. She wished to encourage him. Was she on his mind? Was this a general intention? "*I* think it an excellent plan for you to marry. However, you must choose the *right* woman." Elizabeth smiled archly, "Do you think this wife might dance with you in a London ballroom?"

Darcy held Elizabeth's hand as they twisted through the next figure. His manner had become easier at Elizabeth's words and smile. "And how do you think the *right* woman would behave? What sort of wife do I need?"

Elizabeth bit her lip. She would behave as she always did. He spoke obliquely and deserved a teasing answer. "Why, someone who never teases or quarrels with you. A woman who combines perfect deference on the outside with perfect mercenary greed on the inside. Miss Bingley is your ideal."

Darcy looked like he'd bitten through the worm in a rotten apple. Elizabeth laughed, and at the sound his expression brightened. She saw he loved her laughter. Thrilled Elizabeth spoke, "You need a woman who will quarrel and dispute with you in fun. It ought to be someone pricklier and less pleasant than Jane." Elizabeth finished with a dancing smile, "After all you are not nearly so agreeable or easy as Bingley."

"You have diagnosed my needs perfectly. But she must also be a dear friend and have the most beautiful and striking eyes. While I might dance with her in a London ballroom, such a woman could not be met in one. My only hope would be to meet such a lady in the assembly rooms of some small country town. But I am such a fool that if I did, I would likely insult her."

Elizabeth's heart beat fast. She stared at Darcy and barely noticed that the music had stopped and the dance ended. "And she would be such a fool as to be deeply offended and not see your good qualities at first. But over time — any such girl must come to love you."

Darcy still held her hand in his warm large one. The speech affected him and brought his color high. "Elizabeth —"

"Lizzy — Lizzy." Jane grabbed Elizabeth's arm and pulled her away from Darcy. "Charles is already dozing. We must leave." Jane yawned. "I am quite tired myself, and you were up so early — Mr. Darcy, I apologize for stealing your partner, but I am sure you shall not mind."

Something in Darcy's stare made Elizabeth smile and said he minded very much. Jane added chirpily, "Oh, you look to be in a quite ill mood yourself, you must be tired too. Mr. Darcy, promise me you shall leave right after us and go straight to bed."

Without waiting for a reply Jane started to pull Elizabeth away. Elizabeth disentangled her arm from Jane's and looked at Darcy. It was impossible to leave him like this. She looked longingly into his eyes.

Darcy's brow cleared, and he kissed her hand again while Jane watched them. "Miss Bennet, soon we shall see each other again. I am eager to become friends with your friends in Meryton, and you must see Pemberley. I so want you to see my home. Once you have, we will finish this interrupted conversation. It — there is no hurry, and my home has always been so dear to my heart once you have seen it —"

Elizabeth hoped she understood him aright. "I shall take that as a promise."

Chapter 14

A few weeks later Jane and Bingley removed to Netherfield. Darcy would have followed them immediately with Georgiana, but he still wished to keep her separate from Wickham. The regiment was to depart in the middle of the summer, a fortnight later than its initial plan, and Darcy would bring Georgiana to Netherfield that day. Then after another two weeks they would head to Pemberley.

It was a terribly long time. Two months would pass between the ball at Lord Carrington's, and when he would at last have Elizabeth at Pemberley. Perhaps he was a fool when he did not ride down to Longbourn the day after to seek Elizabeth's hand.

But the argument of January had left him scarred. She had called him cruel and selfish. She had identified the contempt he showed. She had been right. He needed to prove he'd become better. She would see his behavior among her family, and she would see the home he offered her. Then he would ask.

She had as good as promised to accept, but he wanted her to see everything first.

When Lady Matlock, Darcy's other aunt, begged to have Georgiana in her house for two weeks before the season ended, Darcy eagerly encouraged the plan, and, without any further obligations in London, took his carriage to Netherfield.

He would at last see Elizabeth again. He needed to see Elizabeth.

She had been so beautiful at the ball. She had smiled at him so. That beautiful, wide, white toothed smile. The smile of approval and affection. That smile haunted his dreams.

He loved her rationally and passionately. His spirit had placed a luminescent glow around Elizabeth. At the start of their second dance, he had been fatigued, and she made him feel relaxed and happy. He could tell Elizabeth anything. She had become his dearest friend. She saw his flaws and liked him still. She drove him to become a better man.

The road to Netherfield was a little familiar to Darcy. He'd seen those towns and hills before. His mind circled Elizabeth. How would she act when they saw each other? When he first approached her at the ball, surrounded by gentlemen whose eyes lingered hungrily upon her, she had looked about with a smile enjoying the scene. And then she saw him. And her eyes lit up.

Would she smile so again?

When the carriage pulled into the drive at Netherfield, Elizabeth was there. She stood on the portico with Bingley, her mother, and Jane to greet the carriage. Darcy paused before he stepped out to take her in. A pair of white marble columns framed her. She wore a light yellow dress with a wide green ribbon around her waist tied just below her bosom. Curls floated about her forehead, and their eyes met.

Her gaze struck in the core of his being. She looked down and blushed sweetly. Darcy exited the carriage. Elizabeth looked at him with an uncertain smile. His heart beat hard as he smiled back. She met his eyes with a sunny grin.

Bingley greeted Darcy effusively. While Darcy shook his friend's hand and was ushered indoors, Elizabeth kept her eyes upon him. Her admiration made him stand tall and proud.

Once they all sat in Netherfield's drawing room, Mrs. Bennet burst out, "Lord! Mr. Darcy, it is very kind of you — so kind — to host so much of my family — No matter what anyone said, I always thought the best of you. They all claimed you to be rude and silent, but I said: No, Mr. Darcy only shows a very becoming family pride."

Darcy inclined his head though this unexpected speech confused him. No matter what he would be polite to her. He had no idea what to say.

Mrs. Bennet rushed on, "I never believed anything Mr. Wickham said against you. Never — I am sure it would not possibly bother you if I sent off my daughter Catherine along with Jane and Lizzy to your estate. Jane said she could not bring Kitty along as you do not know her, and it would be impolite. But an additional girl could hardly signify. Kitty is so much better natured than Lizzy — I do not understand why my brother invites Lizzy to everything — and Lydia travels to Brighton in a few days. Kitty is so unhappy — she will hardly meet any wealthy men *here*, but some neighbor of yours might take a fancy to her."

Darcy incredulously stared at Mrs. Bennet. Her bold smile made the large unnatural blotches of red rouge on her cheeks stand out. The openly mercenary nature of Mrs. Bennet had not changed. And she denigrated Elizabeth's value. "Madam, I have not spoken three words to your daughter. This is to be a party of friends. An extra will be in the way."

"Kitty will not bother you — she is a well behaved girl who never runs off her mouth to her betters, unlike —"

"*Mama*, I begged you to say nothing," Elizabeth interrupted.

"Heavens. Lizzy, I do nothing wrong by asking. *You* care nothing for your sister, but *I* shall not be silenced."

Elizabeth coloured deeply and fell silent after a pained glance at Darcy. Mrs. Bennet's mistreatment of Elizabeth bothered Darcy more than the impertinent request. Elizabeth's unhappiness at the scene frustrated him, and he replied with a sharp authoritative voice, "Madam it is impossible."

Elizabeth flushed further, but Darcy's object was achieved, and the room fell silent. Elizabeth stiffly stared away with bright cheeks. Darcy was struck by her beauty and the knowledge he'd misspoken again. He had promised himself to not insult her family. How could he hope to make her happy if he always behaved rudely towards them?

Jane spoke, "Mama, I just recalled a matter in the management of the pantry I wished to ask your advice upon. It affects my preparation for the dinner we shall have tomorrow, so it is a matter of some urgency."

"Oh! Of course — I have trained you well" — she smiled at Bingley — "but it is good for you to ask when there is any doubt." The two ladies left the room. Elizabeth did not look up at their departure but continued to stare out the window.

Bingley said, "I apologize Darcy, we did not imagine she would ask you direct on such a matter. None of us — not even Kitty — think it a good idea. We did discourage her."

Darcy waved his hand. "It is of no significance."

Elizabeth was still flushed and would not look at him. Did she wish him to invite Miss Kitty?

THE RETURN

Surely Elizabeth did not wish Miss Kitty to be present. If he recalled the girl right, she was immature and a little insipid. An additional member to their party would take some of Elizabeth's attention. Darcy did not know how Miss Kitty would get along with Georgiana.

He should not assume he knew Elizabeth's mind. Even if she did not wish Kitty's presence he should ask.

Darcy hesitated for an instant as he truly did not wish Miss Kitty to travel with them. "Elizabeth," Darcy flushed when Bingley sat straighter and gave him a hard look, "Miss Bennet, I ought to have treated your mother with greater patience."

Elizabeth looked at him intently. There was a smile. Her eyes were striking and brilliant.

Darcy nearly stumbled to a halt. "Would you — that is do you wish your sister's presence? For if so it would not be too crowded in the carriages."

"No!" Elizabeth beamed at him. "Oh, no. There's little I wish less than to be trapped for many hours while my sister complains how unfair it is that Lydia traveled to Brighton while she could not. It is not only selfish reasons which argue against it — *Kitty* has no interest in the scheme. When Mama suggested it, Kitty thought a big house and a stuffy man" — Elizabeth's eyes twinkled — "or had she said a stuffy house and a big man? Either way, it was a poor substitute for officers and the seaside."

Darcy knew he'd spoken right from the quick turn in Elizabeth's spirits. "Pemberley's rooms are always well aired; I must be the stuffy one. Further, though tall, I am not near so large as Pemberley."

Darcy's heart beat faster at the bright way Elizabeth looked at him. "It was — it was handsome of you to offer. I know you would greatly dislike having a person who was nearly a stranger to you in the party."

"I would. But I would suffer anything to delight you."

Bingley coughed. "I am still here. Darcy that is a terribly pretty sentiment. You don't treat all your friends with that attitude."

THE NEXT EVENING WAS a dinner party at Lucas Lodge. Elizabeth prepared herself carefully. She chose a red evening dress with a wide square chest. It was a daring dress. Darcy's eyes had lingered over her; her slim figure delighted him. Elizabeth flushed with happiness and the familiar arousal that came when she imagined him kissing or touching her. He would hardly look away tonight.

As was his habit Mr. Bennet remained home. It was only a few minutes' walk to the Lucases, and though they did not leave early, they arrived before most guests. The entire walk Lydia and Kitty loudly quarreled. Upon their arrival the girls ceased. Lydia rushed to the punch table, and Kitty went to speak to Maria Lucas.

Elizabeth stayed near the vestibule and conversed with friends as they arrived. But part of her attention was always on the door. At last Darcy arrived with Bingley and Jane. He stood tall with his thick brown hair falling in neat waves and wore a well cut blue coat. His eyes sought around for her. They widened and he stopped as though struck when they lit upon her.

As his eyes lingered, Elizabeth lightly stepped to him to give greeting. "Mr. Darcy, I am delighted to see you arrive *at long last*, I had near despaired." She smiled, "You look to be in fine health and spirits tonight."

Before he replied, Sir William finished greeting Bingley and spoke to them, "Mr. Darcy, welcome, welcome to my home. It is a great delight to have such a distinguished person beneath this roof once again."

Darcy bowed his head in acknowledgement and said, "I am greatly pleased to be here. Your entertainment is always well worth enjoying."

"Your praise graces us. It graces us. You are too kind, far too kind. Like your distinguished aunt, at whose table I have dined twice. She is a perfect exemplar of her exalted rank. As you are."

Darcy nodded, smiled, and attempted to move away so he might direct his conversation towards Elizabeth again. However, as Elizabeth expected, following this show of goodwill from the silent Darcy, it was impossible for Sir William to let him leave so quick. "I had never seen such a great house as your aunt's. And her treatment of my daughter and her husband shows a perfect condescension that should be modeled by all the great in the kingdom."

In like manner Sir William continued, praising Lady Catherine near as effusively as his son-in-law and only pausing to ask such questions as, "The marble lions kept on the dining table, they are exquisite. Know you which master produced them?"

Elizabeth bit her lip. Darcy remained amiable under this onslaught of friendly inanity. Every minute or so he caught her eye and she grinned at him. Darcy did an admirable job of keeping any impatience out of his body language, but his eyes were a little helpless.

It was sweet of him to try to prove he could be sociable and friendly in Meryton. And his discomfort, evident to her, was delightfully charming. Each time Sir William asked a question, Darcy replied with a full sentence and looked at Elizabeth, who would smirk again. After ten minutes, Elizabeth at last pitied Darcy and rescued him.

"And the portrait of your aunt's late husband in the dining room, I measured it with my eye and believe it to be at least eight feet tall. It is a perfect likeness and the most glorious portrait I have seen except at St. James's. Do you not agree?"

"I —"

"I am sorry Sir William, but I just heard a call for music from the other room, and I wish to respond. I must claim Mr. Darcy to turn my pages for me."

She smiled winsomely at both of them

"Capital, capital. There is an excellent idea. Music is one of the greatest of refined pleasures. I shall not delay you."

As they walked to the drawing room Elizabeth said, "I perceived you enjoyed the conversation very much indeed, else I would have interrupted more quickly."

"You perceived that, did you?"

Elizabeth sat on the piano bench and patted next to her for Darcy to sit. "I did, yes. I know how very much you enjoy discussion of the price of your aunt's furnishings. I recall how you went on about them with Mr. Collins at Hunsford."

With that Elizabeth settled a piece of music before her and began. Because Darcy enjoyed her playing at Rosings, Elizabeth of late had practiced substantially more than her usual habit. The opportunity to display was welcome.

He sat quite close to her on the bench, and their arms and knees would occasionally brush. Each time Elizabeth felt a flutter through all her nerves, but her hope to impress kept her from missing keys.

After she finished the performance Elizabeth stood to allow Mary her turn. Turning to Darcy, she asked with a smile, "Well Mr. Darcy, will you at last admit how poor my performances really are?"

Darcy replied with a grave smile, "If I did not know that your vanity had not taken a musical turn, I would imagine that you fished for a compliment."

Elizabeth replied impishly, "And had I been fishing for a compliment, what might you have said?"

"I hardly know. For, to me, your playing has always been perfection itself. There is no performer I enjoy more. Yet, I do perceive you have improved your technical form and execution — Which is an improvement — and yet perfection is that which cannot be improved. Do you perceive my problem?"

"No, for that *was* a very pretty compliment. And to compliment was the task I set before you. You succeeded admirably at *that*. I do apologize for forcing you into a philosophical quandary, but I cannot help you there as it seems an insoluble paradox."

"Ah, well. I am glad I managed a compliment, even if it required dreadfully offending the ghost of my old logic teacher." Darcy paused and added with a little discomfort, "I have greeted the host — should I also give my greetings to the hostess? Where is Lady Lucas?"

"You are most serious about this attempt to rescue your reputation in the neighborhood." Elizabeth smiled brightly. She loved the way he wished to please her, and the way he wished to better himself. "I can tell you this will be no difficult task. Already, Sir William will spend the next month praising your kind condescension in listening to him praise Lady Catherine's kind condescension."

For the rest of the evening, Elizabeth led Darcy from conversation to conversation, helping him to talk with the more sensible (or on occasion entertaining) of her neighbors. While he did not have the skill to find meaningless phrases to fill space, he could greet people politely and *appear* to listen attentively. Elizabeth perceived that when a neighbor made a speech of little interest, he kept her in the corner of his eye.

Darcy was positively amiable and fluent when Elizabeth found sensible and clever persons for him to talk with and kept the conversation on matters which interested Darcy. It was no burden to fill in the gaps in his talk and push the subject towards topics which interested both her neighbors and Darcy. He did not become fatigued over the course of the night, as he had during the ball in London, but amiably conversed the entire time.

She saw what their marriage might be like. Elizabeth had not *cared*, but she'd expected him to be stiff and unpleasant outside of a family circle. It would not be like that at all. Her presence would soften him and help to make him liked in addition to respected in society.

"Catch me, Denny. Catch me. 'Tis such a joke!" Near the end of the evening, while Elizabeth and Darcy talked together, Lydia ran past waving a saber she had stolen from an officer.

Darcy watched with a stiff face. Elizabeth flushed; she hated that Darcy saw this. His affection was such that he would bear it, but she wished her relations were not a burden.

Lydia eventually collapsed into a chair and relinquished the weapon. Colonel Forster frowned at Lieutenant Denny as he eagerly placed it back in the scabbard.

Lydia cried out, "La, I'm so tired!"

Elizabeth glared at her sister. Darcy's voice brought her attention back to him. "She is a bit wild, but really not so very bad. Many girls behave so."

Elizabeth treated Darcy with a hard stare. "I thank you for saying so. I do. But I hope *we* do not need to pretend with each other. She is very bad."

Darcy shrugged. "She is but fifteen." He smiled at her. "No sensible person would judge her siblings harshly for her behavior — I do not claim to have always been sensible myself, but I hope I am *now*."

Elizabeth smiled back at him. That response showed his true thoughts. She had no need to be unhappy about Lydia or anything else. Things were well. Her family might embarrass themselves, but Darcy cared little for it.

"She is to go to Brighton with the regiment?" Darcy's voice was concerned.

Elizabeth threw her hands in the air. "Lord, I tried. But Papa will not listen — he will not. Lydia will make herself into the most determined flirt who ever sought to make herself and her family ridiculous. And he cares nothing about it. He doesn't want to be disturbed by her unhappiness. Quite likely she will marry some penniless officer, who is twice the fool she is, and the rest of us will be left supporting his career for life — and she shall have the joy of living on a too small income."

"Has every attempt been made to convince your father? Did Bingley seek to speak with him?"

"*You* know Bingley; he was *your* friend first." Elizabeth and Darcy shared a look. "His marriage has made him less yielding than he was, but he is hardly a man to move my father to do anything he does not wish. My father is determined. I have sworn to think no more upon it, for it is not my nature to worry over problems I cannot fix."

Chapter 15

Lydia stayed in Darcy's thoughts. If he was to marry Elizabeth, he should care for her family. Mr. Bennet could not realize the danger faced by an effectively ungoverned girl of Lydia's age. If he understood how easily any girl, even one whose manners gave less reason for concern than Lydia's, could be persuaded into ruin, he would act. Any sensible father would. Elizabeth had tried, but many men foolishly discounted the opinions of women.

Perhaps Mr. Bennet would listen to another gentleman.

The next morning Bingley stayed at Netherfield to deal with estate matters, but Jane called upon her family. Darcy rode with her. Elizabeth was out with Lydia and Kitty to call upon their aunt in Meryton. Mrs. Bennet effusively greeted her daughter but showed him cold civility. Though he should wish for greater friendliness from his prospective mother-in-law, Darcy could not mind.

Darcy went to the library where he knew Mr. Bennet usually spent his days. Elizabeth's father sat in a large stuffed armchair with a small glass of port in his hand and a book on a reading stand in front of him. Mr. Bennet was bald, and he had a bright, incisive look in his eyes that reminded Darcy of Elizabeth.

Darcy had always rather liked him. He was a clever man who liked books and solitude. While Mr. Bennet should do better by his family and estate, if Darcy disdained every gentleman who had a serious flaw, there would be no end of it.

Mr. Bennet wore an informal red dressing gown and spectacles. He froze at Darcy's entrance and his eyes did not move. Darcy walked to the middle of the room and waited to be acknowledged. When Mr. Bennet said nothing Darcy at last spoke, "Sir, I wish to discuss a matter of some importance."

The older man closed his eyes and took in a deep, almost pained breath. "So you do." He exhaled. "Well it does no good to put such things off. What question have you?"

"I am concerned about your daughter Lydia's planned trip to Brighton. If you realized the dangers she might face on such a trip, without careful supervision, you would not allow her to go."

"*Lydia?*" Mr. Bennet pushed his book stand away with a shaky hand. He laughed. "Of course it is Lydia you wish to speak of." He pointed at the couch nearest to his chair and said, "Well, sit down, sit down."

As Darcy sat down he understood. Mr. Bennet had expected him to ask for Elizabeth's hand. No wonder he had acted so odd when Darcy first entered the room. She had spoken often about how much her father depended upon her company. It could not be pleasant to lose such a daughter.

Mr. Bennet picked up the book that had been on his reading stand. "Tacitus, the *Annales* — a tale from those early decadent days of the Empire. Not much has changed in eighteen hundred years; men are all much the same, are they not? Still there is an endless fascination in the details of characters. I understand you to be something of a scholar yourself?"

"Far more at Cambridge than at present. I do not make the time needed maintain my skill with the classical languages."

"It is difficult. And once married you shall find it harder. If you wish to reestablish the habit, you should soon." Mr. Bennet put the book aside on a small cast iron table next to his armchair. "So Lizzy set you up to be her champion."

"I assure you Miss Bennet did not send me to you. I chose to come wholly by myself."

"There seems little difference."

Darcy could make no reply to that. Mr. Bennet sighed and took a small sip from his tumbler of port. "I shall give you the same reply I gave to Lizzy: There shall be no peace if Lydia is denied this opportunity, and I see little real harm that could come about from it."

"Do you not fear the way she might embarrass and shame herself? She is a wild girl who shows scant restraint."

"Fear it? It is part of the value of the exercise. Lydia will not be easy until she has exposed herself in some public place, and I cannot imagine a way to allow her the opportunity with less expense and inconvenience than this."

"You wish your daughter to embarrass herself?" Darcy was aghast. He'd thought that, while eccentric and unsocial, Mr. Bennet was at bottom a sensible and responsible man.

"Nothing but a real fear of shame will lead her to quiet herself in public. And a little embarrassment never hurt anybody." Mr. Bennet smiled conspiratorially. "Lizzy has been remarkably improved since her battle with you at Jane's wedding. Eh, Darcy. Don't you agree?"

He'd come to accept their quarrel as having good consequences, but it was not a matter to be made fun of by anyone but Elizabeth. Darcy took a deep breath to push away his annoyance. "Surely, you cannot consider such serious matters with so little concern. It is not embarrassment I fear. Young girls can run themselves into serious trouble when they are detached from proper supervision. I have certain knowledge that at least one of the officers in Colonel Forster's regiment is a very poor character indeed."

"You refer to your Mr. Wickham? He may be a gambler and a spendthrift as Lizzy believes, but that hardly makes him a danger to my daughter."

"He has attempted to seduce at least one gentlewoman of Lydia's age."

"And what was the dowry of this gentlewoman?" When Darcy did not reply, Mr. Bennet said. "I daresay, it was quite large. I have read your friend's character — he is more fortune hunter than seducer. And Wickham is no fool. It would destroy his position in the regiment were he to trifle with a gentlewoman's daughter, and even with what Bingley's generosity might volunteer, Lydia is not worth enough for him to form a serious design upon her. No, there is no danger from that direction."

The mulishness of Mr. Bennet frustrated him. "Surely, you can see that a girl such as Lydia could find opportunity to shame herself in a manner which will bring discredit and shame upon all those connected to her. Does not the welfare of your other children concern you?"

"They are *my* children. *You* are not connected to Lydia. It is no concern of yours how I manage her. She is a foolish girl, but she knows better than to behave in an immoral manner."

The two men stared at each other. Mr. Bennet's informal dress left his neck visible. The muscles were taut with anger. Darcy began again, "I do have a strong interest in her wellbeing, I —"

"Enough!" Mr. Bennet took up again the volume of Tacitus and held it in the air. "I will hear nothing more on the matter of Lydia. No more. If this so concerns you, you should abandon whatever reasons make you care. This conversation entertained me, but the vices of the Roman Emperors call."

Darcy stood stiffly. "I am certain I need not assure you that my attempted interference was well meant."

"Yes, yes — I am sure your intentions are so noble they would put those of a saint to shame. Just tell Lizzy I no more enjoy it when others nag for her than I do when she bothers me direct."

As Darcy walked out the back into the house's garden, he met Elizabeth returned from her visit to Meryton, rosy cheeked and smiling. At Darcy's scowl, her smile fell, "What is the matter?"

He did not reply. Resentment welled again. Mr. Bennet should care. How had Elizabeth turned out so well? She took Darcy's arm. "Come, I have not walked near far enough this morning — have you seen the stream which goes through the tenants fields in the south? It is a pretty sight with a thicket about at parts."

Darcy willingly allowed Elizabeth to lead him. They were silent, but he knew if he kept his anger it would worry and annoy Elizabeth, "What are your favorite views here about? You have asked me so much about Pemberley that I only now realize I have been remiss in demanding a minute description of Longbourn."

"There is less to describe than you imagine. As you can see our gardens are not extensive, and there is barely a full park. We are quite modest. It is the hidden spots along the country lanes that are best worth finding."

"Please describe your favorites."

Elizabeth blushed and described a hidden alcove and bench in a forest on Mr. Goulding's land. They walked along the stream Elizabeth had mentioned then they crossed a small wooden foot bridge.

They fell silent.

She will never be easy until she embarrasses herself. What sort of man could think such a thing? Very likely the result would bring shame upon all connected to Lydia. Had he no paternal feeling? Did he care nothing for his own respectability?

"Please, tell me what bothers you so."

Elizabeth's voice was soft, and her warm eyes begged a response from him. "I spoke to your father about Lydia. I tried to convince him to keep her away from Brighton. He —"

All of Darcy's frustration and disappointment came back. He pulled his arm from Elizabeth's and threw his hands in the air. "How can such an irresponsible, foolish, stupid — how can such a man exist? He wishes — he really wishes your sister to embarrass herself. It delights him — all this time I thought him merely lazy. He is worse, more disreputable, than your mother."

Elizabeth began to sob.

Darcy felt sick. "Elizabeth — Lizzy. I apologize, I should not have spoken so, not of your father." Darcy tried to take her arm, but she pushed him away. Her breath hitched. "Please, don't cry, please. I don't mean it. I shouldn't have —"

"I have already said I do not wish you to pretend. It is true. I know it is. We are all disreputable embarrassments. No sane man would connect himself with any of us. I know it. You have said it yourself."

"Elizabeth, that is not true. I was wrong then. You know I no longer think that way."

"No matter what you think, my father is irresponsible and foolish, and Lydia will embarrass us all, and — oh, I wish my family were better. You will come to hate them. If even my father can offend you so — he must have mistreated you terribly. You will regret any connection to them."

Darcy took her hand. His stomach roiled at Elizabeth's unhappiness. He must have spoken some inner fear of hers. If only he had been less arrogant the previous autumn. If only he hadn't hurt her now. "I never will. I know my own mind. I — my affection, the sources of my esteem, are such that matters like this cannot touch them. No matter what your family is, that will never waver. Please say you trust me."

"I trust you. I do. If I did not..." Elizabeth swallowed and laughed anxiously. "My feelings are silly. I have acted as a goose. I am well again."

His stomach was still knotted with guilt. "I should not have said or thought that about your father. I —"

His apology boosted Elizabeth's mood. "Do not be absurd, you certainly should *think* that. If not the words, at least the sentiment. I said it was a hopeless case, and he was determined to push Lydia towards ruin. But so long as my father cannot change how you" — Elizabeth bit her lip and looked down — "It was sweet that you tried — I am very pleased you wanted to."

"I had some thought — well, many gentlemen are fools who rarely listen to women. I'd thought maybe your father was one, and if another man explained the dangers, he might —"

Elizabeth laughed; the sound removed most of Darcy's remaining anxiety. "You mistook your target. My father will listen to my reasons perfectly well. He is indolent, not dismissive. He just does not care and does not wish to hear reason for care."

They smiled at each other, and Elizabeth took Darcy's hand and squeezed it. "Even though you failed, I could wish no better champion."

Darcy squeezed her hand back, and things felt right between them on the walk back to Longbourn.

THAT EVENING ELIZABETH replied to any attempt by her father to engage her with an offended silence. Why could he not be responsible? Elizabeth was sure Mr. Darcy *had* been treated abominably by her father.

Must every member of her family expose their worst behavior to him? Surely after so much he could not be scared off. But, might some member of her family finally act out in a way that would be too much for Darcy to accept?

The next time Darcy called at Longbourn, Mr. Bennet came out of his library to sit with the family and make teasing insults towards Darcy. Elizabeth begged him to stop that evening, but Mr. Bennet's response was, "So, you fear I'll frighten off your suitor? He is made of sterner stuff than that. He'd be long gone if he were not."

That night Elizabeth had a nightmare which startled her awake, shivering despite the summer heat. The end hung vividly in her imagination. *I should not have married you.*

Lydia had done something immoral and disgraceful in the dream, and Mama praised her for it, saying: *Isn't she such a lively girl.* What had been Lydia's crime? Elizabeth couldn't recall, but the moment Darcy stared into her eyes and claimed he regretted their attachment wouldn't fade.

She needed to trust him. He knew his own mind. She believed him. He would not come to regret her, no matter how horrid her family might behave. She had to believe that.

A silent agreement was made between Elizabeth and Darcy that she would call on the Bingleys with her mother — who insisted on visiting Jane near everyday — and Darcy would avoid Longbourn. With this policy in place things went very well between Elizabeth and Darcy.

Their conversations were like they had been at Rosings again: meaningful, engaging, and enlivening. In comparison to his former habits Darcy had become near a social butterfly, though he only was talkative with a few clever gentlemen he came to like or when Elizabeth was present.

Soon most of the neighborhood came to approve of him. The general expectation that Elizabeth would return from her trip to the north an engaged woman encouraged this shift. A man who would marry one of the local beauties *and* who further made a clear effort to modify his manners to please her could not be so bad.

Lydia left; Georgiana arrived.

Elizabeth liked the exchange. Georgiana was the sweetest dear, and they took to each other immediately. Within a few days they had become Lizzy and Georgie to each other and happily shared laughter and confidences. Though it was no surprise they liked each other: Seldom would two persons meet more eager to please and be pleased.

Georgiana was shy with all persons she was not close to. Watching her helped Elizabeth to understand Darcy's mannerisms better. They were much alike in many ways, and Elizabeth was sure with proper guidance Georgiana would develop a delightful sense of humor.

A few days before everyone departed for Pemberley, Darcy and Georgiana called with Jane and Bingley at Longbourn. Very early the next morning, Darcy was to travel to London for two days to settle matters of business in the capital before leaving the region entirely. Despite the tension between Darcy and Mr. Bennet, politeness required he call once before leaving the neighborhood.

Mrs. Bennet loudly clamped onto Bingley and ignored Mr. Darcy as she always had since he refused her request to allow Kitty in their party. Mr. Bennet attempted a few witticisms, but Darcy resolutely responded politely to each, so he tired of the game and returned to the library.

Elizabeth was tense. She feared disaster every time the Darcys were in the walls of her home. The image from the nightmare had faded, but the awful feeling it gave her flared again.

The call was not intended to be long, but a thunderstorm, which had threatened, burst. The hard rain kept everyone indoors. Mary loved to perform before any new audience, so before anyone brought out cards for a game, she announced her intention to play a concerto for them.

Elizabeth blushed for Mary's overly affected manner as she flourished her hands and sat stiffly in front of the modest instrument. But Darcy had seen it before, and Georgiana was too sweet to be amused. When Mary finished her piece everyone clapped politely, and she immediately began another.

As Mary played Georgiana's eyes lingered on the piano, and Elizabeth fancied her fingers twitched. Before Mary started a third piece, Elizabeth said, "Georgie, do you wish a turn?"

Georgiana blushed and looked at her brother, who smiled encouragingly. She nodded and said in her soft voice, "I would."

Mary made way with a pout. Georgiana settled herself and stretched her fingers before laying them on the ivory keys. She closed her eyes and began from memory. It was a complicated sonata by Beethoven, which Elizabeth would not dare try. The music had intense power. The adagio brought tears to Elizabeth's eyes, and everyone listened spellbound.

Mr. Bennet entered the room, drawn by the sound of Georgiana's playing. His movement drew Elizabeth's attention; he settled next to Mary, who stiffly listened with an intent frown.

When the melody ended with a beautiful crescendo, Georgiana looked about at everyone's loud applause and ducked her head shyly.

Mr. Bennet stood, still clapping. "That was the best playing that has ever been heard in Longbourn. Mary, if only you could play like that, people might *wish* to listen to you."

Elizabeth realized her sister had been near the edge of tears, and at her father's words she leapt to her feet. "I hate you!" She pointed at Georgiana and shouted, "I hate you too!"

Mary sobbed as she ran out of the room.

Georgiana's eyes drew together as she stared about with her hand against her cheek. Elizabeth was quite as ashamed of her family as she had ever been. Darcy sat next to Georgiana and gravely talked to her.

Jane went after Mary. Mr. Bennet grinned at Darcy and said, "Silly girl. She is so excitable. Women always make mountains out of trifles."

Elizabeth saw Darcy's face twitch with anger, and he stared at Mr. Bennet for an instant before speaking again to Georgiana.

"Miss Darcy," Mr. Bennet spoke, "that was divine. Truly divine, might you favor us with another piece?"

The rain had ceased as they listened, and with a brief glance out the window, Darcy said in a cold voice, "That will be impossible. We are leaving."

Darcy pulled Georgiana out of the room without looking back at Elizabeth. She should go after him to ensure things were right, but she felt too awful to move. Her family had hurt Georgiana. What if this finally disgusted him enough to destroy his affection?

Mr. Bennet left the room jauntily humming to himself. Bingley let loose a long frustrated breath. "Georgie is so shy. It will be no good for her to think she can bring other girls to frustrated tears like that. I feel worse for Mary; she tries so hard."

Elizabeth nodded dumbly, too full of her own ashamed misery to sympathize with Mary's unhappiness. It wouldn't change Darcy. He had been frustrated when he stalked away. It was nothing. She trusted him. But her stomach still hurt.

Chapter 16

Darcy sat next to Georgiana in their carriage as it returned to Netherfield. Georgiana spoke, "I had not realized I would hurt her by playing so."

"You did nothing wrong."

Georgiana did not reply. Damn him. How dare Mr. Bennet use his sister as part of his petty vendetta? He intentionally acted to injure two young ladies, one his own daughter. A selfish disdain for the feelings of others. Darcy was not the only gentleman of Elizabeth's acquaintance of whom that could be said.

Darcy nudged Georgiana. "You should not worry. It really was not about you."

Georgiana smiled a little and nodded. Georgiana's acceptance allowed Darcy to relax. He began to ruminate again upon Mr. Bennet.

Georgiana said, "I like Lizzy enormously. She is different from Jane, but she is just as wonderful."

Once back at Netherfield Georgiana changed clothes and sat to play, and Darcy went to the desk he generally used in the drawing room and buried his head in his hands.

Damn Mr. Bennet. He never wanted to see the man again. He hated the thought of being tied to him. He hated the thought of asking him for anything. He didn't want to ask *him* for Elizabeth's hand.

Was he being a fool? Would it be a terrible mistake to become that man's son?

The question made Darcy feel a wrenching horror. He couldn't lose Elizabeth. Nothing was worth that. Nothing. She was worth anything. Georgiana was well, or at least she would be, and — he couldn't even think of allowing anything to separate them. He needed Elizabeth.

He stood up preparing to head back again to Longbourn. He needed to speak to her, to make sure she knew he didn't care about her father's foolishness. She would know, but she would worry. How had she looked as they left? He couldn't leave for London without reassuring her.

Darcy heard Bingley and Jane return and looked out. The rain had started to pour again, and it was late enough in the evening that the light was dying. He shouldn't ride across the three miles.

The door opened, and Bingley entered. Darcy's friend stood awkwardly in the middle of the room and pulled his hands through his hair. At last he cried out, "That was a damned bit of tomfoolery. I am dreadful sorry. Mary should never have acted like that, and she knows it. She apologized most profusely and wanted Georgiana to know that she enjoyed her performance greatly. Jane is delivering that message now." Bingley stammered, "I do hope Georgie is well, and you are not too terribly offended."

"Georgiana is fine. I am not offended by *Mary* at all."

Bingley chuckled. "You did warn me Jane's family showed a lack of propriety. This is quite embarrassing. Mary isn't a bad girl."

"I'm sure she is not." Darcy's anger flamed back into his chest. "Mr. Bennet. Did he apologize? Did he admit how wrongfully he acted? Or does he think his daughter's remorse is sufficient?"

Bingley flushed. "What do you mean?"

"You heard him. He pushed Miss Mary into a tantrum, likely to offend me."

"That explains why she shouted at him." Bingley rubbed his face. "I know not what to say. You do not need my apology. Mary tries hard to improve her playing. It matters a great deal to her."

"My sister practices enormously as well. She would not behave so badly if faced with a superior performer." Darcy flushed. Bingley knew nothing of the incident, but with Wickham, Georgiana had made a mistake of far greater moment.

Bingley did not realize Darcy's silence meant he disagreed with himself and exclaimed, "Dash it. They may not always behave correctly, but the Bennets are my family, and I love them for it. I have never been so happy as I have been since I married Jane. I would deal with twenty such women as Mrs. Bennet descending upon me daily or a thousand girls weeping about something silly to have her with me. I think any man put off by the failings of a lady's family cannot be in love."

In a rush Darcy's anger left, and his concern for Elizabeth returned. He clapped Bingley on the shoulder. "You are right. Completely correct. You have never been so right."

Bingley stammered a bit at Darcy's voluble agreement. Darcy added, "You can see the weather. It would be unwise for me to ride back to Longbourn at present, and I ought to head to London at the earliest moment tomorrow. I know it is improper, but would you deliver a note from me to Elizabeth tomorrow morning?"

"What?" Bingley was surprised into stillness and then grinned widely at his friend. "Of course I shall. With the absolute happiest of feelings."

ELIZABETH FELT WRETCHED the next morning. She had spent half the night unable to sleep. She would not see Darcy for another two days. That made the matter far worse. What was he thinking? Elizabeth had not spoken to her father during dinner or breakfast.

Jane and Bingley arrived together early in the morning, and Elizabeth immediately sought her sister. "How did they seem? Is Georgiana well — Darcy, was he angry?"

"Georgie accepted Mary's apology. She was most understanding. She did not feel well enough to come out with us this morning though." Jane spoke quietly to Elizabeth, "I gathered she wished for a bit of solitude this morning."

"And Darcy?" Elizabeth asked, "How did Darcy appear?"

"Oh, he was much as he always is. He was not angry, and he too holds no rancor against Mary."

At this statement from his wife, Bingley coughed; then, he winked at them and said, "Lizzy, might you step out with me? I have a matter I wish to discuss with you."

Elizabeth looked at Jane who shrugged. Then she followed Bingley into the gardens.

THE RETURN

"I have been charged with the most serious task," Bingley said with faux gravity once the door closed behind them, "A most serious task. Can you imagine what it might be?"

Elizabeth looked at him impatiently.

"A gentleman. Yes, a gentleman gave me a missive to deliver to you. Now as your brother, I am not sure —"

"Darcy left a note for me?" Elizabeth exclaimed eagerly. "Please let me see it."

A little miffed by her interrupting his fun, Bingley said, "I have not named the sender."

"If it was not Darcy, I have no care for it." So saying Elizabeth stuck her hand out. "Stand and deliver."

Bingley laughed. "You eager young lovers — no patience." He pulled a piece of paper from his pocket and handed it to Elizabeth.

Nothing, no consideration could dim the pleasure your presence gives me. I care only for your happiness. I could never regret anything which contributed to it. I wish I were with you now, and you are in my thoughts. Georgiana is well, and for my part, I hate that I must travel away from you, even though it only be for two days. Alas, business must be dealt with, but when I return we shall travel to Pemberley and finish that conversation *your sister interrupted.*

Yours, with the sincerest and steadiest affection,

F Darcy

When she completed the brief message, Elizabeth brought it to her mouth and kissed the signature. All her worries evaporated. She was sure nothing could ever concern her again.

"Well? What did he say? It could not have been horrible or you would not have *kissed* the page."

Elizabeth went bright red. "Bingley *that* is no proper question. I showed *you* greater consideration."

He laughed. "You did. I shall ask no more, but I *am* glad the message pleased you."

Elizabeth carefully hid it in her dress and asked, "Do you think Georgiana might enjoy it were I to call on her. I know she wished solitude, but perhaps the right company would be welcome."

Bingley nodded, "I think that a good scheme. I would not want yesterday to sit on her mind much, and it will be impossible for us to keep her company today. We must finish our round of farewell calls before setting out for Pemberley."

When Elizabeth was announced by the butler, Georgiana met her with a wide smile. "Lizzy, I am delighted to see you. I had been practicing, and with your sister and brother gone for the day, it is a little quiet. I am used to *that,* but I still hoped to see you."

"I am glad to hear it." Elizabeth smiled. "My dear sister claimed you to be resolved against company. I feared I may have acted quite rudely to come nonetheless."

Elizabeth could tell Georgiana wished to speak about the previous day. To encourage her she said, "You played beautifully yesterday. I have heard that piece before, but never so well managed. I am sorry you left so soon, but — I understand. However you should not take it to heart."

Georgiana blushed and looked down. "Tell me truly, did I do anything amiss yesterday? I had no idea I might offend Miss Mary."

Elizabeth smiled. "Of course not, dear."

Georgiana shook her head insistently. "Do not dismiss my concerns — I hope I can trust you not to spare my feelings. Fitzwilliam will say whatever he thinks will increase my confidence in company, yet how can I be confident when I do not know whether I give offense? Jane said I had nothing to worry about and that my behavior was perfect in all respects, but she is so nice she would not see me as having acted wrongly even if I behaved in a quite horrid manner."

"*That* is a true portrait of my sister. I salute you on it." Elizabeth laughed and squeezed Georgiana's arm. "You did nothing wrong. Let me explain what did occur."

"Whilst Jane is perfection, and the Gardiners are excellent people — the rest of my family is not entirely what they ought to be." Elizabeth let out a slow breath; it was unpleasant to expose her family so. But Darcy already knew what they were, and Georgiana's distress demanded she explain.

"My sister Mary — it is partially mine and Jane's fault as we always were tightly bound and did not bring Mary into our games. Mary always has been a little isolated, and — as my mother tells her at length — Mary is not quite so pretty as the rest of us. She chose to seek distinction by being more studious and accomplished than the rest of us."

"So when my playing was so much superior to hers she felt bad? It meant she was surpassed in the one area she sought to excel. I knew when I sat down that, while her playing was by no means bad, mine would be superior. So I did act wrongly, at least in that."

Elizabeth let out a breath and forced herself not to smile at Georgiana's concerned expression. She really was a sweet dear. "Georgie, a little vanity and pleasure at the skill developed through great practice cannot be reprehensible. It cannot. You intended no harm and have nothing to feel poorly about. My sister and father were entirely to blame."

"Oh yes, it was quite horrid of him to say that. I cannot imagine how poorly I would feel if Fitzwilliam spoke that way to me." Georgiana blushed. "I should not insult your father."

Elizabeth laughed. "You should not. But as I am vexed with Papa myself, *I* shall not be offended."

Chapter 17

When he arrived back at Netherfield two days later, Darcy came in by a side door and scrubbed the dust off his face and hands. The butler informed him that Elizabeth and Georgiana were in the drawing room, while Jane and Bingley had called at Longbourn.

"Can't we make it four out of seven?" Darcy paused in front of the doors to hear Elizabeth's wheedling voice. "I near won that game."

"Nay, nay. We had agreed on three out of five. I win." There was a pause and Georgiana started giggling. "Do not act like that," she said as she continued to giggle, "you shall pick the next game."

Darcy had worried Georgiana would be lonely while he was gone, as Bingley and Jane would be often busy during their last few days in the county. He should have expected Elizabeth would keep his sister company. Darcy knocked on the varnished oak door and entered. Elizabeth had stuck her tongue out at Georgiana and was flicking cards at her. Georgiana was red-faced from giggling.

The two immediately straightened at his entrance. Elizabeth gave a smiling curtsy, and Georgiana jumped up and hugged him before stepping back with a blushing glance at Elizabeth.

"I can see you did not terribly miss me while in London."

Georgiana exclaimed, "I did too!"

Elizabeth said, "I've kept Georgiana company when my sister and Bingley call at Longbourn; today my father and Bingley are out shooting while my mother gives Jane advice on how to pack for the trip. I came to play cards with your sister — I would say delightful sister, except she won."

Georgiana giggled. "Don't be a sore loser."

Elizabeth laughed; her face glowed. Darcy felt a rush of tenderness at the easy banter between his sister and the woman he loved.

"Did you plan to stay long? I thought to call on Longbourn this afternoon to give my regards a final time before we decamp tomorrow morning."

"You wish to visit Longbourn? It is not necessary." Elizabeth's eyes were stuck on him.

"They are your family. I want to show them every respect and friendship."

A broad smile spread across Elizabeth's face. Darcy felt like her happiness pulled his heart from his chest and nestled it against hers. Turning to Georgiana, Darcy asked, "Do you wish to come to Longbourn?"

Georgiana looked about, glancing at the piano and the bound volume of a novel on a table near her. "I suppose I ought."

Elizabeth smiled at Georgiana. "Are you certain?"

"I am. Hiding from awkward situations will do me no good. Let us go now."

In the carriage Georgiana was a picture of nerves as she picked at her gloves. Darcy was not sure what to say. Telling Georgiana, again, she had done nothing wrong did not promise to help.

Elizabeth sat across from the two siblings. She grabbed Georgiana's hand and squeezed it.

Darcy made his own attempt to comfort Georgiana. "You are calling upon the family of dear friends. There is nothing to be concerned about."

"I know, but I ought to have returned earlier. It was dreadfully rude to hear Miss Mary's apology and not return to Longbourn to accept in person."

As Darcy searched for something to say, Elizabeth said, "I know how awful it is to think you performed some horrid *faux pas*. But this is nothing to worry about. Mary will not hold it against you."

"I know, yet..." Georgiana trailed off with a confused face.

Elizabeth laughed and squeezed her hand again. "I can only advise you so far." Elizabeth gave Darcy a pretty smile. "Your brother believes everyone to have their own particular failing — mine is not excessive shyness. Perhaps were you to pretend yourself to be me for half hour it would go well."

Darcy smiled. "Like when you dined with Lady Catherine?"

"Very much so. And *you* shall paint the scene for your sister."

Darcy raised his eyebrows and smirked at Georgiana, who now appeared more curious than nervous. "Our dear Miss Bennet had the previous day expressed her view that the names of reigning English monarchs made the best Christian names — which was as a cruel blow to me as there has not been, and most likely never will be, a monarch named Fitzwilliam."

"Now, if I remember this conversation aright, you were expressing deep sadness that you had not been named after Agamemnon, or Oedipus, or some other similarly unfortunate figure."

Elizabeth's eyes sparkled, and her pretty mobile mouth turned up delightfully. Darcy replied, "Madam, you had demanded *I* be the one to tell the story. And you are most mistaken, I'm quite certain I never expressed that opinion."

"Oh, that is right, you had not. I recall now, clear as day, the disappointment, the awful tortured disappointment in your countenance when Lady Catherine convinced you that Fitzwilhelmina would be a poor name for a daughter."

"Fitzwilhelmina?" Georgiana dissolved into giggles, which were only enhanced by Elizabeth's winks at her and Darcy's pursed lips as he shrugged at Georgiana. "I confess the name came from my mind. Though I recall quite clearly Lady Catherine had *not* convinced me to abandon the scheme."

Elizabeth laughed.

"I tell you, I am serious. The more I hear it in my mind, the better it sounds — and you convinced me I should avoid names from antiquity."

Elizabeth appeared aghast before she dissolved into giggles. "And to think I once believed you knew not how to laugh."

"Nay," Darcy insisted, "'tis no joke, Fitzwilhelmina has a special ring to my ear."

Elizabeth's eyes were delighted, but Georgiana was worried and said, "That would be an unkind name to have. It would show family pride, but no girl would like such a name."

"Then as your advice corresponds with that of your aunt, I must take it. Though it is an unhappy blow."

Elizabeth grinned at him. "I daresay, you shall not cease to insist you like that name anytime soon."

"For I do like it — familiarity wears away the great strangeness, but leaves the monument to my vanity." He suddenly saw a pregnant Elizabeth, her belly swollen with his child, laughing as he insisted he really did wish to name the child Fitzwilhelmina if a girl.

Only the awareness of Georgiana in the carriage kept him from kissing Elizabeth right then.

They were quiet. Elizabeth and Darcy stared at each other, their eyes speaking what they could not say aloud in Georgiana's presence.

Georgiana plaintively asked, "Tell me the rest of the story. How did Lizzy act with Lady Catherine?"

"Ah, yes — so our dear Miss Bennet the previous day had expressed her opinion that classical names were best avoided, while those of reigning British monarchs — such as Elizabeth or Georgiana — were excellent. I was unconvinced, but aware of my own fallibility in this matter, I suggested Miss Bennet ask my aunt for her advice." Darcy leaned close to Georgiana. "As you know, our aunt is a great giver of advice."

Elizabeth smiled. "As she did not perfectly agree with my pre-existing sentiments, I am not inclined to agree with you. For if she were a good giver of advice, she would have replied to me with what I wished to hear in the first place."

"I see your point. However I claimed her to be a great giver of advice, not a good one. That single word makes the difference. We *do* agree that Lady Catherine should not be approached if your desire is to hear what you already thought."

Elizabeth gave a pretty bob of her head in agreement.

"Miss Bennet asked our aunt her opinion when we all dined together the next day. Though — you were more deferential to Lady Catherine *then*. You said you would do as she wished."

"She agreed that the names of reigning monarchs were excellent choices, even if not superior to other aristocratic names. And, though I do love you dearly, and Georgiana is an excellent name, in most cases a girl should not be given a man's name with a feminine ending. I was honest when I told Lady Catherine I would name within the constraints she suggested."

"Lady Catherine doesn't like my name?"

It was wonderfully sweet the way Elizabeth leaned across the space between the seats to pat Georgiana on the hand. "I'm sorry my dear, but it is true. I'm sure if you ask, she would own it directly. She does not blame *you* though — if it helps you to bear up under the weight of your aunt's preference, *I* like your name."

"Oh, I do not care. I'm always terrified of Lady Catherine; I would never dare ask her a question — even if it were serious."

"She is an impressive woman," Elizabeth agreed, "and very sure of herself. Your brother did defend your name. Quite valiantly, he directly argued with your aunt — which I would not have done without closer acquaintance to her than I had."

"I did promise her not to name my daughter Fitzwilhelmina — a promise I may need to break. And what will be left of my honor then?"

Elizabeth laughed.

The carriage rolled up to Longbourn, and Darcy quickly stepped out, so he could help each lady to the ground. Darcy smiled for the short walk to the door. Elizabeth entangled her arm sweetly around his, and her thumb rubbed at his wrist. He glanced at her face as they knocked. Her clear eyes and pert smile promised future joy.

ELIZABETH WOKE ELATED the morning they started the trip to Pemberley. She was sure that in two weeks' time she would be engaged to the best and handsomest man in Britain. It had been so kind of him to visit Longbourn once again after all that had occurred. Everything felt perfect. Even Mr. Bennet, while he did not apologize, made a real attempt to be amiable towards Darcy.

Darcy had accepted with grace her mother's civility and challenged her father to several games of checkers. He had been too willing to engage with Papa. *She* would not be happy till Mr. Bennet admitted wrong doing. Darcy showed that while he might not *approve* of all of the Bennets, he could treat them as family.

Happily, Mary and Georgiana properly befriended each other. They had gone outside to talk, and when they returned, they smiled and practiced a duet. Elizabeth asked Mary about it after the Netherfield party left, but all Mary said in reply was that Georgiana was very good and kind.

When the Gardiners arrived shortly before supper, Darcy greeted them with real enthusiasm. Elizabeth knew they had dined together several times in London, and she loved the way her uncle and Darcy enjoyed each other's company.

When the plans for the parties were arranged, Elizabeth managed to place herself in the Darcy carriage while Mr. and Mrs. Gardiner rode with the Bingleys. It was a happy party. They talked and exchanged stories and played games.

After the stop for lunch Elizabeth asked, "How do you entertain yourselves on long rides?"

"In general we talk, like now, or read," Darcy replied.

"That is boring, and I'll not allow you to continue with it. When it is me and Jane in the carriage, or the Gardiners, we always play riddles and ask each other conundrums." Elizabeth gestured back towards the carriage following a dozen yards behind theirs. "Unless Bingley has some terribly clever plan which persuaded Jane to betray our tradition that is what they do now."

Darcy raised his eyebrows. "I can vouch that Bingley has no terribly clever plans to pass the time. Though we have posed puzzles to each other. Most likely your guess about what they do is correct."

Georgiana said in a nostalgic voice, "You used to invent stories for me."

"I did? — Oh yes, I recall. That was several years ago."

Darcy appeared slightly embarrassed, and Elizabeth begged for more details.

"It was after father died," Georgiana answered for him, "I was miserable the first year when we traveled to London to gain the attention of a renowned music master. I spent an hour crying on the first day, and Fitzwilliam had no idea how to comfort me."

"I remember now, I knew you enjoyed stories, so I retold the first one that came to mind, which was Othello."

Elizabeth bubbled at the image of a much younger Darcy comforting a small, teary eyed Georgiana. "Othello? That is hardly the tale I would choose if I needed to comfort a crying child."

"Which is why he invented a new ending." Georgiana smiled at Elizabeth. "Halfway through he started to change what happened. The lieutenant saw through Iago's plots and convinced Othello of Desdemona's innocence. There was a battle of wits where Desdemona used a clever stratagem she had learned from Othello's stories to save him from Iago. Iago repented and became a traveling priest who gave sweets to children — it was very good."

Elizabeth laughed and said to the blushing Darcy, "*That* is a most charming story."

Darcy tapped Georgiana's knee. "I fear my sister was terribly disappointed when she later saw Othello performed."

"I was not — I knew perfectly well you made up the ending."

Every story, every habit, every small matter she learned about Darcy made her affection grow. "You said he invented stories, was this the only one?"

"Oh no, I insisted he tell more, so the next time he told about a princess Georgiana. Until the year I first went to school I always begged him to tell me stories on carriage rides."

"That was sweet of you. You will one day make an excellent father."

Darcy flushed and smiled. "I hope to." He then added, "I do look forward to taking little Fitzwilhelmina on my knees and inventing stories for her entertainment."

Chapter 18

Pemberley was a long beautiful building, with rows of windows and an imposing set of marble columns guarding the entrance. However, despite the structure's beauty, as Darcy led her up the long staircase to the entryway, Elizabeth looked longingly out at the park.

A nearby trail ran direct under a pretty set of woods, and she could see a stream burble along next to another path. In the distance was a pretty hill with a small temple atop it. Elizabeth could see hints of gazebos and statues and benches half hidden by the groves of trees.

She'd spent most of the past two days inside the carriage and desperately wished to stretch her legs and ramble freely for a good hour. The house was beautiful, but the lands around it were the prettiest she'd ever seen. None of the great houses in the vicinity of Meryton showed anything like the perfect combination of nature and taste displayed here.

The summer flowers were in full bloom, and their perfume wafted about; the trees were heavy with green, and bees buzzed amongst the vines and plants emplaced around the walls of the stairs. A motion caught Elizabeth's eyes. It was a deer. A gentleman in the neighborhood of Meryton kept a park where the deer were fed and would quite willingly accept the approach of people. Darcy had once mentioned something similar.

Darcy squeezed her arm to get her attention. "Unless I am greatly mistaken, you wish a long walk after our sojourn in the carriage."

"Will you think me terrible if I acknowledge it? For a preference for gardens and trees after a long carriage ride, instead of pretty rooms and a bath, is not refined. But I confess that preference, and confess it openly. Despise me if you dare."

"Will it shock *you* terribly if I confess the same preference? Though gentlemen are not supposed to long for pretty rooms, so I have the better of you." Darcy smiled. "I shall get up a party for such a walk."

The house had been built in the style of the previous century and with a massive entry hall. Ten foot tall paintings whose styles crossed a hundred years decorated the walls. The floor was a pattern of black and white marble squares, which gave off a hard sound when stepped upon. A huge gold chandelier hung from the roof. The banisters on the double staircase gleamed.

It made Elizabeth feel overwhelmed. Was she really to become mistress of all this? Was that merely a dream or delusion? She looked at Darcy. His eyes were warm, and he smiled at her. "I must admit it is ostentatious."

The approval in his eyes and the way he was glad to see her in his family house made Elizabeth feel safe and washed away her sense of smallness. "I love this room. I shall hear no attack on it. The decorations and furnishings are beautiful and exactly as they should be."

Darcy grinned at her. "Ah, but we do not disagree. It *is* exactly as it should be — the ballroom is behind those doors," Darcy pointed to the top of the staircase, and my great-grandfather wished to ensure he would not be shamed when a Duke should attend a dance. To create an entry hall worthy of a duke requires ostentation."

Elizabeth laughed, and Darcy said to everyone, "I know we all wish to rest from the journey — I'd thought a picnic on the grounds would be an excellent plan for lunch in two hours. Afterwards, we could tour the park or the house — those who are not Bingley will appreciate the chance to see everything. If any of you wish to join me, in ten minutes I plan to take a walk around the park to stretch my legs after all this time in the carriage."

Elizabeth immediately expressed her intention to be part of that group. Georgiana curtsied, but said it she wished to visit her room again. Jane and Bingley also chose to retire to their rooms for the next hour. Unfortunately for Elizabeth and Darcy, Mr. and Mrs. Gardiner announced they would join them.

Darcy asked, "Are you certain you are not tired from your journey? And the rooms which have been provided are well appointed — please do not think I would take it as rude if you did not join me. I assure you, Miss Bennet shall the company enough."

Mrs. Gardiner smiled. "We shall not be terribly in your way, but you know I saw your park as a girl. I have longed to wander those woods again since our plans were made."

Butterflies played in Elizabeth's stomach. He'd wanted to get her alone. Might Darcy have asked her at last if not for her aunt and uncle? And even if he had no such plan, could she have convinced him to adopt it? She had wanted to kiss him for such a long time.

Elizabeth followed a maid to the room which had been assigned to her and rapidly readied herself to walk about on such a fine sunny day. If it did not happen naturally within the next few days, she'd contrive some plot to be alone with Darcy.

Less than ten minutes later, Elizabeth stood in the garden which had been appointed for their meeting. She wore tightly laced boots and a wide brimmed straw bonnet to keep the sun off. The garden was gorgeous, and Elizabeth looked every way attempting to identify exotic plants, many of which she had never seen, even during her visit to the Royal Gardens.

She'd been alone for less than two minutes when Darcy joined her. He stood several feet off and smiled at her. His light coat was thin enough to show the muscles in his shoulders, and the multicolored cravat set off the image perfectly.

The experience of being here at Pemberley with its master seemed pregnant. They looked at each other frankly, stepping closer but not speaking. Elizabeth felt the special meaning of the moment. "So beautiful," Darcy breathed out stepping closer to her, "prettier by far than the flowers."

Elizabeth's eyes were fixed on his, and a magnetic attraction between them drew her closer. Her aunt and uncle entered the square, and Darcy and Elizabeth blushed and looked away from each other.

Darcy bowed to his other guests and with admirable self-possession gave a friendly greeting, "Shall we set off?"

He immediately took Elizabeth's arm, but before they set off, Elizabeth pointed to a plant she had looked at and asked Darcy its name.

Darcy hmm'd and said, "I have no idea, it is exquisite." Taking his arm back from Elizabeth, Darcy pulled out a knife and carefully cut off a yellow and white blossom. "My mother loved to collect plants from exotic locations and see whether they could be made to thrive in our England climate. My gardeners know all there is to be said on each, but I never did memorize it all."

Holding the flower that he had cut by its stem, Darcy smiled at it and twirled it back and forth. Then he held Elizabeth's head and pushed the flower into her hair. Darcy brushed his fingers softly over her forehead before he stepped away. "Perfect."

Her stomach flipped at the proximity, and she near forgot the presence of her aunt and uncle. Mr. Gardiner stepped up and said approvingly, "That is a good look for you Lizzy." Then with a mischievous smile Mr. Gardiner took Elizabeth's arm and, gesturing at Mr. Darcy, he said, "Pray, which of these pathways shall we start upon first?"

The frustrated expression on Darcy's face made Elizabeth smile mischievously at him as he resigned himself and gallantly offered his arm to Mrs. Gardiner.

DARCY'S MIND WAS TOO full with Elizabeth's proximity to sleep well. While dressing him, his valet told Darcy that Mr. and Mrs. Bingley had woken more than an hour ago and were seated at breakfast. When Darcy arrived, not only were the Bingleys down, but also his sister and the Gardiners. It was unusual as most mornings Darcy awoke the first out of his party.

Bingley looked up from his meal when Darcy entered the breakfast room and said heartily, "I see you have woken at last — why, I've been awake these six hours at least."

Jane poked her husband's side. "We've not been awake nearly that long."

Bingley grinned. "It is most unlike you."

Bleary-eyed, Darcy grimaced at his friend. Georgiana poured him a cup of tea as he collected several rolls and pastries onto his plate. "Is Miss Bennet still abed?"

"Lizzy was asleep when I asked her maid a half hour ago," Jane replied.

Georgiana exclaimed to Jane, "When she comes down I wish to give a real, proper tour of the house. We had so much fun yesterday there was no time to look it over. I talked to Mrs. Reynolds — she knows even more of the history than I do — and she will be at our disposal for several hours."

"That sounds like a lovely plan." Jane smiled at Bingley. "I know you have seen the house in detail before. Will you and Darcy go out shooting this morning?"

"Certainly not," Darcy spoke before Bingley could, "what tour of the house can be complete without the master attending?" By no means would he lose an opportunity for Elizabeth's company.

Elizabeth knocked on the door and entered wearing a pretty light blue dress that left her arms bare. Darcy immediately stood and gave her a small bow.

She curtsied, turned mainly towards Darcy. "It was terribly decadent of me to not wake earlier — yet I was far too comfortable in the room you provided. I must argue that the blame should be shared."

Elizabeth showed him her challenging smile and set about collecting food onto her plate. Darcy replied, "Most mornings I am up by 7 o'clock — my rooms do not force one to sleep until nine."

Mr. and Mrs. Gardiner smiled at each other, and Bingley exclaimed, "Pray, do not believe him — he was asleep this morning near as late as you."

Elizabeth dimpled as she sat down next to Darcy, her plate loaded with one of each type of pastry provided by his cook. "Shame on you Mr. Darcy."

"That does not affect my point. For it was not the rooms which kept me abed — and everyone else was awake much earlier. The cause must be particular — not general to the house."

"Perhaps you go too far, maybe it is the interaction of the house with a particular circumstance. Had this been Longbourn, I would've been walking about by 8 o'clock. I have found Pemberley's one flaw: it is too comfortable." Elizabeth's eyes were bright, and her smirk delightful as she finished, "Deny that if you can."

Darcy asked, "You hope to make me claim Pemberley to be uncomfortable?"

Elizabeth's mouth was full with a lemon tart, and she swallowed before delicately wiping her lips with her napkin. "That" — she tapped the remains of the pastry — "is delectable. Your cook is not a flaw of your house. I told you that you would be unable to deny it."

"I must confess defeat then. I do love my house dearly, so I can be forgiven for agreeing it is too perfect. Though, while its perfection may lead you to sleep late on occasion, its other perfections will prevent the growth of decadence." Darcy had Elizabeth's eye. "You shall see."

Elizabeth blushed and boldly keeping his eyes said, "I look forward to the discovery."

Mr. Gardiner spoke, "Lizzy, the plan is for us to be given a proper tour of the house this morning. "

"That is a fine plan, I shall never be happy until I have seen every nook and cranny of this beautiful building and know its story!"

Seeing her here, in the halls of his ancestors, in his home, was everything Darcy had hoped for it to be. She belonged here. And after one last, sadly necessary, trip to Longbourn she would live here. Her eyes had sparkled yesterday as they toured the park.

Soon as breakfast finished, Mrs. Reynolds joined to help guide the tour. Darcy enjoyed the clever questions Elizabeth asked his housekeeper and saw the beginning of mutual respect grow between them. Elizabeth's questions were detailed and sincerely interested, and both Darcy and Georgian enthusiastically retold all the old stories. As a result their progress was quite slow.

They had tramped up and down the halls for two hours when Bingley whispered with Jane and then shouted out, "We must finish this another day. Jane is a little fatigued, and she wishes to sit down."

Darcy felt a little shamed. He had been so intent on watching and speaking with Elizabeth that he had failed to attend to the rest of his guests. It was hardly the best behavior for a host. "What have you in mind?"

Bingley gave a small shrug, "For myself, I would like to begin our planned fishing expedition. Gardiner, you recall what I said about that spot by the stream — you do not wish to delay longer I am sure."

Darcy did not wish to be separated from Elizabeth, but he had promised Mr. Gardiner an opportunity to enjoy the excellent possibilities for fishing at Pemberley. It would be ungracious to delay unnecessarily.

In twenty minutes he was out with his friend and Mr. Gardiner. The branches of the trees extended over the stream and formed a shaded area that his father had found to produce excellent results while fishing. A small gazebo had been built to provide shelter when it rained, and they had a set of excellent lounge chairs.

The three men were mostly quiet, and Bingley and Mr. Gardiner appeared to concentrate on the task in front of them.

Darcy's mind was on Elizabeth. He wanted to leave them and look for her. But it would be rude (though he trusted both Bingley and Mr. Gardiner to take it in good humor). Besides, if he did so too quickly, she would tease him for it.

Darcy lasted more than an hour and caught several trout himself. However, when he glanced back towards the house, he detected movement. It was two women traveling from the house towards the orangery. He thought it was Elizabeth and Mrs. Reynolds, though the distance made certainty impossible.

Darcy had no ability to resist such a temptation, and he made an excuse to Bingley and Mr. Gardiner. He promised to return shortly, but if Elizabeth *was* in the orangery, he would define the terms of the promise quite liberally.

When Darcy reached the glass building, he saw Mrs. Reynolds and Elizabeth. Elizabeth sat on a bench and intently examined the roots of one of the citrus trees that flourished in the carefully controlled conditions. Darcy opened the door and stepped in.

Mrs. Reynolds curtsied while Elizabeth stood. She said with a bright smile, "Your fishing expedition cannot be very good if you abandoned it this soon — and after you praised Pemberley's ponds so high to my uncle. And you brought Bingley into the deception as well. Fie on you both."

Darcy smiled. He had known Elizabeth would tease him for leaving them. "I have regularly fished there since boyhood. My attention could hardly be so fixed upon it as your uncle's. I spied you walking towards the orangery, and it was impossible for me to not follow."

"Aha, I see. You think my company to be more tempting than that of the fish. Until now I believed you to be the perfect gentleman. But the gentlemanly pursuits of writing, fishing, and hunting are to be paramount. You should be ashamed, Mr. Darcy, ashamed."

"My dear Miss Bennet, you must blame yourself. If Pemberley is too comfortable, you are too tempting."

Elizabeth blushed, but her smile showed her delight at the compliment. Darcy said to Mrs. Reynolds, "You must have some task which might command your attention. I would not claim my knowledge to match yours, but I know enough of the orangery and the history of its plants to give Miss Bennet a creditable tour."

The servant looked between the two, and when Elizabeth smiled at her, she gave a curtsy and left. Darcy felt in his entire being that he was alone with Elizabeth for the first time since they arrived. A taut tension vibrated in the air between them.

Elizabeth broke it first, "How shall you entertain me? I just learned about those trees" — she pointed to the middle of the room — "and heard two delightful stories about you as a child. Shall you share your own childhood reminisces with me? Something horridly embarrassing I hope."

She smiled sweetly. She was far too tempting; he wanted to kiss that smiling face and hold her body tight against him forever. Darcy's heart hammered, and he stepped close to her.

He could tell she was affected too from how her lips trembled, and her eyes were fixed upon his face. She did not step back at his approach. He'd had a vague idea that he wished to wait and ask her in the last few days of the visit to Pemberley. That was an obviously foolish scheme.

Their faces were only a foot apart, and Darcy's stomach squirmed with unexpected anxiety. He said in a low voice, "Elizabeth —" he paused and swallowed unable to continue. Elizabeth nodded fractionally, her eyes not deviating from his. Darcy began again, "Elizabeth would you —"

The door to the orangery slammed open, and Jane ran in. She grabbed her startled sister in a tight embrace, crying out, "Oh, Lizzy, she's run off! She's run off."

A cold pre-sentiment froze Darcy's irritation as Elizabeth snappishly quizzed her sister, "Who ran off?"

Then Elizabeth went pale in realization, even before Jane replied, "Lydia, she's run off! With Wickham. She's run off with Wickham. Here, read." Elizabeth's lips trembled as she smoothed out the paper Jane thrust into her hand and began to read with wide eyes.

As Elizabeth read, Darcy sought details from Jane, "When did this happen? Are they married? Has Wickham made any demands?"

"Oh, I hardly know — Papa does not think they went past London, though Lydia expected them to go straight to Scotland. I cannot believe Wickham is so bad as to run off with Lydia if he had no intent to marry her." Darcy and Elizabeth shared a look. Neither had any trust in Wickham's good character. "Oh! Charles will tell you everything — I sent him to prepare our carriage, I must find my aunt. Poor Lydia!"

Darcy frowned and paced back and forth. The scent of the fruit laden citrus trees wafted about. Poor Lydia indeed! Was there any hope she could be retrieved without needing to marry that scoundrel? He must find Mrs. Younge. She was his easiest hope. Wickham did not have very many friends who might help him. Men had kept tabs on Mrs. Younge, and her address was filed both in his London house and here.

Having established a plan to hunt down Lydia, Darcy exited his preoccupation far enough to look at Elizabeth. She had finished the letter and stared at him. Tears had begun to leak from her eyes. Darcy desperately wanted to place arms about her and hold her tight until she felt warm and secure and happy again.

If only Jane had sought her aunt before her sister!

He could not finish his proposals while a family disaster loomed over them and Elizabeth wept so. He clenched his fists and turned his face aside, so he could not see Elizabeth. He must control his urge to embrace and kiss her. He did not yet have the right to hold her so intimately.

"What news does the letter contain?"

Elizabeth's voice was anguished, "There is no sign of the roads north of London! No sign. My father delayed his express until his first attempts to search for them had failed. We would have known yesterday. There is no sign. Oh, poor Lydia! To have her life ruined so. And to implicate us all in her shame."

Darcy looked back at Elizabeth. She wept, covering her eyes with one hand and holding the crumpled express in the other. He felt an intense tenderness. Her blotchy cheeks were beautiful. He took her hand and softly pulled the letter from it. "Please, is there anything I might do? A glass of wine? A handkerchief?"

Darcy forced his handkerchief into Elizabeth's other hand, and when she took it and blew into it, he said, "I promise, this shall somehow come out aright."

"Poor thoughtless Lydia!" Elizabeth burst out, tugging at her hand. "It cannot. Not when Wickham is the one who chose to take advantage of her stupidity. You know as well as I that he shall not marry her without a substantial sum. This disgrace must affect us all, even Jane and Bingley. Oh! I cannot wish enough to be paid, and Wickham will not be reasonable — I feel sure he does this in part for revenge."

Darcy dropped Elizabeth's hand and looked away unhappily. Yes, Wickham sought to gain revenge upon him by hurting Bingley and Elizabeth. This was his fault, had he managed Wickham better Elizabeth would not be in pain now.

Elizabeth added, "Yet, if they do not marry, Lydia's character will be ruined forever. Oh! Why did this need to happen? My family has now proved itself immoral. It shames me. I am ashamed, so ashamed."

"You have no reason for shame. You did all you could. You attempted to protect your sister. It — no shame lies on you. You could do nothing. Do not blame yourself."

Darcy paced again. His mind was full of the situation. "But must they be made to marry? Is there no other possibility? To be connected so to that man" — Darcy shook his head — "that would be terrible indeed."

Lydia was a thoughtless girl of fifteen; she did not deserve to suffer her entire life from such an irretrievable choice made now. The failure was her father's far more than her own.

Elizabeth buried her face in her hands and sobbed. It was a small choking sound, and she visibly struggled to keep from loudly weeping. Darcy watched her, his heart in his throat. Now, when Elizabeth was so distressed — in part due to his own failure — he realized more than ever before how much he cared for her.

Another minute and he would have embraced and kissed Elizabeth. Bingley burst into the conservatory. Red-faced and agitated, he shouted out, "Darcy, I must have your help. Have you any idea where that scoundrel Wickham may have gone to ground with my sister in London?"

Darcy opened his mouth to reply, but Bingley spoke over him, "Quickly man — I plan to ride within the half hour. I need your help. That scoundrel has run off with my sister, and Jane says he has no plan to marry her. I swear I'll shoot him if he doesn't."

Elizabeth made a distressed gasp. Darcy spoke, "Don't be a fool! That creature is not gentleman enough to be dueled. Of course I shall come with you."

Bingley's scowl lightened. "Of course you shall. I should have known. Of course you shall. Come now, it is a hurry. Lizzy, your aunt and Jane are in the drawing room with that view of the hedge maze in the gardens. Jane is distraught. Your presence may comfort her."

Could not Bingley see that Elizabeth was distraught as well? Lydia was her sister, also. Elizabeth nodded, though Bingley did not see it as he was already rushing out the door.

When Darcy did not immediately follow him, Bingley shouted back into the orangery, "Come, quickly."

"There is a hurry, but might I do anything for you before I leave?" Darcy looked worriedly at Elizabeth. Her cheeks were covered in tears. She shook her head without looking up at him.

Bingley's voice called from the hallway, "I've ordered one of your people to saddle your horse and prepare a bag. Hurry! A certain speed is essential. Mr. Bennet delayed too long before he called us to London."

Elizabeth at last looked at him with a forlorn smile and gestured towards the door. "Go. I shall be fine and must find my sister."

It was impossible to leave without a final gesture, Darcy seized Elizabeth's hand again and kissed it. She still clutched his handkerchief. "I swear, I shall make this well for your sister."

Chapter 19

With Mr. Darcy and Mr. Bingley gone ahead, there was little reason for the ladies to rush. Still they packed and prepared quickly, and it was early in the afternoon when they set off for London.

What had Darcy meant? *To be connected so to that man. That would be terrible indeed.*

For a while, Elizabeth distracted herself with the rush of packing and muttering in a low voice about the dire probabilities of a good outcome with Mr. and Mrs. Gardiner. They had split the party so everyone would have be able to stretch out during the journey, and Elizabeth was in Mr. Bingley's carriage, with her aunt and uncle, while Jane rode with Georgiana and Mrs. Annesley in the Darcy's carriage.

Elizabeth was too anxious to hold her part of the conversation. Mr. and Mrs. Gardiner shifted between silence and repetition of speculations already well-worn. This could not keep Elizabeth's mind away from Mr. Darcy. His manner had been so odd, and Elizabeth could not settle for herself what it meant.

He had been about to ask her for her hand. She was sure of that. Then Jane interrupted them, for a second time. If Elizabeth was not miserable, she would laugh. Then he turned and paced while she read. That was simply his manner when absorbed in thought.

After Jane left, he looked at her, then he clenched his fists and stared away from her. What had been his meaning? She'd been crying. She should not distrust him, but it was then Elizabeth wondered if the behavior of her family had finally destroyed his regard.

She had begun to weep, and he immediately tried to comfort her. He had been so eager to hold her hand. He had assured her that this did not lower his estimation of her at all.

THE RETURN

Some thought made him drop her hand. Then, without looking at her, as his footsteps took him back and forth between the orange trees, he said it: *But must they be made to marry? To be connected so to that man. That would be terrible indeed.*

Darcy hated Wickham. She did not know the real source of his dislike, but for a moment, Elizabeth was convinced that while the immorality of her family would not scare him off, he would refuse to connect himself to Wickham.

She had begun to weep again. Darcy had seized her hand again before Bingley dragged him off, but he tried to comfort her by swearing things would be well *for her sister*. Was that merely because he believed her distress was entirely due to Lydia?

Lydia's situation affected her not nearly so much as the fear that this at last would drive Darcy away. It was selfish to care mainly for herself in a time like this, but Elizabeth never claimed to be anything else. Any man but Darcy would certainly be driven away.

But Darcy was honorable. He cared for the substance of things and not appearances. *He* would care more for the joy they found together. He would remember the way she softened his mood and made him smile. Lydia's behavior, a connection to Wickham, could not end his desire to make her laugh and his hopes for a settled home.

Darcy would not hesitate at the scandal or unhappy connection. He was too wise to destroy their future happiness over such a thing.

She must trust him. She must believe that he expressed unhappiness for Lydia and fear of what her life would be once she married Mr. Wickham.

Mr. and Mrs. Gardiner asked if Darcy had told her anything about his plans. She had little to say, beyond that he had promised to make things well for Lydia. Elizabeth's heart beat uncomfortably the entire afternoon, and her stomach was too unsettled to allow her to eat that evening.

It was a miserable, quiet party at the inn that night. The next day Elizabeth and Mrs. Annesley switched places. Now it was Georgiana, Jane and Elizabeth in the Darcy carriage.

Jane had awoken in an optimistic frame of mind and, after they had been on the journey a while, said, "The situation no longer seems so poor to me. I know you think very ill of him, Lizzy, but Wickham cannot be wholly bereft of proper feeling. He would not have gone off with Lydia if he did not feel real affection for her, and so long as papa and my husband guarantee them enough to live upon, he should willingly marry her."

Elizabeth stared at Jane. Rather than goodness this was hopeless innocence.

"You are wrong. Entirely wrong." They both looked at Georgiana. "That worthless, vile man will never marry your sister. Not without a great sum of money. He has *no* proper feelings. He feels nothing but lust or greed for her."

Jane appeared shocked. Elizabeth now understood. The realization felt like a limb had been torn from her body. Darcy hated Wickham and would refuse to connect himself in any way to Wickham because he had terribly hurt Georgiana.

Jane blinked. "Surely he cannot be *that* bad. Those are very harsh terms."

"Do not doubt me. I know what I speak of!" Georgiana refused to let Elizabeth take her hand. "You may not wish to acknowledge me once you learn the truth. I was foolish, imprudent, and nearly immoral."

Elizabeth could see how distraught Georgiana was, and despite the chill she felt, she needed to comfort the girl. Jane and Elizabeth had sat on the seats facing opposite from Georgiana, and Elizabeth, holding her hand against the vibrating wall of the carriage to steady herself, jumped to the other side and pulled her arm around the shrinking girl.

"Georgie, you need not speak if you do not wish. I promise that nothing he may have done will change my affection for you."

Georgiana had started weeping, but allowed Elizabeth to hold her and Jane to squeeze her hand. "I must speak. You must hear what sort of man he was. Do not promise that this shall not affect your regard until you have heard. Wickham convinced me to elope with him last summer at Ramsgate. I would have done it. I thought I was in love with him. It was only the barest luck that my brother arrived the day before we were to execute the plans. I would not hide the scheme from him."

"It would have been imprudent," Jane said, "but not immoral. Wickham, perhaps, did hold you in some real affection. It had been very wrong for him to encourage you to marry without your families approval, but —"

"He did not. He said he hated me! I hid to overhear his conversation with Fitzwilliam, and he openly owned that he had only sought to attach me for my dowry and revenge against my brother."

Jane clapped her hand over her mouth. "Oh! That is horrible. And to have overheard that, it must have hurt you so." She moved to the other side of the carriage, and Georgiana was tightly squeezed between the sisters.

Georgiana sobbed. "I don't deserve your friendship. I was a horrible girl and sister. You both are so good, and I know you would never act so foolishly."

Elizabeth would have told the story, in a manner to make Georgiana laugh, of how Wickham had deceived her, and how she gained her revenge on him, but it reminded her of Darcy. Of their argument, and of how he cared for her.

That would be terrible indeed.

Her breaths came fast. He would not connect Georgiana to the man who'd hurt her so. He wouldn't. But he had no choice. He had near enough promised to marry her that his honor was engaged. Even if he regretted it, he still must ask her.

Elizabeth saw years of Wickham able to bother Darcy and Georgiana because she had connected him to them. She could not do that. She had to let him go. She felt tense and numb, almost as though it was someone else's arm that held Georgiana.

"Lizzy, what is the matter?" Georgiana's voice seemed distant. The girl gasped. "You can't! You can't let me stop you marrying Fitzwilliam. He loves you. Don't hurt him that way because of me. I know you can't want me for a sister but send me off instead. I'll live with — I'll even live with Aunt Catherine."

Georgiana's anxious plea snapped Elizabeth out of her panic. She pulled in a deep breath. Then several more.

Georgian spoke again, "Promise me you'll marry him. We were all so happy, you can't let my immorality destroy it."

"Georgie, you did not behave immorally. Even if you had, it could not damage my affection for you. There is no one I would wish more than you to have as another sister. But — if Lydia marries Wickham, surely you would not wish him to be so closely connected to you and Mr. Darcy. Would not such a connection be terrible indeed?"

"How can you think I would care? It is a quite distant connection in any case, and I would never need to meet him. Even if I thought it would hurt me, you cannot think me so selfish as to wish you and Fitzwilliam to be unhappy over it."

"Yes, but — does your brother feel the same way? Good sense must rebel against becoming the brother of such a man as Wickham." Elizabeth added in a forlorn voice, "He must come to regret the connection."

Georgiana recoiled away from Elizabeth with an open mouth. "You cannot think that. My brother loves you, surely you understand that. He is not so disloyal."

"But he said — he said: 'But must they be made to marry? To be connected so to that man would be terrible indeed.'"

"He felt sorry for your sister. *Obviously.*" Georgiana crossed her arms and tried to get as far away from Elizabeth as she could by squeezing against Jane. "How can you doubt Fitzwilliam?"

Georgiana's anger reassured Elizabeth. She knew her brother well. Elizabeth let out a long breath and slumped against the red cushions of the carriage. Much of her panic drained away, leaving a dull unpleasant residue in her stomach. She was mostly sure Georgiana was right, and she had promised to trust Darcy. She must trust him.

Elizabeth closed her eyes, and the carriage was silent for several minutes. Elizabeth opened her eyes again, Georgiana still glared at her, and Jane's eyes were concerned.

Elizabeth smiled at Georgiana; her hand trembled as she touched the girls shoulder. "You are right, I must — I do — trust your brother. It is only that I am distraught. My emotions are unsettled. I have been tense and fear some disaster. I will not be happy until…" Elizabeth blushed. She would not be happy until Darcy smiled at her again and assured her that all was well.

Georgiana's anger immediately ended, and the girl now attempted to comfort her, hugging her again and saying, "Oh, Lizzy, this must be so hard for you. It will be well, I am sure of it. Fitzwilliam loves you."

THE RETURN

Georgiana's words did comfort. Elizabeth knew Darcy loved her. But the chill did not disappear, and she still needed to offer to release him from any obligation he felt.

DARCY AND BINGLEY HAD made good time on the road from Derbyshire to London, and they arrived at Darcy's house in town several hours before dusk the day after Mr. Bennet's express was received. They had gone by horseback the entire way and were sore, dirty, and smelly. They rode the previous day until it was quite dark and then set out before dawn in the morning. Darcy drooped with fatigue.

No express had been sent ahead, and it would have arrived only a few hours before them if they had. His housekeeper and butler were surprised to see the master and his friend arrive. Still, even though food, a bath, and a change of clothes were not immediately ready, the house — and its stuffed chairs and sofas — was a sight for sore bodies.

Darcy and Bingley both collapsed in one of the smaller rooms, leaving the dust covers draped over the sofas so they would not be stained with their clothing. Neither spoke for a good twenty minutes. They did not stir when the butler entered and left behind a tray of cheese, rolls, and sliced fruit with a decanter of wine.

On the road the two decided to see if Mr. Bennet had discovered anything further before Darcy sought out Mrs. Younge. They had no note from him when they arrived, and at last Bingley roused himself with an effort. "I suppose I must go by my uncle's place to see if a message is left from Mr. Bennet there."

Darcy grunted and forced himself to sit up. He had never ridden such a distance in such a short span of time. Once or twice before he had ridden between Pemberley and London. But it had been comparatively leisurely. "Refresh yourself first" — Darcy gestured at the tray left by his butler — "a few minutes more or less can make no difference."

Bingley nodded and pulled the tray close to himself. He took a thick wedge of cheese and several rolls and quickly ate them with little show of manners. Darcy immediately joined Bingley in stuffing the food into his mouth as quickly as he could eat. The two friends then shared a quick glass of wine before Bingley pushed himself up, holding a last roll, and said, "I am off, wish me success and good news."

Darcy waved his friend off but was too sore to stand. It was unlikely Mr. Bennet found anything, and he needed to search out Mrs. Younge's address. Ten minutes after Bingley left, Darcy stood and rang for the meal to be cleared.

His back and thighs throbbed with each step, and they would feel worse the next morning. Darcy slowly worked his way up the stairs like a much older man. All of the papers related to Wickham were kept in the safe, and Darcy pulled them out as a group.

That worthless creature. Darcy thumbed through the yellowed notes which described what had been laid out for Wickham's education each year. More than half that generous allowance had gone to disreputable women and gambling. On the bottom was a copy of the receipt for the three thousand pounds Mr. Wickham had been given in exchange for renouncing right to the Kympton living.

He had received so much and had so many opportunities, and yet he still was angry at his betters for not giving him limitless support. And now Wickham had to be dealt with again. And in a situation which would permanently connect Darcy to the man.

Darcy found Mrs. Younge's address. After Georgiana's near elopement Darcy had hired investigators to track her for several months. He wished to ensure she would attempt to tell no stories. Also the entirety of her prior connection with Mr. Wickham had been discovered. Darcy copied out the address and then stared at the paper, tired and unhappy.

Eventually the lack of sleep the previous night combined with the food and wine caused Darcy to nod off as he sat in his comfortable desk chair. Darcy shook himself awake and tried to plan how to approach Mrs. Younge. However his mind could not concentrate, and after a few minutes, he slid into sleep.

He was woken from a dream where he kissed Elizabeth while threatening Wickham with a gun.

Bingley shouted greeting from the door, "Sleeping at your desk? Fortunate for you. I wish you'd been the one to head out. The hackney cab I

THE RETURN

found had a terrible driver, all jolts and rough stops. Shook my sore muscles about horridly. No chance for sleep."

Darcy's neck hurt, and his body did not want to stand. He rubbed at his eyes and looked at his friend. "You do look beaten-down. Pray, did you find Mr. Bennet? Any news?"

"It is about what we expected." Bingley sighed. "I found my father. He has discovered no information about Lydia. He confirmed no sign of them is present on the roads north of London."

"No messages sent? No calls for a meeting?"

"No, I was thinking, if Wickham hopes to gain money, he would wait until I was positively identified as being in town. Mr. Bennet has rather little he can directly give."

Darcy nodded, rolling his head around to try to work the pain and stiffness out. "Go to bed. If Wickham has told Mrs. Younge where he is, I can bribe her for his location without you. I'd rather, in any case, for Wickham to know he must deal with me if any arrangement is to be made."

Bingley grunted. "Surely, he must expect I would call for your aid."

Darcy shrugged. "I doubt he knows how close friends we are. Most families would instinctively hide news of such an event for as long as possible."

"I'm coming with you. Lydia is my sister, not yours. Your help is appreciated — but the duty to deal with her... The duty is mine."

"No, Wickham's ability to act with any credit is in part my fault, and I wish to take a full part in resolving this."

"Do not be ridiculous. This is Lydia's fault — and Mr. Bennet's. And mine. I ought to have pushed Mr. Bennet not to let Lydia go to Brighton and offered an alternative. Jane and I knew full well it was not wise to let her go. Though, I held to Jane's counsel in the matter, and she never would have imagined her sister would elope in this manner."

He hoped to marry Elizabeth, and Bingley ought to have figured that out by now. If money must be given to Wickham, he would pay the lion's share. "Bingley, I *do* have a very strong interest in this matter."

"Oh yes. I thought so. But, ah, have you and Lizzy... Are you two just being sly?"

"I wished to allow her to see Pemberley before I spoke. Had *your* wife delayed another five minutes, I believe it would be well and settled." Darcy frowned. "Bingley, could you not see that Elizabeth was distraught? You sent her right after Jane. Lydia is just as much her sister."

Bingley rubbed a hand against the back of his head. "I suppose you are right. But — we held off telling everyone because we expected a *different* announcement." Bingley paused and then grinned as brightly as Darcy had ever seen him. "Jane is with child. I do not wish her to be bothered more than necessary at such time."

Darcy took his friend's hand and shook it heartily. "I am delighted to hear that. You shall make an excellent father." Darcy opened the bottle of whiskey he kept near his desk and poured a tumbler for both of them. "Here. We must drink to your child and your wife."

Soon the memory of the task before them returned. Darcy said, "Let us head off to Mrs. Younge. If you insist, have it your way and come along. Promise me this: If we encounter Wickham, allow me to speak most."

A small chaise which the Darcys kept at their London home had been brought out of storage and prepared for use while Bingley sought Mr. Bennet. It was near the high point of summer, so the day ended late, and the glimpses of the red glow of the setting sun Darcy received through the buildings were beautiful. Despite the scene it was a typical London evening in the summer: loud, horridly hot, and a truly awful stench exuded from the open cesspits.

By now, the exodus of the very rich triggered by the worsening smell and end of Parliament's session was mostly complete. Yet, that did little to lessen the crowding of the streets. Most of the teeming masses of London were not gentry and their servants, but workers, merchants, and apprentices. It was the greatest city in the world and had the greatest smell and greatest traffic.

Not that Paris, Berlin, or Vienna would be any more pleasant late on a summer evening. Most likely they would not be. The stories he had heard from acquaintances in the employ of the East India Company claimed the great trading cities of the Orient were worse. And there were slave pens in the East Indies. The world was a terrible place, filled with immoral sorts like Wickham and Mrs. Younge.

Bingley fell asleep a few minutes into their trip. As Darcy's house was in a very different part of London than Mrs. Younge's location, it took them almost an hour to travel across the city. When the carriage pulled to a stop in front of the soot covered three-story building with peeling paint, Darcy gently shook Bingley awake.

He stretched, winced, and clutched at his back. "It does not look like much," Bingley noted.

Darcy nodded and slammed the knocker hard against the dilapidated door.

The door was opened by an untidy middle-aged maid with thick arms and a red face. Her surprise at the presence of two richly dressed gentlemen outside this establishment was evident in her expression, and she made a poor caricature of a curtsy before asking their business.

"Is Mrs. Younge in? I must speak with her." Darcy handed her his card.

"What do you wish to talk to the mistress about?"

"That is my business," Darcy replied gravely. "Take us to her." The woman hesitated. Darcy had little patience; he hoped to have some positive news to comfort Elizabeth when she arrived the next day. Darcy pulled from the purse kept in the inner pocket of his coat a half crown and let the woman see it.

Her eyes widened at the amount of money, which was far more than he would usually offer as a bribe in a situation of this sort, and she gave another curtsy, equally awful but with more sincerity, once Darcy handed her the coin.

Mrs. Younge was a well-educated woman, who, despite her worsened circumstances, maintained an elegant manner and dress. A little like Mr. Wickham himself in fact. She went pale when she saw Mr. Darcy. "I have done nothing against you — nothing. I've spread no stories, neither true nor false, and have only sought to provide for myself by running this establishment. You have no cause to bring against me. None. I haven't said anything about your —"

"We are not here about that." Darcy cut her off sharply and glanced at Bingley, who looked a little curious. "Pray tell, has Mr. Wickham contacted you recently, my friend wishes to find him."

"Oh." She released a nervous laugh as she realized Darcy was not angry at her. She sat down heavily in one of the only rickety chairs in her small sitting room. Mrs. Younge chuckled and said to Bingley, "Run off with your sister did he?"

Bingley startled and replied, "How did you know?"

"Don't give her unnecessary information."

Bingley flushed, and Mrs. Younge chuckled again. "I've seen the girl, are you sure you want her back? She is the worst sort of rich child. No sense in her head, none at all. Completely believes in Wickham — thinks it will be a great joke to marry before most of her sisters."

"You've seen them." Bingley stepped forward eagerly. "Do you know where Mr. Wickham is? Please tell me."

"Pray, why should I betray the location of my friend? I've known Mr. Wickham for years — he's always been good to me. Except…" She scowled at Mr. Darcy, "No, I shall not tell you."

"How much?" Darcy wished the interview over so he could sleep before hunting Wickham down the next morning.

"Mr. Darcy! How dare you suggest I am anything but a respectable woman? How dare you suggest I would betray friendship for some small pittance?"

Darcy pinched his nose tightly between his fingers. He was tired and hated that he must play these games. "I understand madam. I should not have insulted you and will seek some other method to find your friend." He stiffly bowed. "Good day."

Bingley was shocked as Darcy walked towards the door. "But, you said she was our best opportunity to find Wickham easily! *She knows where Lydia is.* Time is of the essence, if we find them and make them marry quickly, the scandal will not be nearly so bad. You can't give up so quickly! Madam, it is no betrayal of your friend, for he will benefit as well. Can you not understand how, as a concerned husband, I must see my wife's sister safe, and her character restored? My friend is tired, and I apologize for his insult. We are desperate, and you are our only hope: Can you not find it in your heart to help us?"

Darcy stared at Bingley in amazement. Mrs. Younge caught the look between the two of them and laughed uproariously. "Ha, ha, ha — such a good joke. Such a joke. I'll tell this one for years."

"What is amusing?" Bingley asked.

Darcy rubbed his forehead. A headache was coming. Mrs. Younge said, "I am your only hope, Mr. Darcy. Ha, ha, ha! I'd known you really wanted my help but not that you were desperate for it."

Darcy did not reply, but Bingley at last realized what he had done, "You had no intention of leaving — did you? Damn! I have no skill at these things; you know that."

"Which is *why* I did not wish you present. At least stay silent when we speak with Mr. Wickham. Your amiability and good humor are not assets here."

Darcy's voice had been harsh, but Bingley took no offense. "I shall take your advice and speak not a word in his presence if you do not prompt me."

Mrs. Younge laughed again and said, "Mr. Bingley, how much is the reputation of your wife's beloved sister worth to you?" Bingley opened his mouth but stammered and said nothing. Mrs. Younge continued, "Do not be cheap — every minute that passes the story of her running off with our fine handsome friend spreads."

Before Bingley actually named a number, Darcy stopped him, "Do *not* say anything." Bingley flushed with embarrassment, and Darcy added, "If you ever should purchase that estate you must find somebody else to negotiate the price for you. You are perfectly unqualified for the task."

Darcy frowned and thought; Mrs. Younge knew they had no other options and would feel that she could demand very much. Yet, she also knew there were limits. He needed a number, high enough for her to take seriously — and which would put a leash around her hopes — but low enough to keep him from giving the foul woman more than he must.

Before Darcy spoke, Mrs. Younge said, "Come Mr. Bingley, helping your sister must be worth at least five hundred pounds to you. Surely, you cannot find such a sum excessive."

"Do not be ridiculous," Darcy replied immediately, cutting Bingley off. "My friend is not nearly so well-off as I am. He cannot afford such expenditures so easily."

"Can you not, Mr. Bingley?" She looked Bingley closely in the eye. "I think you can, and — you are a man who deeply loves his wife. You do not wish to tell her, when next you see her, that you would not help her sister because you were greedy."

"Well," Bingley stammered.

"Mrs. Bingley is with child. Bingley would not wish me to explain to her how he took a substantial amount of money away from their future children to give to a disreputable woman. Miss Lydia has already thoroughly ruined herself. Another day, or week, or even month would not make a stupendous difference. After enough time has passed that Lydia's reputation is irretrievable, Mr. Wickham will approach us himself. So you are not, in fact, our only hope. Find a nicer number — thirty pounds."

What followed was a half hour of circling negotiations that left Bingley one hundred and fifty pounds the poorer — Darcy planned to cover more than two thirds of whatever they gave to Wickham, but *this* expense would come out of Bingley's pocket — and one address the richer.

Once they left Mrs. Younge's quarters, the two decided they would return to Darcy's house and then attend on the wayward couple at 7 o'clock the next morning. It would be early enough for there to be no chance they had gone out already, yet late enough that even Wickham should have returned to his lodgings.

And they would gain the advantage that Wickham would be the dreadfully tired one.

It had long since turned dark when they exited Mrs. Younge's building. For the first minutes of the carriage ride the friends maintained a silence. It was annoyed on Darcy's side — had Bingley not been there fifty pounds at the absolute most would have been paid out — and thoughtful on Bingley's. At last Bingley said, "That was an education."

Darcy grunted.

Though he could not see it, as they had not lit the carriage lamp, Darcy heard the smile in Bingley's voice as he replied, "Nay, I know you are terribly annoyed at letting that woman get anything. Yet, the story alone was well worth a hundred fifty guineas. I am not unhappy."

Bingley was irrepressible. Darcy said, "Keep in mind, the sums of money Wickham shall try to gain will be far greater than the value of any anecdote."

Bingley hummed in reply, and Darcy added, "I really should be the only one who negotiates with Wickham."

"I must be there, but I promise I will say nothing."

Darcy sighed. This was the best he could hope for. "Be sure that you do not."

Chapter 20

It was before lunch the next day when Elizabeth arrived at Darcy's house. It was a beautiful building, fronted with marble columns and neat rows of windows. The garden in the square was surrounded by a fence with lamps atop each post, and a few persons sat on the benches beneath ample clumps of oak and beech trees.

Would she and Darcy one day sit together on those benches? She'd had the nightmare again last night: *I wish I had not married you.* She trusted Darcy. She would talk to him; he would reassure her; and she would feel well again. Yet her nerves skittered.

The butler informed them that the master and Mr. Bingley had returned the previous night a little before midnight and left again at 6 o'clock this morning. A note had been left by Mr. Darcy, but he only said that they followed an excellent lead.

Mr. and Mrs. Gardiner immediately left to visit their house and talk to Mr. Bennet. The rest of the group settled into the first floor drawing room.

Everyone's spirits were too depressed and nervous for much conversation. After several minutes of dull sitting about, Georgiana went to play. It was a mournful song, and each cadence made Elizabeth more convinced of disaster. Jane may worry for Lydia, but Elizabeth fancied she knew her sister's fate. Mr. Darcy would find Wickham and pay him off, and Lydia would marry him.

But then? Georgiana might expect it, but would Darcy still wish to marry her? Now that her family had proven to be not merely improper, but immoral. Now that it would connect him to Wickham.

The melancholy air Georgiana played, and Jane's occasional attempts to say something cheerful gnawed at Elizabeth. She could not stay here with them and wait for him to return.

Elizabeth stood. "Georgie, I must be alone. My thoughts are whirling, and — your brother said the library here is half as good as that at Pemberley, where might I find it?"

Georgiana and Jane let Elizabeth withdraw. The library was a beautiful well-appointed room with shelves that went ten feet high and three rolling staircases to reach the top shelves. There was a handsome marble fireplace in the wall opposite the windows, and the upholstered chairs were many and comfortable. Small mahogany and rosewood tables were spread about for books and drinks to be placed on, and a globe taller than Elizabeth stood in a corner.

He would decide he no longer wished to marry her and be relieved when she offered to release him. Everything she knew about Darcy said he'd not change; that his affection was too durable. But now that she was alone, her hands shook with anxiety.

What if they married, and he someday regretted it like Papa did. What if she made him unhappy? What if he made her unhappy? Maybe she should leave the house and walk to her aunt and uncle's and never let Darcy see her again.

She sat next to a window and cried for twenty minutes. She didn't move but slipped off her shoes and pulled her legs onto the chair and wrapped her arms around them. It was a bright sunny day. The room was stuffy from the unavoidable heat. She felt miserable.

Elizabeth had her reticule and pulled out the note that Darcy delivered through Bingley the morning he went to London. She'd kept it carefully stored in her bag and read it often. Darcy had written: *I care only for your happiness. I could never regret anything which contributed to it.*

Elizabeth smiled and kissed the paper again. It would be well. Despite her anxiety, she trusted him. Frightened obsessing would do no good. Elizabeth selected a copy of a novel she knew well from the rosewood shelves and forced herself to read.

SHE DID NOT NOTICE his entrance, so Darcy paused to look at her. Elizabeth's feet were drawn up under her, and her nose was barely visible above the book. She reached a hand up to rub at her forehead and saw him.

"Mr. Darcy!" She put aside the book, rising before Darcy could stop her. "You look tired." Her eyes were concerned as she stepped closer to him, she poured him a glass of wine from a decanter on a side table and pushed him onto a chair. "You ought to go to bed immediately after dinner."

Darcy smiled at her stern expression; he attempted to mimic the lisp of a schoolboy, "Yes, ma'am."

Elizabeth smiled, but it did not reach her eyes. Her spirits were visibly low. Hopefully the news would improve her mood, though it could not make her happy.

Darcy drained his glass of wine; fatigue and soreness covered him like a thick blanket. He gestured for Elizabeth to sit down. "You must wish to know what news I have."

"Only if speaking of it won't distress you."

"I am tired, not —" Darcy spread his hands an explanation. "No, while the situation is poor — the news is as good as it could be. I have found them, but it proved impossible to convince Lydia to abandon Wickham. However, while there are still details to be negotiated, I convinced Wickham to marry her for an almost reasonable sum."

"So that is the best we can hope for, that she marry such a man. Wickham is to be my brother." Elizabeth sighed unhappily. She was beautiful, and he wanted to make her happy. But nothing could change the situation.

Darcy spoke rapidly, "It is unfortunate, but do not worry so. We shall — do not worry. We will keep an eye on Wickham and ensure that some of the money settled upon them goes directly to your sister. She will not be mistreated. He will take a commission in the regiment of a close friend of Colonel Fitzwilliam's — Lydia will face no worse than an imprudent husband who really cares nothing for her. It cannot be what you wish for her, but a great many people face situations quite as bad without becoming really unhappy."

Elizabeth silently cried, and tears rolled down her cheeks. Darcy grabbed her hand. "Elizabeth, please don't cry. It will be well — I promise you."

"I am being ridiculous, but I feel so anxious." Elizabeth pulled her hand away from his to take a handkerchief from her reticule to cry into. It was the one he had given her the last time they spoke. Darcy retook possession of her hand and gripped it tightly. She squeezed his hand back.

Darcy settled himself closer to Elizabeth, dragging the armchair he sat in forward with his weight. He pulled Elizabeth's hand up to kiss it briefly and then covered it with his other. It was impossible for him to undo the consequences of Lydia's imprudence, but he wished to share as much of Elizabeth's pain as he could.

For a moment, he feared he may have acted amiss. The sobs which had begun to relax redoubled; however, when Darcy moved to pull his hands away from Elizabeth's, she murmured for him to stay and gripped him tightly.

At last Elizabeth ceased crying. She clutched Darcy's wet handkerchief in her free hand. She attempted to pull her hand away from him. Darcy did not let her. Elizabeth turned away with a blush. "I should not cry over what must be. I should not have imposed upon you so."

"There is nothing I desire more than for you to impose upon me."

Elizabeth looked him full in the eye. "I sincerely thank you for that. I do. I cannot help but think about all the other ways my family has imposed upon you. You have my deepest gratitude for your goodness."

Darcy squeezed her warm hand tighter and began to speak, "Elizabeth, I — you must know that —"

"Wait." Elizabeth closed her eyes and clenched her free hand. Her face was pained. "I have something I must say. I must. Before you say anything else — Georgie told us how Wickham attempted to use her. I now know why you hate him so. You could not — you said it would be terrible to be connected to Wickham. You could not wish Georgiana to be attached in any permanent way to that man. I know you have — much of what you have said of late was in the nature of a promise. And I — if you no longer wish to —"

"Don't be ridiculous" — Darcy's chest tightened with anger — "I shall not let you say such words. I shall always wish to marry you. How could you think my heart might change? How could you imagine Wickham might make me love you less? I could never wish to abandon — you cannot think my feelings so shallow."

"I know you love me. I know it wouldn't affect *that*. But you'll regret it someday. You will. Like Papa. We won't always feel so much as we do now, and one day you'll find I'm not so young, and Wickham will make some insolent demand, and you'll regret it. I cannot do that to you."

Like Papa. He hated that she could feel uncertain, but she needed his affection now more than ever. "Oh, Lizzy." Darcy leaned close and pulled Elizabeth near, so he could kiss her forehead. "Oh, my dear sweet Lizzy." He kissed her again, on her cheek and then on her nose. "It is not your person but your soul I love. Age shall only strengthen its appeal. We shall grow old together and tease and love each other more than ever. You are my dearest friend, and there is no companion I could want more. If I have you by my side, I shall never regret it."

Her beautiful eyes looked at him. They were red and wet. She nodded. "I know. I was ridiculous. But —"

"You were not." Darcy said softly, "Elizabeth Bennet, will you take my hand for life? Will you marry me? For I ardently admire and love you."

Her eyes stared into his, and she said, "Yes, oh yes! I love you. Your manner, your face, your quirks, your presence has become unspeakably dear to me. All my affections; all my hopes of happiness are bound up with you."

This speech moved him, and as they spoke, their heads had come so close. At last he kissed his Elizabeth.

The door to the library slammed open, and Jane entered, shouting, "Lizzy, Lizzy — my husband has brought good news — they have found Lydia, and she is at our aunt and uncle's. Mr. Wickham will marry her!"

Elizabeth and Darcy jumped apart, and Darcy could feel that his face was as hot as Elizabeth's looked.

Jane realized what she had interrupted and, with an embarrassed "pardon me," quickly backed out of the room and closed the door.

Elizabeth gave an exasperated huff. "If she continues to interrupt us so, I shall grow very cross with Jane. I never interrupted her so when Bingley was courting her. I have desired to kiss you for close on six months now."

Elizabeth's frustrated scowl was adorable, and Darcy laughed, soon joined by Elizabeth.

"I confess," Darcy said, "I spent at least a full half hour upon the road cursing that your sister had not delayed five minutes before she interrupted us in the orangery. Had she waited another minute, I would have requested your hand."

"Only a mere half hour" — Elizabeth smiled cheekily — "and what, pray, absorbed the rest of your thoughts?"

"You, my dear." Darcy took Elizabeth's hand again and looked into her smiling eyes. "Deeply as your sister annoyed me, I believe I thought mainly of you."

Darcy could see Elizabeth was affected by their closeness, and though she attempted to keep her voice light, it trembled as she leaned her face ever closer to him. "Now that — that is a topic of contemplation I approve greatly of."

Darcy kissed her.

Far before Darcy would've liked Elizabeth pulled away. She sighed, "We must rejoin the others — else Jane will think the worst of us. And, I wish to share the good news."

"Do not be absurd — Jane will never think the worst of us. Even if we deserve it." Elizabeth giggled, and Darcy kissed her again as she laughed.

They stayed in the room long enough that if Jane suspected the worst of them, she would now be certain. At last they stood to leave the library and find the others. As they did Elizabeth said, "I hate that such a matter intrudes on my mind, but you talked with Lydia. In what manner did she behave?"

"She is unrepentant. She was quite angry at me. Her head is filled with tales of my crimes against Mr. Wickham, and she is devoted to her dear Wickham. The impropriety and immorality of her situation has no hold upon her. She was quite as bad as you imagine her to have been."

They paused outside the drawing room, and Elizabeth sighed. "I suppose — I suppose it is best, since she will marry him, that she takes her husband's side. Still..." Elizabeth shook her head and reached to open the door.

Darcy stopped her with his hand and whispered, "This conversation has made you look a little unhappy." He gave Elizabeth a quick kiss and was delighted to see how her cheeks flamed.

"They are right in there," she said, pointing her head towards the door.

"Elizabeth, I must have you look the part of the blushing bride. I cannot let our family think you are anything but happy. Your embarrassment is an advantage in this situation."

Elizabeth's mouth formed a silent 'O'; she leaned up on her toes and, lacing one hand through his hair, kissed him soundly. "There, now you look properly unsettled as well."

Chapter 21

The next morning Elizabeth awoke in one of the Gardiners guest bedrooms. Things were not perfect, which was for the best. If one had no cause at all for unhappiness, then fate would conspire to bring sorrow. Lydia still was to marry Wickham, and she was separated from Darcy by more than a mile of city streets. So, Elizabeth had no need to fear that she was too happy.

Elizabeth jumped out of bed and, punching the air in delight, danced a fast jig in her stockings and nightgown. She was *at last* engaged to Darcy. They had spent a full twenty minutes kissing in the library. It was even more sensual and perfect than her fantasies. Soon they would marry, and she would live with him at Pemberley and tease Darcy into his brilliant smiles every day.

Maybe, she *was* too happy.

The previous day Jane suggested that as Elizabeth and Darcy were engaged, it would be improper for them to sleep under the same roof. She really would become vexed at Jane if she continued to interfere with her and Darcy. Jane had been apologetic when Elizabeth glared at her. Darcy laughed.

In the hour after they joined the others, Darcy yawned often. Rather than let him accompany her to the Gardiners, Elizabeth forced him to go to bed after they had a quick evening meal. He would come this morning to call on her and ask papa for his blessing. Elizabeth herself went to bed after a short evening with her family.

It was enough time for her to find Lydia unrepentant and resentful of her father. Mr. Bennet appeared dispirited and alternated between melancholy silences, where he stared at Lydia or pretended to read his book, and angry lectures when Lydia said something particularly foolish.

Now that Elizabeth's happiness with Darcy was positively settled, she could begin to properly feel for her sister. Her father also received her sympathy. It had been his irresponsibility that left Lydia prey for Mr. Wickham, but he felt the depth of his failure.

Elizabeth came down to breakfast. Her father and Mr. and Mrs. Gardiner were already seated around the table. Her father read Mr. Gardiner's newspaper, more it seemed to avoid conversation than from any real interest in the contents. He lowered the paper and looked at Elizabeth over it before returning his eyes to the broad pages.

"Good morning, Papa," Elizabeth said chirpily. Her manner was too happy for the somberness of her father's mood, so she attempted to school herself to show more of the emotion she ought. "I am sorry for your troubles. It must have been terrible. You went through much stress and difficulty while you searched for Lydia."

Mr. Bennet looked at Elizabeth, folded his newspaper and put it to the side, saying, "Not nearly enough. My sufferings were too little. I have erred and erred greatly. Some part of the unpleasantness ought to be mine. No, this affair has turned out far better than I could have expected, and with less cost and scandal — all thanks to your young man, for Bingley alone could not have arranged matters so tightly."

Elizabeth blushed at the reference to Darcy. "You must not be too severe upon yourself."

"It is sound for you to warn me against such; the nature of many people is to criticize themselves to excess. That is not my vice. Let me for once in my life feel how much I have been to blame. I'm not afraid of being overpowered by the impression. It will pass away, sooner than it ought."

"Things are not so bad, I do not believe Lydia will be really unhappy — even should she discover for herself what sort of man she has married — and the situation has been managed so that there should be no ill effects on Kitty or Mary."

Mr. Bennet raised his eyebrows in response. "And you have no worry for yourself?"

Elizabeth blushed at the look in Mr. Bennet's eyes but did not respond.

Mr. Bennet looked at his coffee. "Lizzy, I bear you — and Mr. Darcy — no ill will for being justified in your advice. Considering the event, it showed some greatness of mind."

Elizabeth squeezed her father's hand. She was too happy to resent her father's mistakes and had learned too much of her own flaws to judge others harshly.

Lydia pranced into the room, wearing one of Mrs. Gardiner's lace caps. "La! I shall look so fashionable dressed as a matron." She modeled herself for them, turning one way and the other to let them see her head from each angle, and exclaimed to Mrs. Gardiner, "Lord! Your styles are so boring — not nearly enough lace and trim. I shall make my dear Wickham buy me something much prettier as a present when next I see him."

The night's rest had convinced Mr. Bennet that lecturing his daughter further was futile, and he simply grunted and picked up the newspaper next to his plate and, after he shook it out, began to read again.

Mrs. Gardiner spoke, "Dear, it is well for you to wish nice things — but you shall be living on a limited income. You will need to make do with a fewer caps and less lace than you are used to."

"La! Do not be silly. My Wickham shall buy me whatever I wish, and if we should need more money for necessities, I will just ask Jane to provide us more. She and Bingley have so very much — they can have no objection to giving us a little every so often. Especially since Bingley insists on remaining friends with that nasty Mr. Darcy. It was his fault my dear Wickham is in such straits."

How dare she insult Mr. Darcy! Why, he had shown more true care for Lydia's well-being than either herself or her father. If Lydia did not end wholly miserable in life, it would be solely due to Mr. Darcy's kindness. Elizabeth leaned forward. "Mr. Wickham's troubles are of his own devising — Mr. Darcy has only ever acted with honor and a great excess of generosity towards him."

Elizabeth flushed as she saw Mr. Bennet look from around his newspaper to give her a knowing smirk.

"La, Lizzy you are so silly. Whatever makes you trust that nasty, ugly Mr. Darcy over my handsome, friendly Mr. Wickham."

Elizabeth glared at her sister, while Mr. Bennet said mildly, "Lydia, whatever you may have against Mr. Darcy, you cannot claim him to be ugly — it is *that* which annoyed your sister most."

Lydia made a face and replied, "Perhaps not. But he ought to be ugly — after he was so mean to my Mr. Wickham. Lizzy, what think you of how this cap looks?"

"Far better on your aunt. Perhaps if you had it trimmed with more lace." Elizabeth threw her napkin on the table, stood, and gave a halfhearted curtsy. "Excuse me, but I do not feel hungry any longer."

How dare she be such a foolish Lydia! And after Mr. Darcy had shown so much goodness towards her. Elizabeth quickly put on a pair of walking boots and stepped out of the house to go towards a nearby park. She'd gone barely one hundred yards, railing in a low voice at Lydia the entire way, when the clatter of the carriage stopping made her look up. It was Bingley and Darcy. Darcy had already climbed out and come to her side.

"I was just come to call upon your father." He smiled at her with concern.

Elizabeth's tension and annoyance melted away, and she grabbed Darcy's arm tightly. "Walk with me first. I was in a poor mood and have no desire to return to *her* anytime soon."

"I am always and wholly yours to command."

The serious way he said that drained Elizabeth's remaining unhappiness. "Oh my! That is a substantial gift. Always. I shall need to think on some way to abuse it horribly. Perhaps something inspired by courtly romance."

Darcy replied with a steady voice, "How could you possibly abuse my obedience, when any task done for you — no matter how silly or ridiculous — shall be its own reward, as I do it for your love."

Elizabeth blushed brightly. "Goodness — that was a pretty speech!"

"I'm glad it pleased you. I shall endeavor to find other extravagant means to express my regard."

As they strolled into the park Elizabeth smiled and nestled herself closer to Darcy, enjoying the feel of his arm and coat. The day had already warmed, but was still pleasant to walk about in, and the smells of the park muted much of the unpleasantness of the city atmosphere. Birds flapped, cawing at each other. Everything but the wonderful man she was to marry seemed distant.

"What did Lydia do to annoy you so?"

"Oh." Elizabeth thought back to her frustration. "I hate that she insults you and believes every word Wickham speaks against you. How she can believe, and even fancy herself to love, that worthless, false, superficial man and not see your goodness?"

Darcy made no reply but a small snort of aborted laughter. Elizabeth looked at him. He suppressed a smile. "What amuses you?"

"I had best not speak of *that* and simply say that your fierce defense of me pleased me greatly."

Elizabeth huffed. "Speak, I can see in your eye you half wish to, and if you do not tell me what amused you, the curiosity will eat at me."

"Well, I merely thought you should not be so harsh at your sister for preferring Wickham's words to mine as she is not the only lady of my acquaintance to have done so."

Elizabeth flushed with embarrassment. She had changed so much since then. "I was a fool then. So foolish and blind."

"And I was rude and acted selfishly. I should not have told you what I thought."

"I'm pleased you did, and my philosophy is to think only on the past when it gives pleasure or offers useful lesson. Perhaps I should not judge Lydia so harshly, but she frustrates me."

"I daresay, the interview Bingley and I held with her yesterday morning was not the most pleasant hour of my life."

"From her manner, she enjoyed it no more than you." Elizabeth was silent for a brief time, then peevishly burst out, "She said you were nasty and ugly. Ugly! You. Is she blind?"

Darcy chuckled, and Elizabeth quickly joined him. "Tell me truly," Darcy asked, "was the insult against my appearance what drove you to your walk?"

"It was the immediate cause." She laughed heartily at herself and said gaily, "You must know I marry you to be universally envied. If anyone should deny the great superiority of your appearance, my triumph will not be complete. For you are very handsome."

Elizabeth grinned as Darcy stood just a bit taller at the end of her speech. "Ah," he said, "so Lydia offended an important point of your feminine vanity. I understand."

Elizabeth cried out, "Is this to be how you treat me. I had thought it was the place of a husband to always puff up his wife's virtues beyond any reasonable bounds."

"I know enough of your mind to guess at the corollary to your idea of how a husband should act; pray, is the wife to tease and quarrel with her husband as often as may be?"

Elizabeth giggled at Darcy's expression. "Oh, very much so. You shall have no cause to repine, for a wife who flattered your every belief and never found cause to disagree with you would not be much to your liking."

"Certainly not. I have been, unknowingly, in the pursuit of the most charmingly disagreeable wife possible."

Elizabeth looked at Darcy's face. She wished they were not in a public place; she wished Darcy could kiss her again. He caught something of her mood. He looked at her with intense eyes and played with the fingers of the hand she had upon his arm. He said in a breathy whisper, "When you look at me in that way, I desire so terribly to kiss you."

Elizabeth breathed back, "I wish that as well."

They exchanged a long impassioned look. At last Darcy said with a smile, "We should return to your uncle's house. You shall have Jane to share Lydia with, and I have a conversation with your father which I am most eager for."

DARCY OPENED THE DOOR and quietly entered Mr. Gardiner's study. Mr. Bennet sat in a large armchair looking out the window. A book was in his lap, but for once Mr. Bennet did not read. He held a glass of port and had a half empty decanter next to him on the side table.

"Please, sit — sit." Mr. Bennet gestured for Darcy to pull up another armchair close to him. The manner he poured a glass of port for Darcy was sober enough to allow the conversation. "Drink with an unhappy man."

Darcy accepted the glass and settled into the indicated chair. Mr. Bennet said, "I never paid much attention to the younger girls. They were always so much sillier than Elizabeth and Jane. It was my duty and I failed."

Darcy waited to see if he wished to say more.

"You are not one for empty banter or comforting a man who ought not be comforted. I should thank you. You attempted to turn me from this path. I ought to have treated you better, and I am sorry for it. The event proved I have been purely a fool."

Darcy replied, "It is easy for a guardian to fail in some important respect. Even if they try to be diligent."

"That will not do to reduce my guilt, for I did not try, and I ought to have."

Mr. Bennet drained the rest of his glass and said, "I see you do not disagree. Well out with it, you must have sought me for some particular reason."

Darcy placed the glass down and steadied himself. "Mr. Bennet, I wish to ask you for the hand of your daughter Elizabeth in marriage."

Mr. Bennet took in a sharp breath, then he exhaled. "I expected it to be that. Well, I shall miss her. However, I have seen too much of you two together to doubt her happiness with you."

His face became pained. "I owe you another apology. I had hoped — it was even more foolish of me and very wrong, but I had hoped — not consciously, I could see your feelings were too strong for such a stratagem — but in my heart I had hoped that if I behaved unpleasantly towards you, your mind might change. Derbyshire is so far away, and I will miss my girl very much."

"I suspected as much. You can visit despite the distance. The turnpikes have made travel not so bad as it once was, and our library is grand indeed." Darcy could not feel really angry at the man who had raised Elizabeth and was now to lose her companionship. "You should not have involved Miss Mary and Miss Darcy in your game."

"I know it was wrong. I am glad they ended friends during that last call. Mary will be glad to see your sister again. By the by" — Mr. Bennet smirked — "Lizzy defended you most fiercely this morning from Lydia's repetition of Wickham's accusations against you."

Darcy smiled. "She said as much to me."

"Well, no use to put it off." Mr. Bennet reached across to shake Darcy's hand. "You can marry her with my blessings, and I am sure you will prove to be a better father and husband than I have."

"Thank you, sir." When Mr. Bennet said nothing further, Darcy stood so he could return to the drawing room and Elizabeth.

"No, wait." Mr. Bennet filled both of their glasses from his decanter of port. "Let us first toast to my Lizzy."

Darcy nodded and with a happy smile clinked his glass against Mr. Bennet's. "To Elizabeth."

Chapter 22

It was nearing midnight the night before Darcy's wedding, and he sat with Bingley and Colonel Fitzwilliam around a card table in Netherfield's billiard room. The table was piled with bottles of expensive spirits and empty crystal glasses. Colonel Fitzwilliam had insisted that Darcy drink with them for the last night of his bachelorhood. He had become quite tipsy, and the glass of brandy he sipped now was to be the last of the night. No matter how amusing his cousin would find it, he was not going to attend his wedding with a hangover.

Bingley had imbibed more heavily and, with his hand weaving unsteadily, explained to Colonel Fitzwilliam how Darcy had met Elizabeth. "It was at the assembly rooms, the day after he came back with me from London. Now, I had heard ever since I arrived in Hertfordshire how pretty the Bennet girls were, but believe me — Jane was even prettier than I thought possible. Than I had imagined possible. She is an absolute angel."

Bingley leaned into Darcy's face and, with the smell of the alcohol clear in his breath, demanded, "Admit it Darcy, my Jane is the most beautiful creature in the world."

Darcy's tipsiness let him respond belligerently. He pushed his nose close to Bingley's and roared, "You are wrong! Elizabeth is lovelier by far."

Bingley recoiled. Darcy sat back and firmly smacked his hand on the wooden arm of his chair. "Your Jane is nothing to her sister, nothing!" Darcy waved his hand in pain. That had hurt.

Colonel Fitzwilliam guffawed and exclaimed, "I must join this game — my new mare King Charles the First is the prettiest girl I know."

Bingley replied immediately, "Unsay that! My Jane is prettier than your horse! Admit it."

"I daresay, your Jane is prettier for a human, but my King Charles is a better looking horse."

Darcy asked, "Why? Why would you name a mare King Charles?"

"It was in honor of our aunt — you know how she hates Cromwell." At Darcy's flat stare Colonel Fitzwilliam coughed in embarrassment and said, "Well, it seemed funny at the time."

"Were you drunk?"

"Maybe — you have no right to judge. Remember when you let Georgiana name your horse Brownie?"

The cousins glared at each other, and Bingley burst in, "I must finish my story. Then you can fight about proper horse names — by the way, humans are prettier than horses, so Jane is prettier than King Charles — so Darcy, in that stiff, upright, too tall for anyone to approach manner he has — you know what I speak of —"

Colonel Fitzwilliam nodded energetically. "Oh I do — I certainly do."

Darcy had a mildly annoyed frown as Bingley continued, "Darcy was not dancing, so I approached him. I said, 'Darcy you stuffed shirt, you powdered wig, you exceptionally tall and noble looking gentleman, I must have you dance.' Of course, Darcy replied, 'I do not wish to dance.' So I said, 'don't be a fool Darcy, some of the girls here are uncommonly pretty — you may even decide to marry one of them — why right there is the very pretty sister of my partner.' Don't you agree Jane happens to be the very, very prettiest girl in the entire world?"

Colonel Fitzwilliam laughed uproariously as Bingley gestured wildly and spilled a little brandy. Darcy watched the floor absorb the liquid: A bottle that excellent deserved better. He stifled the urge to refill his almost empty glass.

Bingley continued, "And Darcy looked at Elizabeth for half a second, and I remember what he said clear as day — it was the night I met my darling Jane, and I remember everything from it clear as day." Bingley pantomimed pulling himself as tall as he could and spoke with a much deeper voice, "She is tolerable; but not handsome enough to tempt me."

Darcy blushed and quickly finished his glass to hide his embarrassment as Colonel Fitzwilliam laughed. "I daresay your opinion has changed."

"That it has, that it has." And pulled by the alcohol, and his genial mood, and the fact Fitzwilliam and Bingley were his closest friends, Darcy added, "She overheard that conversation."

"So that was how you insulted her? And she still will marry you?" Colonel Fitzwilliam laughed. "Your tall noble mien must have greater effect on the ladies than even I had realized."

Darcy replied smugly, "Elizabeth does have a proper appreciation for the excellence of my features."

Colonel Fitzwilliam replied, "Some men have all the luck: rich, and handsome, and tall. Though not charming, that belongs to me — and you Bingley."

"Elizabeth enjoys my company."

"That is because she is perfect for you. Or more, you are perfect for her. With the manner she looks for clever ways to poke fun at everything, she needs a husband who is as clever as she. Fine a woman as she is, I'd go mad after three months with her trying to tell when she was laughing at me and when she was serious. Besides, she likes to argue."

Darcy smiled as he thought of the ways he could bring Elizabeth to laughter. He loved her; he loved her light manners, her sharp sense of humor, and her clever ability to make any situation better. He loved the charming way she argued with him. Every day since their engagement had been a wonderful new opportunity to learn more about her mind.

"Look at him" — Colonel Fitzwilliam pushed Bingley hard in the arm — "sitting with that silly grin. He's thinking about her: That foolish face is the sign of a man in love. I hope I never look so."

Bingley replied, "Marriage to a beautiful woman you love is worth anything. Even looking remarkably silly in front of your friends. Say Darcy, how did you apologize to Elizabeth for her hearing that?"

"Well, first we argued about it."

Bingley waved his hands about. "So *that* was what the famous argument between you and Elizabeth after our wedding was about?"

Darcy shrugged. "We discussed other things."

Colonel Fitzwilliam laughed again. "I recall when you told me of that argument. You said you no longer had any affection for that girl. Hahahaha."

Colonel Fitzwilliam poured himself and Bingley a refill, but when he moved to pour more for Darcy, Darcy covered his cup with his hand and shook his head. Colonel Fitzwilliam nodded. "Wise, I'd not want to face Elizabeth after turning up drunk for her wedding either. She is mostly proper in company, but you can tell she has a temper when offended."

"I have discovered that myself."

The three pondered that. Bingley said, "Say Darcy, aren't you terribly glad I ignored your advice last winter and married Jane?"

"I have been pleased you did not follow it ever since I saw how happy you were together."

"Yes, yes, I know *that*. You admitted a long time ago your advice was wrongheaded, and you only were concerned for my welfare. Yes, yes. No, but for yourself — you'd not be marrying Elizabeth if I hadn't brought you two together. So the credit for your happiness goes to me. If I hadn't realized that for once you were a fool, you'd be miserable."

"No, she would have visited Mrs. Collins without your interference. I would've met Elizabeth again while at Rosings. So I do not depend upon you ignoring my advice for my present happiness."

"Ha! That is where you are wrong. Elizabeth still would have been mad at you for your rudeness. You may have asked her then, but she would have refused you. And then, you would have left Rosings and likely never met her again. And I would have been most melancholy without Jane, and Jane would have been most melancholy without me, and you would have been most melancholy without Elizabeth, and Elizabeth still would have been mostly happy."

"And I," Colonel Fitzwilliam cried, "would have been available to drink with both of you. And properly too. I tell you, in Spain we would've laughed at any man who got drunk after such a little amount."

"I am not drunk," Bingley slurred back.

As the two quarreled good-naturedly, Darcy thought about Bingley's question. If he'd met Elizabeth again at Rosings, he would not have known that she disliked him. She would have discovered that he had helped to separate Bingley from Jane, and she would have believed Wickham's lies. His manner would have been most ungentlemanly. He would have asked her to marry him, but she would have refused him.

His own foolishness could have so easily prevented his current happiness. "Bingley — I admit it. I am damned glad you did not listen when I advised you not to marry Jane Bennet. Damned glad."

A Request

Elizabeth and Darcy lead charmed lives. When we finish a story, we know Elizabeth will not die a year later in childbirth, and we know her children will escape the diseases that killed so many. She is a fictional character, whose wellbeing is protected by the will of the author.

The real persons in Regency England had no such guarantees. My research suggests one in two hundred full-term pregnancies ended in the mother's death. At least a fifth of children would die before they became teenagers in rich families.

These facts should be a sad part of history. But they are not. They are a terrifying reality. More than a billion people today live without access to medical care. Right now there are places where pregnancy is still among the most common ways for a woman to die; places where one in five children do not see their sixth birthday.

Each month I give money to Doctors Without Borders. I enjoy knowing my actions may keep another human alive. You should support them, or another organization that provides healthcare in the poorest countries. Donate ten dollars a month, or twenty dollars a month, or one percent of your paycheck, or two percent — or any amount you feel comfortable giving. But donate something.

If we act, in twenty years, there will be a mother who survived childbirth because a doctor stopped her from bleeding to death. She will feel nostalgic, yet happy, as she watches her child, who survived an ear infection because of antibiotics we paid for, fall in love for the first time.

http://www.doctorswithoutborders.org/our-work/medical-issues/womens-health

Get the FREE 12,000 WORD STORY, *Darcy's Dance with Jane* **when you sign up for my mailing list. It is an exclusive bonus for people who sign up for my mailing list.**
Click here to sign up![1]

---

1. https://b23331fe.sibforms.com/serve/MUIEACtEGcyB1mBRgetKCa7501H-7auzCuuUQhz42YJgF_bLN1ZMzqy3NRY7V1fJmZcxmWJNk6I1blWAreFP0s8eOEy8AO7wVuvIDWiTw5oeQkBaLv06tKhEqQd6aoAfsqkFvGECjHqDaGiWkq4oebsFboz1qe-9coQZd_1-ZR8JEykNZzQS5xpwOrZnPalnMZ1uyb_qZgsp7x71

Also by Timothy Underwood

A Dishonorable Offer
The Return
Mr. Darcy's Vow
Colonel Darcy
The Trials
Too Gentlemanly
The Missing Prince
A Compromised Compromise
Mr. Bennet's Daughter
Elizabeth's Refuge
Writerly Ambitions: An Elizabeth and Darcy Story
Overhearings Less to the Purpose
Reader I Married Him

Made in the USA
Coppell, TX
05 February 2025

45394695R00115